PEGGY ROTHSCHILD

Evernight Teen ®

www.evernightteen.com

Copyright© 2015

Peggy Rothschild

ISBN: 978-1-77233-561-3

Cover Artist: Jay Aheer

Editor: Melissa Hosack

PEGGY ROTHSCHILD

DEDICATION

For Richard. Always

ACKNOWLEDGMENTS

My sincere thanks go to The Sunday Morning Writers—a smart, talented, perceptive group—who read this manuscript in its many iterations and shared their insights: Ann Brady, Anne Riffenburgh, Howard Rosenberg and Tam Spiva. Thanks also to Melissa Hosack whose editorial talents made this book shine, and to everyone at Evernight Publishing and Evernight Teen for their hard work in bringing this book to publication.

PEGGY ROTHSCHILD

PUNISHMENT SUMMER

Peggy Rothschild

Copyright © 2015

Chapter One

Maybe if I hadn't downed that last shot of tequila, I would've noticed Dad sitting at the desk as I climbed through my bedroom window. Instead, I tumbled over the sill and thumped to the floor with all the grace of a 118-pound bowling ball, my nose landing inches from a brown loafer. Dad's brown loafer. Uh-oh.

I rose to my knees and swayed. My brain scrambled. How could I talk my way out of this one? The frown twisting Dad's mouth didn't help in the inspiration department. My stomach lurched. I stumbled to my feet and ran for the bathroom, managing to lift the toilet lid as my insides volcanoed out.

When my Mount St. Helens impersonation wound down to dry heaves, Dad spoke from the doorway. "Clean yourself up, Nicki. Then get packed." His voice sounded as cold as the tile beneath my knees.

I grabbed the rim of the toilet bowl and looked up at him. "What?"

Dad's face loomed pale in the hall light. "I said you need to pack your stuff. Now."

"But, it's the middle of the night."

"I know. Why do you think we're having this conversation?" He took a noisy breath. "Listen up. You're going to your grandfather's for the summer and I don't want to hear any argument. Pack your boots, wool socks, and that heavy jacket of yours. It's cold there."

Caught somewhere between the tequila fog and reality, I rubbed my face. It sure felt real. "Why am I going to Grandpa's?"

"We talked about this. But you broke the rules anyway. Again." He crossed his arms over his broad chest. "I know you snuck out two weeks ago."

"I—"

"I don't want to hear your excuses. Obviously, grounding you isn't getting the job done."

I slumped back on my haunches. Though most of the booze was out, Dad's words twisted my insides. "So, you're shipping me off to Grandpa's? I screw up and you send me away? How's that fair?"

"Fair?" Dad stepped into the bathroom, his voice rising to a roar. "You want to talk about fair? In a fair world, I'd have two daughters. In a fair world, you'd have two parents. Life isn't fair. You should know that by now." His large hands balled into fists and he grimaced. In the half-light, he no longer looked like my dad. "Get packed. You've got fifteen minutes."

I staggered to my feet and leaned against the sink. After rinsing my mouth and face, I tottered back to my room, ripping off my top on the way. I grabbed clean clothes from the dresser and pulled on a tank top then covered the eight-inch scar running along the inside of my right arm with a long sleeve shirt.

Inside the closet, I pushed aside the shoes piled on my duffle bag. Then the grizzly in my gut bit down and I doubled over. After several deep breaths, the pain eased. I straightened and wiped my damp upper lip. Whenever Dad roared, the gut grizzly roared, too.

Dad knew I wouldn't dig in my heels. I may have been the queen of the late night sneak-out, but I was no fighter. Dad was the one always ready to rumble. Normally I was pretty good at hiding the kind of stuff that set him off. Not that we spent much time together. I hadn't seen him this mad since—

My stomach twisted again.

No. Thinking about that was a mistake. My insides were like a giant knot already. I took a deep breath, wiped the tears from my cheeks, and started shoving clothes inside the duffle. Before hauling my bags to the back door, I tucked my iPod into the knapsack's outer zipper compartment then patted my pocket to make sure my phone was still there.

I must've set some kind of speed record for packing. Dad hustled me, my duffle, and my knapsack out to the car fifteen minutes later. Once I got belted in, it hit me: I'd crossed the line Dad cared about most. A deep crease bisected his forehead. His jaw looked carved from stone. I closed my eyes, wishing I could hit 'rewind' and get a do-over for the night. The party hadn't even been fun. At least not for me. Watching Gemma with her arms around my sort-of boyfriend wasn't my idea of a good time. It was also why I drank so much.

A stay at Grandpa's looked unavoidable. But, getting sent away for the whole summer because I snuck out twice? Over-react much? Typical Dad move. I slid a glance his way; he looked mad enough to chew concrete. It'd be better to wait until he calmed down before I tried pleading my case.

To show him I was mad, too, I tried forty-five minutes of stony silence as we sped north through the pre-dawn darkness. I wasn't sure he noticed. Somewhere along the way, I nodded off. I woke when Dad pulled into a drive-through south of LAX. Without a glance in my direction, he placed our order.

After exchanging money for food at the next window, he finally spoke to me. "Here." He passed me a breakfast burrito then zoomed out of the shopping center, one hand holding his meal, the other gripping the wheel.

The last thing I wanted to do was eat. At least half my inner knots were still securely tied. The night's beer and tequila binge wasn't helping my stomach either. Slumped, knees against the dashboard, I pinched off a small circle of tortilla. Steam rose, carrying the smell of cheese. My stomached lurched. I rewrapped the burrito and set it on the floor near my knapsack. Dad hadn't bothered to tell them to hold the cheese. I stared at his iron jaw then looked out the passenger window. The sun was cresting the horizon, turning the housing tracts pink and gold as we whizzed by.

North of Bakersfield, tall glass buildings gave way to squat stucco homes, every mile bringing me closer to a summer with Grandpa. The knots in my midsection tightened. I tried to breathe past them. When Dad was good and pissed, fighting back never fixed things. That much I knew. Maybe I could talk him into reducing my sentence, only spend half the summer in exile. Get home before Gemma helped Scott forget all about me. I gulped then turned to look at him. "I shouldn't have snuck out and gone to Gemma's. It was stupid. But I didn't know it would turn into a party. And I'd already spent the whole first day of vacation cooped up in the house. I only wanted to have some fun."

"Fun?" The car veered into the next lane. A horn blared. Dad jerked the wheel, bringing us back between the lines. "You and your friends were drinking, smoking pot. I saw the photos."

I'd rip Gemma a new one for posting those. Talk about stupid.

Oh no. A fuzzy memory took shape: me laughing my ass off while Gemma and I huddled over her iPhone. Had I been idiot enough to help her? Talk about the dangers of alcohol. "You should see the stuff other kids post."

"Other kids aren't my concern. You are."

When I wasn't grounded, Dad gave me a lot of freedom. I chalked that up to his sadness over our Incredible Shrinking Family. But pot and alcohol were a big constant 'no.' Last summer, when I turned sixteen, he'd grown increasingly rabid on the topic. The result of Single-Surviving-Child Syndrome. Okay, not a documentable condition, but real in my world. Still, maybe this was fixable. "You're right. I'm sorry. It was immature." Dad liked me to strive for maturity.

"Immature? Try stupid. Try dangerous. This isn't the first time. Or the second. I hoped that you… After what we've been through…" He shook his head. "I can't even talk to you right now."

So that was that. No turning back. Chugging along in Dad's Smart Car with everything I owned – well, everything I was able to pack in fifteen minutes – shoved behind my seat and in a knapsack at my feet. Heading to some kind of midpoint for the state: Nowheresville, California. Dad says I met Grandpa when I was four, but I don't remember. Obviously he didn't care much about me – he never sent birthday cards or presents. Never called. Not even after the fire.

* * * *

I jerked awake, stared out the dirt-spattered window. The two-lane road was empty except for our car parked on the shoulder. No nearby buildings, just a lot of trees and bushes. I checked the time. Over six hours had passed since we left home. My brain banged against the inside of my skull. I should've asked Dad for an extra soda when we stopped for gas. Or not drunk so much last night. "Where are we?"

"Your grandfather's picking you up here." Dad checked his watch. "We're a couple minutes early."

I must've dozed through half the state. Hard to believe I fell asleep with my feet jammed under the knapsack and tension pretzeling my guts. "You can't be serious about this. I screwed up. But sending me off with a stranger… That's way too harsh."

"He's not a stranger."

"Right. I feel super-close to the guy. I don't even know what he looks like."

"You're staying with your grandfather. End of discussion." Dad pulled off his sunglasses and massaged the bridge of his nose. "When he gets here, don't try to drag things out. He hates coming in to the city."

I glanced at the dusty road and scrub-covered hills. "What city?" I gave my knapsack a kick. "This is so un—" I caught myself. I didn't want to hear another rant about fairness. "Uncool."

Dad snorted. "I'm doing this for your own good. Use this summer to grow up. Not play at being grown up – like your friends. Take on some responsibility. Try to figure out who you are."

"Sending me to Grandpa's will do that for me?"

"Nicole, nothing and no one will do that for you. You've got to do it yourself."

"Whatever." I slumped down, which was tricky considering the lack of legroom.

A gray pickup pulled onto the shoulder in front of Dad's car. Dust filled the air, making it hard to see the driver. When he stepped from the cab, he looked eight feet tall – at least from where I slouched.

"Wait here." Dad climbed out.

If this meeting went badly, Dad might take me home.

The two hugged.

Crap. Not a good sign reprieve-wise. They talked for a few minutes before Dad signaled me to join them. I sighed. No stay of execution. I yanked my bag from the narrow space behind the seat, pulled down the cuff of my sweatshirt jacket, then hoisted my knapsack onto my shoulder and dragged my feet and the duffle across the dirt.

Grandpa wasn't actually eight-feet-tall. Dad had a couple inches on him – and he was six-foot-six. He was dressed in a plaid flannel shirt, sleeves rolled to his elbows, ropey muscles showing along his forearms. With his iron-gray curls shooting out around his head, he looked a little crazy. Grandpa's gaze flitted from me to the highway, like he was anxious to get a move on. His gray-green eyes were a match with Dad's.

"You've grown a lot since I saw you last, Nicole. What are you – five-six, five-seven?"

"I go by Nicki. And I'm five-seven-and-a-half."

He nodded. "Is that all your stuff?"

"Everything I had time to grab." I glared at Dad. Grandpa hoisted my duffle like it was empty and tossed it into the back of the pickup. I held on to my knapsack.

"Be good." Dad leaned down to give me a kiss. I turned away. His lips grazed the side of my head. "See you at the end of summer."

I swallowed the lump in my throat, climbed onto the passenger seat, slammed the door, and didn't look back.

Grandpa made a U-turn then gunned the engine. We rocketed along the empty road. Away from my dad. Away from my life.

Chapter Two

I'll give him this much, Grandpa didn't try to buddy-up on the ride. The man barely spoke, his attention focused on the road and rearview mirror. I spent a good chunk of the time chewing my lower lip. Though I still felt sick, it wasn't due to the booze. Dad's willingness to send me away hurt. But it was only for ten weeks. I'd gone through worse things than this.

After a three-hour drive along tree-lined roads, we pulled off the highway and shunted onto a series of bumpier and bumpier lanes until we left all paving behind. Towering pines surrounded us, blocking out the sun. I grabbed the dashboard as we rolled over a narrow bridge that looked made from Popsicle sticks. When Grandpa turned onto an unmarked track cutting through a swath of forest, my stomach sank. "Where the hell are we going?"

"Watch your language, missy. It's all right for an old fart like me to swear, but not for a young girl like you."

"That sounds fair."

"Out there in America, it's a democracy. In my house and my truck, I'm the king and the law. Deal with it."

"Like I've got a choice."

"Glad you figured that out."

The truck lurched across a deep rut. "How much farther?"

"'Bout forty miles. Relax while you can."

That didn't sound good. Since curiosity would imply interest, I didn't ask what Grandpa meant. An hour later, he pulled into a clearing. In the center sat a faded red barn plus a log cabin. Metal stilts rose from the cabin roof, supporting what looked like a silo. A large vegetable garden filled the area in front where, in a normal kind of place, a lawn would grow. To the right of the cabin, chain link surrounded a shed along with a rectangular patch of bare ground. The place looked like something out of that old TV series Dad liked to watch, *Northern Exposure.* At least the sun reached below the trees here. "This is where you live?"

"Yep." He maneuvered the truck into the barn. "And for the summer, you do, too."

"Crap."

"Remember what I said about your language?"

Heat blazed across my face, but I knew where anger led. Two deep breaths and I managed to shut off the feeling. "Right."

"Grab your bags." He climbed from the truck. An enormous German shepherd bounded over. Grandpa crouched, ruffled the dog's fur, and then stretched his back. "Come on."

The dog chugged to my side of the cab, tail wagging. The thing was huge. I'd not been around many dogs – and never one as big as this. After one more deep breath, I opened the door and stepped down. The dog pushed against me. I froze.

"Relax. Let Queenie sniff you. Once she knows you, you'll be part of her pack. Hurry up with those bags."

I tried not to bump the dog as I lugged the duffle from the truck bed. Grandpa waited for me then pushed the barn door shut. Clucking came from the enclosure at the side of the yard.

"You've got chickens?"

"Yep. Hurry up now."

With the knapsack over my left shoulder and the duffle clenched in my right fist, I humped my belongings to the cabin, the dog trotting by my side. Grandpa led the way into a bare bones kitchen. On the left, the kitchen opened into the living room, where a stone fireplace covered one wall. Dead deer heads hung everywhere and the place smelled like smoke and fried fish. Our house was no picnic but, even though the missing and dead shadowed our rooms, we never mounted their heads.

"Please tell me you've got indoor plumbing. Running water. A toilet. Shower."

"Yep. Back there." Two doors divided the rear wall of the kitchen. "Got a water-pumping windmill that keeps the tank on the roof full. A cistern holds water for the shower and toilet. Got a septic tank, too. Your grandma insisted. Said she'd live in the woods, but not like an animal. We're fully civilized."

I looked again at the animal heads on the walls. "Right."

Dad never talked about his parents, though I knew Grandma died before I was born. I tried to imagine a grandmotherly-looking woman making this stack of logs her home. The picture wouldn't come into focus. I dropped my bags. "I need to use the bathroom."

"Sure thing. You had a long drive." He pointed to the leftmost door. "Right in there."

The bathroom was small, but the toilet and sink both looked normal enough. A weird little gate stood to the left of the toilet, in front of a shower curtain. I unhooked the latch and pulled back the sheet of plastic. "Holy fuck." I stared at the crude wood steps leading down to the shower. Three tin walls finished off the enclosure. Up above, a barrel perched, supported by metal brackets. A hose snaked down to the shower head.

Since the barrel was round and the shower enclosure square, a blue triangle of sky peeked through at each corner. "I don't believe this shit."

As I washed my hands, I checked my reflection in the medicine cabinet mirror. I hadn't brushed my hair all day and it now looked like a long, blonde tangle. "Great." I dried my hands on my shorts and went out to face my new life.

Grandpa looked up from where he crouched by the kitchen table petting Queenie. "You got a choice of where to sleep." He gestured to the sofa. "This thing folds out. You sleep here, you gotta fold it up each morning. I won't have the place looking like a sty."

Right. Like the place was some kind of palace. "What's the other choice?"

"Up there." He pointed at a loft on the far side of the living room.

I stared. The ladder leading to it looked like stripped branches lashed together with leather.

"That's more private. If you're one of those people who gets up to pee in the middle of the night, all blurry-eyed and confused, the sofa's safer."

"I'll take the loft."

"Sheets are on the end table. Go get settled. Take your bags up, too."

"Where do you sleep?"

"There's a bedroom back there." He nodded toward the other door in the kitchen's rear wall. "I'm an old man and I'm not giving up my Posturepedic for a young pup like you. Go on now. When you're done, we'll go over the house rules."

It took me three trips to haul all my bags and bedding. Each climb up the ladder made home feel farther away and weighed down my heart. But each time

I reached the ground floor again, Queenie greeted me like a long-lost friend. By my second trip down the ladder, the press of her damp nose against my calf no longer startled me. I ruffled the fur behind her ears. Her tongue lolled. Maybe I should've claimed the sofa – a lot less work and Queenie could keep me company at night. Still, I didn't care if the old man was my grandpa. For all I knew, he liked to stroll around downstairs during the night. Though slant-roofed and cramped, I would stick with the loft. I grabbed the sheets and blankets and climbed up again.

The head of the bed butted against the three-foot-high railing running along the loft's edge. Next to the bed sat a crate to stow my things, but no dresser. I changed my ultra-short shorts for a pair of semi-short shorts, pulled a fresh long-sleeve cotton shirt over my tank top, and left the rest of my clothes inside the duffle. Unpacking would make this real. I dug out my brush and tackled my hair. When I climbed down the ladder, as soon as my feet touched the hardwood floor, the dog leaned against me. Her coat was rough and warm against my leg. At least one thing about my summer here would be nice.

I pulled out my phone. No reception. "Crap." I scanned the downstairs area: no sign of Grandpa. That was lucky. I'd need to watch the swearing. With Queenie at my heels, I headed for the door. Maybe I'd find a signal outside. A strange swoosh-thunk came from behind the cabin. Queenie trotted toward the noise and I followed. As I rounded the corner, Grandpa hoisted an axe and swung it down, splitting a log.

He straightened. "You can put that thing away."

"Huh?"

"One of the nice things about living here is there's no cell towers, no cell phone service. Keeps things quiet."

I stared at my lifeline to the world. Useless. "There's got to be a signal somewhere."

"On the roof of the general store. You can check it out when we go in tomorrow. Dennis will let you climb up there after I introduce you. There's supposed to be one corner where you can make calls. We need to go to town anyway. Get another block of ice. Pick up supplies. You can find out if your phone works there and check out some books."

"Check out books?"

"Dennis runs a little lending library at the back of the store. I know you kids like entertainment."

Uh-oh. I ran back to the cabin door, yanked open the screen, and stepped inside, staring at my surroundings.

The screen door squeaked again then slapped shut. Grandpa's heavy tread crossed the hardwood floor while Queenie's nails tapped a lighter rhythm.

I glanced over my shoulder at him. "You got a TV in your bedroom?"

"Nope."

"Probably don't have a computer in there either."

"Nope."

This was bad. I had the feeling something worse was coming. I studied the kitchen, the living room. Something bugged me. Something more than the dead animal heads hanging there. Got it. No overhead lights. No lamps. Oh no. No wall outlets. An oil lantern on the kitchen table. Another on the end table by the sofa. "You got electricity?"

"Nope."

Oh God. How was I going to charge my phone? My iPod? My Kindle?

"All unpacked?"

What the hell had Dad sentenced me to? I shrugged. "As unpacked as I need to be."

"Then make yourself a peanut butter sandwich." He pointed at a loaf of bread and open jar on the kitchen table. "And take a hike. You can have your lunch al fresco."

"What?"

"You been sitting around, getting driven here and there. I'm not one to let a youngster sit on her keister all day. You need to get some exercise. Make yourself a sandwich and get going."

Outside the kitchen window, at the edge of the clearing, pines grew thick like a brown and green fence. "You want me to hike in the woods? By myself? Aren't there bears and stuff?"

"Queenie will keep you company. You'll be fine. I told your dad to make sure you packed your boots. Those'll keep the snakes from nibbling your ankles." He smiled, but his face still looked carved from some kind of rock.

Was he kidding? I couldn't tell. No point taking chances. I climbed to the loft, changed my socks and pulled on hiking boots. When I came down again, Grandpa handed me a leather belt with a canteen and sheath hanging from it.

"Wear this."

My mouth went dry. I pointed at the knife handle. "What's this for?"

"You can use it to cut away brush. Not likely you'll run into any animals, but having that should make a city girl like you feel safe. I made you a sandwich while you changed." He handed me a wax paper bundle. "Filled the canteen, too. Now get going. You can eat while you walk." He led the way outside and pointed at one of the

21

tree-covered slopes. "This is all my land on the east, at least until you get to the forest. On the north side, it's best if you stop ten to fifteen feet from the crest. The hilltop marks the property line. You'll know you're almost there when you see my windmill. The Wilders live on the other side. It's best if you avoid them. On the west, when you reach the road, that's the end of my land. We'll take the track south tomorrow when we go fishing."

"I thought we were going into town tomorrow."

"Yep. We'll fish first thing in the morning then head to town. We don't buy our food here. We grow it or kill it. Now get going."

"What about Queenie's leash?"

"This is the country, girl. And my land. You don't need a leash."

Tall trees surrounded the clearing. How was I supposed to know when I reached the forest? It probably didn't matter which way I went – everything looked the same. I started walking. Queenie trotted beside me like we were old friends off on a grand adventure. As bad as I felt about getting sent to the boondocks, I had to smile at the dog. "Come on, girl."

Cushioned by a layer of pine needles, the ground beneath the trees was spongy like the track at school. In the deep shadows, saplings scrambled for sunshine amongst the towering pines. It was like another world. Queenie bolted after something in the underbrush. "Don't go too far, girl." Without the dog by my side, my courage waivered, but I kept on following the narrow trail up the hillside. The smell of sap mixed with the scent of vanilla and earth. Running track kept me in pretty good shape, but the climb worked my muscles in a new way.

What was Dad thinking sending me here? Plunking me down in the middle of a forest? Just because he didn't like my friends. He had no idea how tough it was fitting in. How awkward and long a school day could be without a crowd to hang with. He'd no clue how hard I'd worked to not end up known as the girl with the dead sister and the runaway mom. Or the kid with the scorched arm.

I realized I was practically running. I slowed and caught my breath. Something rattled a shrub to my right. I froze. "Queenie?" The thin branches rustled again. "Queenie!" The dog trotted down the hill. She leaned against me and my fear melted away.

Whatever was out there must have high-tailed it, because the branches stopped shaking and Queenie didn't seem interested in investigating. "Good girl." I ran my fingers through her coarse coat then started walking again. A bird darted between the trees. I jumped. Queenie looked at me. I swear I saw sympathy in the dog's eyes. "Yeah, I'm a tenderfoot. Going to take some time getting used to this place. You'll help me, right?"

Queenie barked.

"Okay then." We continued up the hill.

Chapter Three

The windmill stood in the center of a wide clearing. The squeak and whirr of its spinning blades filled the air. A few feet shy of the crest, I sat on a downed tree to unwrap my sandwich. Tears blurred the greens and browns of the tree line. Why couldn't Dad cut me a break? This was so like him. Blowing up over nothing. Sure, I screwed up. But, didn't he get how important my friends were? How much I needed them? If Mom was still around…

I shook off that thought. Mom had been gone for ten years. Who knew how she'd react to what I'd done? Queenie settled next to me and gave a high-pitched whine. I tore off a chunk and held out my offering. "Make that last. I need to check with Grandpa about what's okay for you to eat." Queenie wolfed the tidbit and looked at me again, her dark eyes hopeful. "Sorry, girl." I wiped my eyes, then bit off a mouthful and listened to the sounds of the windmill and the forest. The peanut butter stuck in my throat. I gulped several mouthfuls of water from the canteen.

Queenie sat up, ears alert. I set the canteen on the ground. The hair along Queenie's back rose. She gave a low growl.

"What is it?" Leaves crunched behind me. Heart thumping, I turned. The dog seemed focused on the tree line past the clearing. The noise grew louder. Something big was moving through Grandpa's woods. I dropped the sandwich and stood. My right hand settled on the knife hilt while I hoped to God I wasn't about to meet a bear. I held my breath and waited.

A dark-haired man appeared between two broad trunks.

Queenie growled again. I stepped back. He kept moving across the treeless area. The guy wasn't much older than me. Eighteen? Nineteen? Dressed in blue jeans and a T-shirt, he looked like the kids back home. Better than a bear, right?

"No need to sic your dog on us. We're not dangerous."

Another boy stepped from between the trees, this one blond. He stopped at the fringe of the clearing and nodded, but didn't speak. Though Dark Hair claimed they weren't dangerous, Queenie's body language said otherwise.

"Who're you?"

"I could ask the same question," Dark Hair said with a smile. "And I'm betting that whoever you are, you're trespassing."

"You'd lose that bet. This is my grandpa's land. You're the ones trespassing."

The blond finally spoke. "Come on, Ben, let's get out of here."

"Shut up." Dark Hair turned back to me. "You're old man Smith's granddaughter?"

Smith? What was he talking about?

He walked a few feet closer. Queenie growled again. "I'm Ben. Obviously. And that's my brother, Todd. We're your neighbors. You here for a visit?"

Someone close to my age lived nearby? Things were looking up. Good thing I brushed my hair before leaving the cabin. Ben was cute, too. So was the blond, the one named Todd. Guilt fluttered through my stomach as I pictured Scott's sea green eyes. No way was he hanging out by his lonesome while I was stuck here in the mountains.

Queenie let out another low growl. Her shoulders bunched, ready to charge, her eyes focused on Ben. The guy looked normal to me, but Queenie sure didn't trust him. I tugged my right sleeve to make sure my wrist was covered and took another step back. "I'm staying for the summer."

"Sure that's a good idea? A whole summer with your gramps? He's a grouchy old coot."

"He's okay." It was one thing for me to think Grandpa was odd, it was another for a stranger to badmouth him. Getting pissy with the guy seemed a bad move. Who knew if I'd meet anybody else close to my age here in the middle of nowhere? "So, what do people do for fun around here?"

Ben smiled again. "Hang out with friends, hike the trails, fish, swim. Outdoor stuff, you know? We're not big on mega-malls up here."

Was he implying I was some kind of bubblehead only interested in shopping? My years of experience learning how to fit in told me this guy wasn't interested in making a new friend. With the way Queenie was still standing rigid, eyes trained on him, maybe that was for the best.

"Come on," Todd said, "we gotta get going."

"We got plenty of time."

"No we don't. We're already late."

Ben checked his watch. "Huh, the dimwit's right. Hope I run into you again sometime."

I wasn't sure I felt the same. "One of us will probably be trespassing if you do."

Ben laughed at my weak joke. The two boys retreated into the woods. Queenie's body stayed rigid, her ears pricked forward.

"It's okay, girl. They're gone." Even as I said the words, my gut argued. My lunch spot at the fallen log no longer seemed private. I picked up the canteen and wrapped what was left of my sandwich inside the wax paper. "Let's go." We started walking, paralleling the ridge.

Queenie and I hiked until a chill crept into the air. On the downward slope, she flushed several large birds then trotted to me, looking pleased with herself.

When we got back to the cabin, Grandpa set me to work in the vegetable garden, pulling weeds.

"I'll call you when it's time to clean up for dinner."

Queenie settled in a sunny patch. I gave the dog a pat before sliding on Grandpa's gloves. My hands swam inside them, making my movements clumsy, like my fingers couldn't follow what my brain told them to do – a feeling I hated. I didn't mind dulling some things – like my emotions – but after losing sensation in one part of me, any additional loss of control creeped me out. I pulled off the gloves and continued weeding barehanded.

By the time Grandpa called me, my nails were caked with dirt and the knots in my stomach had loosened. Though I dreaded spending two months in the wilderness, the grizzly that regularly gnawed on my insides seemed to be sleeping. Until today, running was the only thing that sent the bear into hibernation. Being out and about with Queenie seemed to settle him down as well.

After washing up, I joined Grandpa at the oilcloth-covered table where two steaming bowls awaited. Grandpa started eating, so I dipped my spoon in and tasted. "This is good." I took another bite. "What is it?"

"Venison stew."

"You mean, like deer meat?" I looked up at the antlered heads on the kitchen wall.

"Yep. Bambi stew. Enjoy."

I stared at my bowl.

"Oh get over it. It's food. Tomorrow I'm gonna take you fishing. Later in the week I'll teach you how to shoot, give you a chance to try your hand at hunting. Out here, if you want to eat, you gotta hunt or fish."

"Bambi stew it is." I scooped another bite and chewed a tender chunk. "While I was hiking, I ran into a couple guys. Ben and Todd. Ben claimed they're your neighbors. Queenie sure didn't like him."

Grandpa's mouth twisted like he had found a spoiled bit of Bambi in his stew. "Those are the Wilder brothers. You stay below the ridge like I told you to?"

"Yeah. They came into the clearing where I was eating."

"Well, stay away from those boys. That whole family's trouble."

"They're really brothers?"

"Yep."

"Sure didn't look like each other."

"Half-brothers." Grandpa swallowed. "Different mothers, same father. And their old man's a menace, so stay off his land and away from those boys." He wiped his mouth. "Since I cooked, you're on KP tonight."

"KP?"

"Clean up."

"That's CU."

"It's short for kitchen patrol." He shook his head. "When I cook, you clean. When you cook, I clean."

"I'm going to cook?" I looked at the cast iron stove.

"Your choice. You can do all the clean-up far as I care." Grandpa set his spoon in his bowl. "Don't you cook at home?"

My spoon clanked against the side of my bowl. I dropped my hands into my lap then wrapped my left hand around my right wrist. "I microwave. Heat stuff in the toaster oven." I looked at my half-empty bowl. "Nothing like this."

"You'll learn. Other house rules: We get up with the sun, go to bed after it goes down. Unless you're sick. That happens, you get a day of bed rest. Your dad tells me you get twenty dollars a week allowance."

"Yeah." His tone of voice gave me a bad feeling. I leaned back. "So?"

"What do you do for it?"

"How do you mean?"

"What do you do to earn it?"

"I … I make my bed. Go to school."

"That won't earn you an allowance here. Here you help hunt, clean house, cook, take care of the chickens, collect the eggs, work the vegetable patch. That earns you an allowance. And twenty's too high. Like I told your dad, I'll pay ten dollars a week. As long as you keep up with your chores."

The grizzly in my gut stirred. I pushed back from the table.

"Where do you think you're going?"

"To my room. The loft."

"Uh-uh. You haven't been excused. We may live in the wild, but we still got manners."

I rolled my eyes and scooted forward. In case he missed the eye action, I used a saccharine tone and over-enunciated each word. "May I please be excused?"

"In a minute. You don't want to be here. I get that. Try to think of this as an opportunity. You can make this a good experience if you want. Learn. Grow from your time here."

Heat flashed across my face. "How would you know what's good for me? You don't know me. I mean, I screw up and Dad sends me to live in the woods with a stranger. Believe me, I've already learned something from the experience. And it's about Dad, not me."

"I get that you're mad—"

"You've never been a part of my life. What do you know about me?"

Grandpa leaned his forearms on the tabletop. "I know you broke your arm when you were six. I know a boy kissed you in second grade and you kicked him in the shin. You won the school district spelling bee in 7th, 8th and 9th grade. You didn't enter last year or the year before. You made the Girls Varsity team for Track and Field every year—even as a freshman. I know your dad doesn't like those new friends of yours from high school. And I know how you burned your arm rescuing the cat. We may not have spent time together or talked, but I know a lot about you."

I rubbed the damaged skin on my right arm through my cotton shirt. Grandpa left out the part where the paramedics sedated me when I found out the cat wasn't the only one still inside the house. "How do you know all that? You never visit. Never call. Never write. When Dad handed me over, you guys talked for all of two minutes."

"Your dad and I talk on the phone every six weeks. We've done that since you were about two years old."

"What?" Dad never talked to me about Grandpa. Never. The familiar guilt hit and the food inside me rebelled. I swallowed hard. "How come you don't talk to me when you call?" I hated how pathetic I sounded. Not sure I wanted to hear the answer, I crossed my arms and looked at Grandpa.

He shrugged. "With my situation, phones are tricky. I gotta call your dad when he's at work. There's a payphone in town I use. Inside the general store."

"Every six weeks?" Some of the tension left my shoulders.

He nodded.

Four weeks before the end of school, I came home drunk from a party and got grounded. Didn't even get to go to prom. Of course Scott had no problem finding a replacement date. Then last night, I got stupid and snuck out to party at Gemma's. "When did you talk to Dad last? I mean, before today."

"Two weeks ago. He filled me in on the situation, asked if you could spend the summer with me."

"So, this had nothing to do with last night?"

"The plans were made, but I don't think you can say it had nothing to do with it."

I huffed. "He could've warned me, given me time to pack properly. I don't believe this."

"Before you get in a self-righteous lather, let me ask you something." Grandpa pointed his rolled up napkin at me. "If your dad warned you what was coming, would he have found you in your bed this morning?"

My stomach lurched again. Good thing I'd stopped eating. "I don't know."

"Neither did he."

"Did Dad ask you to lecture me, about what I did?"

"No." He shrugged again. "Look, about the drinking and drugs … I'm no saint myself. And I'm sure you get why he's upset. I'm obviously no expert about the internet, but I'll say this much… When there's a record of how you messed up – whether it's photos of you drinking or stoned – it don't matter if it's in print or on everybody's computer, it's still gonna follow you. Your dad thinks this'd be a good time for you to get away from those friends of yours. Spend some time on your own. Figure stuff out. That's the lecture. We all make mistakes. Hopefully you'll learn from the ones you made these last few weeks." He pushed back from the table. "You're on clean up. I'm hitting the shower."

* * * *

A broken web swayed from the eave above. The mattress where I sprawled was narrow and full of lumps. I turned on my side and reviewed my situation. I was stranded in the middle of the woods. Living with some kind of mountain man. Doomed to a chore list every day. My allowance cut by ten dollars a week. Though – reality check – what was I going to spend money on here?

And what should I make of the fact Dad talked to Grandpa regularly and never told me? That Grandpa knew all this stuff about my life while I knew nothing about him? And where did Dad get off telling Grandpa my friends were no good? Dad was the one who moved us four times since the fire. Didn't he understand how lucky I was to have gotten in with a new group halfway through high school? Plus, the timing for my exile sucked. The prospect of Gemma using my absence to hook up with Scott was more than likely. Worse was the strong possibility I'd lose Gemma, too. She wasn't known for her long attention span. Me being gone for the whole summer would give her plenty of time to cultivate someone new. And Gemma was the queen of our group. Without her, I could wind up friendless right before the start of senior year.

Over the last eight years, the distance between me and Dad had grown. Now the gap felt like a canyon.

Less than twenty-four hours ago, I'd pulled on my favorite shorts – the peach denim ones that barely covered my butt. Though long-sleeved, the neckline of the clingy top I'd chosen plunged a good five inches and showed off my tits. Displaying a lot of leg and cleavage seemed to keep people from noticing I always kept my arms covered from wrist to shoulder. Even in summer. The only exception I made to that rule was when running track – and none of the kids in my group competed or came to the meets.

After unlatching the screen, I'd climbed out my bedroom window and dropped to the dry grass below. The night had cooled from the ninety-degree heat that baked our block during the day down to the mid-seventies. When Gemma had called earlier to talk me into coming over, I'd balked at first. Sneaking out to party at Gemma's while I was grounded for getting drunk at Gemma's seemed like a super stupid idea.

"You gotta come. Everyone'll be here. You already missed prom. You really want to end up getting left out of everything? Besides, Scott's coming."

The idea that I'd wind up 'left out of everything' got to me more than the lure of Scott being at Gemma's party. I caved. She couldn't pick me up, but promised me a ride back home. Though I didn't mind walking to her place, I kept my pepper spray at the ready – just in case.

The street where Dad and I lived was lined with condos. During the day, jacaranda trees shaded the sidewalk, their purple flowers dotting the dying nano-sized lawns like confetti. Gemma didn't live in Orange, like me. Her home in Villa Park was a different world, where two- and three-story houses sprawled across swaths of emerald grass. Circled by the City of Orange, I wondered if the Villa Park residents ever got nervous about being surrounded by us poorer folk. Since Gemma's home would easily win any 'best hang-out' contest, we partied at her place. She had a pool, Jacuzzi, tennis courts, trampoline, and the biggest flat screen TV I'd ever seen.

The throb of the bass had reached me as I turned onto her street. For some reason, Gemma shared her dad's love of Megadeth and 'Into the Lungs of Hell' blasted. Pretty stupid. In a neighborhood like hers, someone was bound to call the cops. Gemma didn't listen to many people, but if I told her to turn it down, she would. A couple kids I recognized were kicked back on the front lawn. I nodded and went inside. The music slammed my eardrums. Before I got my bearings, someone offered me a shot of tequila. Once I downed it, the music started to move with me, not against me. Gemma screamed a hello and shimmied over, laughing. Then I noticed my sometime-boyfriend, Scott, trailing behind her, his fingers entwined with Gemma's. After that, I turned my attention to drinking and getting high. Both of which probably explained the brainfart where I helped Gemma post those stupid pics. And my clumsy return four hours later with me practically landing on Dad's feet.

Dad.

Oh jeez. If Grandpa and Dad talked two weeks ago, that meant I had four weeks to prove how well-behaved I could be. A good report from Grandpa might earn me an early release, get me home before I missed all the summer fun. It might also get me home before Gemma succeeded in seducing Scott. Or before she found someone besides me to hang out with. Four weeks. I could do it. Be the good kid. Impress Grandpa. Hell, I was a good kid. Drinking and drugging with Gemma were my only infractions. I got good grades, did my homework. I could still fix this.

I focused on the swaying spider web. I'd hauled a Coleman lantern up to my 'room'. In the flickering light, the web seemed to stretch then tuck up tight. I looked at the dancing spear of fire. Though trapped behind the safety of glass, the closeness of the flame still made me feel like ants were crawling across my skin. The thought of letting the darkness smother me felt worse. I grabbed my Kindle from the crate by the bed and pressed the power button. Nothing. The damn thing was dead – with no hope of recharging it.

"What next?"

Hard to believe my pre-dawn packing flurry happened today. It already seemed like ages ago. My cell phone sat useless atop the crate. The only one of my electronic devices that still functioned was my iPod. To make the charge last, I would need to play it sparingly.

Because, even if I got sent home early, I still had to survive the next four weeks.

Chapter Four

Cold. So cold. The current swirled around my calves. Snow melt, according to Grandpa. The kind of cold that burned. Burned deep. Sharp rock dug into the soles of my feet. Why the hell was I doing this? Trying to prove I could be well-behaved shouldn't hurt this much.

I took another step into the swirling water. My toes met soft mud. Definite improvement. I moved forward again. The river bottom dropped away. By the time my foot touched down, the icy current reached above my knee. I bit back the 'sonofabitch' on the tip of my tongue. No matter that the flesh was getting frozen off my body – Grandpa would fuss if I broke his 'no swearing' rule. Dammit. "Yikes."

Grandpa paused in the middle of pulling his line. "Whoa there. No point risking frostbite for the chance at some gill-breathers. We'll buy you a pair of rubber boots when we go to town. Better get back on shore. If you were staying through the winter, I'd get you some of these." Knee-deep in the river, his legs and chest were safely encased in olive green waders. "During summer, the water level's low enough that a good pair of gum or hip boots'll work. We'll pick you out a sturdy pair today."

That morning I'd moaned about rising at daybreak for chores and the planned drive to Grandpa's favorite fishing spot along Rattlesnake River, but none of that seemed to shake Grandpa's good mood. Before heading out the door, he had pulled on a ratty-looking canvas vest. I'd covered my nose against the reek coming off it. The thing was stained with God-knew-what and had at least eight million pockets. "What the hell-eck are you wearing?"

"The hell-eck?" He turned and gave me a forced-looking frown.

"It's an expression."

"Right." He ran a hand across the vest's front. "This here's my lucky fishing vest. Got a pocket for my lures, hooks, line – everything I need. Caught a thirty-eight pound salmon wearing this."

"And you stole it from the fish? 'Cause man, that thing stinks."

He chuckled as he herded me out to the truck.

Soon after we took off, I stopped complaining. Not only because whining wasn't going to impress Grandpa. No. The simple truth hit hard. I had nothing better to do.

After Grandpa parked a few yards back from the riverbank, I'd climbed down and spun in a circle, Queenie dancing by my side. My world was cities and suburbs. Streets and sidewalks. Air conditioning and water rationing. I had never seen anything like this before. Slender trees grew near the bank, leaning over the river and swaying like dancers, leafy branches shadowing the current. Between the dirt track and the river, redwoods stretched toward the sky. Water frothed across boulders in the river's center. Frigging awesome. I stopped spinning and patted Queenie's flank.

On the drive in, Grandpa had told me how trout faced upstream, waiting for food to come down on the current. If I was to catch one, my fly needed to land up river then travel down to the fish. Queenie apparently knew the drill and had settled near the base of a tree midway between where Grandpa waded into the current and where I'd stood on shore. So far, Grandpa had caught four good-size trout. In spite of his many pointers, I was batting zero for a hundred. Leastways the ache from my arm made it seem like I had cast that many times. Frustration had finally pushed me to follow Grandpa into the water, in hopes that close-up, I would find it easier to copy his casting style. No such luck. By the time I got back on shore, my feet ached with cold. Though I might not catch any fish, at least this way I would get back to the cabin without freezing off a toe.

"Remember, you gotta keep your cast level," Grandpa called over the rushing water. "Think of it like this, your elbow's on a shelf. Can't move it up. Can't move it down. Trust me. That's the only way the loops are gonna fly tight."

I tried another cast. My line landed with a plop downstream.

"I'm trying real hard not to be a cranky old fart, but you're all over the place. Look at what you're doing. You gotta move your forearm without twisting your wrist. Watch me, all right?" He pulled in his line, cast again. "Hear that?"

I nodded.

"Listen for the whoosh. If you hear that, your cast is good."

After hauling in my line, I made another attempt. Elbow level, no wrist twisting. Focused on making a big letter C with the line. The fly flew upstream. I heard the whoosh before it landed without a splash. Right where I aimed.

"Nice one. Like I said, if you don't flail your arm around, the line lands true. Now, move on downstream, slow like. And keep back from the bank so the fish don't see your shadow."

I edged along the riverbank, trying not to hurt my bare feet more than I had already. My line started moving against the current.

Grandpa's eagle eye seemed to miss nothing. Right away he called out, "Go easy now. Raise the tip of your rod before you start to pull."

"Okay." I followed his instructions, surprised to feel the solid weight of a hooked fish.

Grandpa yelled more pointers and, after a five-minute battle, I hauled a silver-speckled trout near shore.

Grandpa waded over, scooped the fish into his net. He hefted the struggling trout. "Caught yourself a real beaut. Looks like he's at least fourteen inches." He smiled at me. "Good job."

A part of me wanted to keep my mask in place, to look annoyed by the whole ordeal of summering with Grandpa. A bigger part was excited and proud. Though stranded in a strange world, I had managed to conquer a small part of it. I smiled back at him.

"I think we've done enough fishing for one day. Let's get these beauties home then go in to town."

* * * *

After we got back to the cabin, Grandpa told me to stow the fish in the icebox.

I pointed at the wood cabinet near the kitchen sink. "That thing?"

"Yep. Put the trout on the bottom right. Anytime you put uncooked meat inside, always stow it there." He pulled the icebox handle. "Look. Milk goes on the bottom left. Fruits and veggies up top on the right. Leftovers go on the second shelf. Got it?"

I nodded and fitted the day's catch behind some unidentifiable meat. More Bambi?

"Hurry up and get changed."

Queenie waited at the base of the ladder while I changed up in the loft. Eager to get to town and resurrect my phone, I skidded down the ladder, entering the kitchen at the same time as Grandpa.

"You ready?"

I nodded.

"Let's get going."

Inside the truck's cab, Queenie wedged herself between Grandpa and me. Within minutes of starting along the dirt road, she stood, front paws on my lap, her nose jutting out the window.

"Queenie, sit," Grandpa said.

"I don't mind."

"Well, I do. Don't want my dog forgetting her manners."

Queenie settled on her haunches, swaying her snout between our two open windows. All I smelled was pine; Queenie's twitching nostrils obviously scented something more exciting.

When we reached the T in the road, Grandpa turned left. The narrow track through the trees felt ten times bumpier than the one we took to the river. Branches scraped against the side of the truck with the occasional leaf poking through the open window. "Sure this is a real road?"

Grandpa's laugh roared through the cab. "Not only is this a real road, it's a piece of history. In the old days, this was the stage coach track."

"Well, the day of the stage coach is gone. Long gone. Maybe it's time somebody put this road in a museum or paved the sucker over." I noticed Grandpa smiling at my sass and kept going. "The town would probably get a few more visitors if you put in a decent road. And posted a sign or two."

"Maybe. Folks 'round here aren't all that crazy about outsiders. We like our privacy."

Outsider. The word fit the way I felt. It also reminded me of something. "Yesterday, I told you how I ran into the Wilder brothers."

"What about it?"

"They called you Mr. Smith." They really said 'Old Man Smith,' but I wasn't going to repeat that. "Why'd they think your name's Smith?"

Grandpa cleared his throat. "Because it is."

"Then how come Dad and I are Steeles?"

He took one hand from the wheel and wiped his forehead. "Your grandma and me decided your dad should take her last name."

"Why?"

"Uh, well, I been boring old John Smith all my life." Grandpa tapped his fingers against the steering wheel. "The world's full of Smiths. The name Steele gave your dad a better chance of standing out."

"You could've hyphenated. Steele-Smith. Or Smith-Steele. That's pretty memorable."

Grandpa harrumped. "No thanks."

Twenty minutes later, we bumped from beneath the trees onto paved road. Grandpa accelerated. We rounded one bend, then another. A handful of buildings came into sight. The truck slowed and Grandpa finally spoke again. "Here we are." He parked in front of the lone gas station.

My mouth dropped open. Four crummy buildings. One was two stories tall with a sign that read General Store. Probably qualified as the town skyscraper. Beside the combination gas station and Laundromat stood two other buildings, but neither had a sign out front. "This is the town?"

"Yep." Grandpa pointed to a large, hand-painted sign that read: Welcome to Punishment, California. Population 82.

"That's the town name? No wonder Dad sent me here."

"Well, it's not an official town. But that's the name all right. They stretch the truth on the population. My cabin's outside Punishment. But they include all us outliers to get that big number. Probably more realistic to say about twenty people live in town." Grandpa climbed down from the truck. The dog followed then leaped into the empty truck bed. "Queenie stay."

I slammed the truck door. This summer wasn't just going to be long, it promised to be endless.

Chapter Five

The general store had seen better days. At least I hoped this wasn't the place at its peak. Patches of green paint had peeled away from the wood siding, revealing a gray layer underneath. Did Dad know what he'd sentenced me to, what this place was like? I trailed after Grandpa. A bell jangled when he opened the door.

The store smelled like leather, dust, and tobacco. Inside to the right sat rows of feed bins: chicken, rabbit, horse, and goat. Who knew there was such a thing as goat chow? A large chart hung on the wall, listing prices for grass hay, oat hay, alfalfa, and straw. Western wear and horse tack filled the next section. People food was located at the back, along with the lending library.

"What size shoe you wear?"

I stared at a shelf holding cans of bear spray. Was that to attract bears or drive them away?

"You listening to me?"

"Huh?"

"What's your shoe size?"

"Eight-and-a-half."

"I'll see what they got in the way of boots." Grandpa waved over a man with a deeply lined and tanned face, gray hair, and wooly sideburns. "Dennis, I want you to meet my granddaughter, Nicki. She's staying with me for the summer. We need to get her some boots for fishing."

"Hi." Dennis smiled, revealing a chipped front tooth. "Let me show you what we got." A Tootsie Pop of a man, he was skinny except for the potbelly straining against the buttons of his denim shirt.

"Is it all right if Nicki goes up on the roof while I pick out some boots for her? She's going crazy not being able to use her phone."

Crazy was a bit of an exaggeration. Since the initial shock, I thought I'd been pretty good about not complaining.

"Sure thing." Dennis pointed to the back corner of the store. "Stairs are over there. You'll find the spot on the roof easy enough." He turned to Grandpa. "One of the Wilder boys went up there with a can of paint and marked the place where the signal's strongest."

"One of them did something useful? Wonders never cease."

I left them to the task of finding me a pair of boots and hurried to the back of the store. The metal stairs moaned with each step and I clenched the rail with both hands. At the second floor landing, I enjoyed the sensation of solid ground while I looked around. There were lots of heavy jackets and foul-weather gear, along with shelves of things I couldn't hope to identify. I climbed the next flight to a narrow door, pushed it open, and saw the rooftop. My pulse returned to normal when I stood on tar paper instead of the wobbly staircase. I shielded my eyes against the morning sun and scanned the roof. The store owner was right. The good cell reception area was easy to spy: a red square decorated one of the corners of the flat roof. Curious, I tested my phone where I stood. No reception. I tried once more within five feet of the marked spot and got a few signal bars. When I stepped inside the painted square, voila! My phone lived again.

Right when I thought the call would go to voice mail, Gemma picked up.

"Nicki? That you? You know what time it is?" Her voice sounded hoarse.

I pulled the phone from my ear, checked the time. "Yeah, it's 9:30." Huh. Half-past nine and Gemma was still in bed. I'd already tidied the loft, helped cook breakfast, gone fishing, and come to town.

"I only got to bed five hours ago. And I'm hung over. Call me later."

"No. Wait. I can't call later."

"Why not?"

"It's a phone thing. I only get reception in town."

"Since when? Something wrong with your phone?"

Gemma didn't know. How could she? "No. I'm not at home. I'm at my grandpa's."

"What?"

"Dad sent me to Grandpa's house. For the summer."

"Since when?"

"Since yesterday."

Gemma gave a long yawn. "Where's he live?"

"In the Mendo. Northern California. On the edge of the Mendocino Forest."

"Guess that means you're not coming to Scott's party this weekend."

Scott. My almost-boyfriend. He'd cooled toward me after Dad forced a last minute cancellation of our prom date, and I'd hoped we'd get back together over the summer. I didn't like the way Gemma's voice perked up when she said his name. Nor how she didn't sound super-sad at the prospect of me not making the party. But the worse part? She didn't sound bummed about me being gone. "No."

45

"Too bad. I'll take some pics and send them to you."

"Don't bother. Doubt I'll be able to get them." The silence stretched. My thoughts raced through the things I had seen and done over the last twenty-four hours. None of that translated to my life at home. How could I explain this place to Gemma? Was it worth the effort?

"Well, I need to catch a few more zees."

Huh. My reluctance to share with Gemma seemed matched by her lack of interest. "Right. Guess I better get going, too."

"Okay." Gemma followed this with another loud yawn. "Talk to you later."

I stared over the short wall that ran along the roof's edge. There was no traffic on the road below, just Grandpa's truck parked in a patch of weeds. I kicked a pebble across the tar paper roof. I'd hoped for sympathy when I told Gemma about my summer banishment, counting on her to join me in railing against the unfairness. Talk about off the mark. She never even asked why I got sent away. Shit. Was she already phasing me out? During the year I'd known her, she'd done it to two other girls. But I was her best friend. Or at least she was mine.

Useless. That's what Dad called the new friends I started hanging out with at school after our last move. He didn't like any of them and didn't try to hide the fact. He said they were a bunch of self-involved, spoiled brats.

But Gemma was the one who had rescued me from solo lunches and empty afternoons. Maybe she was feeling cranky from her hangover.

I scrolled through the contact list on my phone. Less than a day here in the mountains, it was way too soon to call Dad and ask to come home. Even when things were normal – as normal as things got at our house – most days we barely spoke. He wouldn't expect me to call him this quickly. And me calling to complain about the overall weirdness of the town wasn't likely to sway him. After a few more weeks, he might relent about making me stay the entire summer. But from my talk with Gemma, it didn't sound like I had a whole lot to rush home for.

When I climbed back down to the first floor of the store, Grandpa was negotiating with Dennis. I wandered the aisles until I came to the lending library. Some of the mysteries looked interesting. I read the self-check-out rules and left the lending cards for four books on the counter with my name penciled in next to the date. Grandpa and Dennis continued to talk.

Outside on the porch, I considered crossing the road to sit with Queenie in the back of the truck, but the store porch was shadier. I sank onto the wood step, staring at the town. The road continued on past the gas station. Probably the way to civilization. Something outside of my reach right now.

I opened one of the books and started reading. At page five, a shadow fell across the text. I glanced up. A man towered over me. The brim of his hat shaded his face, but the sheriff's department insignia on his tan uniform was easy to spot. I tugged my right shirt sleeve over my wrist.

"You're new around here." His words came out slow, like catsup from a bottle, and held a note of suspicion.

"Yeah." I leaned back to get a peek at his face. The dark-haired deputy wore sunglasses, but I could tell he was checking out my tits. Ugh. He had to be at least thirty.

Behind us, the door jangled and creaked. I turned. Grandpa held out a brown paper bag. "Got your boots. Let's get a move on."

I stood and took the bag. Grandpa scowled at the deputy before walking toward the truck.

The deputy stared at Grandpa's back, his lips pursed like he'd bitten into something sour. Though neither said a word, the silence felt as fierce as one of Queenie's growls.

The dog greeted me like we'd been separated for days instead of forty-five minutes. I ruffled the fur behind her ears before she bounded into the cab. The back of the truck was already loaded with supplies: a block of ice, a burlap bag marked 'rice,' canned goods, and several containers of lamp oil. I climbed onto the seat next to Queenie. Grandpa revved the engine then pulled onto the road. I looked back through the open window. The deputy still stood on the front porch of the store, staring at Grandpa's truck. "What's wrong with him?"

"Who?"

"That deputy."

Grandpa shook his head. "You know what they say, it's best not to turn your back on crazy."

"Who says that?"

"Me."

"So how come we didn't walk backwards to the truck?"

"It's called a metaphor. Don't they teach you nothing in school these days?"

Chapter Six

Queenie raced after a gray squirrel and I continued along the narrow path that cut up the slope east of Grandpa's cabin. After a full week of hiking the hills, I was less edgy when the dog left me on my own, yet my shoulders loosened when she returned.

Squirrel successfully treed, Queenie loped back to me.

I rubbed her flank. "Good girl."

"Whatcha doing?"

I jumped. Queenie growled, the fur along her spine jutting up like a picket fence. I turned toward the voice. Surrounded by towering pines and silent trails, I'd thought Queenie and I had this bit of woods to ourselves.

A few yards away, a dark-haired boy leaned against a thick tree trunk. The boy I met my first day at Grandpa's. Ben. That was his name. The rude one. Right. I checked to make sure my shirt sleeve covered my right wrist. "Where'd you come from?"

"Home." He gave a smirk. "How about you?"

"You know what I mean. Been here long?"

He shrugged. "Saw you heading this way, so I waited."

Ben waited for me? Weird. He acted so cold when we met six days ago. Maybe he was in a bad mood then. "Why?"

"Thought you might want to join me for a little Eco Warrior work."

"Some what?"

"Eco Warrior. That's what me and Todd do. In our free time, we hunt through the woods for illegal pot farms." Ben moved down the hill toward me.

Queenie growled again. The dog either disliked or didn't trust Ben. I hadn't spent much time with her around other people. Was this normal behavior? When Ben moved close, an uneasy feeling settled in my gut. A reaction to the dog's attitude – or something else? "Queenie. Stop that. You've met Ben before." I took a step back. "Hold out your hand, let her sniff it."

Ben tucked his hands in the front pockets of his jeans. "I'll pass. That dog's mind is made up. She doesn't like me. Sniffing my hand's not gonna change that. But I don't mind if she comes along. She doesn't have to like me. As long as you do."

Like him? Was he kidding? I hardly knew him. Maybe he was used to girls throwing themselves at him. By anyone's standards, he was handsome. But I wasn't about to start drooling over the guy. "So, you're like anti-weed?"

"No, but this grower's hurting the land." Ben stared at his dust-covered boots. "These guys come in here and cut down trees to make a grow space. Steal water from the river. Use a ton of chemicals on their plants. Let the run-off wind up in the creeks and rivers. My dad's a farmer. He says the whole thing's ruining the ecology. And, in order to keep animals from eating their crop, they spread this arsenic-based bait around the plants. That's why the deer count's gone way down over the last few years." Ben turned toward the hill then spoke over his shoulder. "You coming?" He started to cut through the woods at an angle.

I looked into Queenie's brown eyes, wishing I could see what she saw. What bugged her about the guy? I trotted after Ben. As long as Queenie was with me, I should be safe. "Where exactly are we going?"

He pointed. "See that bird? That's my spirit guide."

Above, green leaves and pine needles fluttered along brown branches. Bits of blue sky peeked through the trees. But no bird. "I don't see anything."

"You wouldn't. You're not Wintun-Wailaki like me."

"Win what?"

"Wintun-Wailaki. Native American. I'm half Indian. Of the Wintun-Wailaki tribe. On my mother's side. The Cooper's hawk is my spirit guide. I follow and he leads me to what I need to find."

With his straight dark hair and tan skin, I bought the Indian part, but the rest sounded like a load of garbage. "And this invisible bird will take you to an illegal pot farm?"

"He's not invisible. You don't know how to see. The bird will take me where I need to go. Right now, I need to find where the pot farm's moved." His tense tone told me it was time to shut up.

We hiked in silence for ten minutes. At the hill's crest, Queenie nosed my hand. I crouched and petted the dark saddle of black along her back. "Let's go, girl." Ben hadn't stopped when the dog and I did and was now a good five yards ahead. I hurried to catch up. We followed him down the other side of the hill. A gray bird flew past, disappearing into the trees. "That your guide?"

"Nah. I told you, my bird's a Cooper's hawk. They're tan and white. And a lot bigger than that."

Finally, an opportunity to talk. "So, this pot farm you're looking for moves around?"

Ben sighed. "Here's the deal. We got a big problem with pot farms in the Mendo. Every now and again the cops attack, scatter the workers and tear out the plants. A few hands might get arrested, but not the guys in charge. And, once the cops go home, the grower sets up in a new spot inside the forest. Nothing really changes. No one knows for sure how many fields are hidden out here in the woods, but I've heard there are at least fifty. The one I'm trying to find is near our stretch of land. We want this new farm gone."

"Your plan is to find him? And do what?"

"I'm gonna find the farm and turn in its location to the cops. If I keep doing that over and over again, they'll finally get the message to set up somewhere else. We don't need that kind of crap here."

"Isn't reporting them dangerous? I mean, don't you worry they'll figure out you're the one turning them in?"

Ben turned to face me. "I keep to the trees, stay quiet. They don't see me, but I see them. Far as they're concerned, I'm invisible."

The pollution part sounded real, but the rest sounded like bullshit. Like his spirit guide. "Can't the guy in charge find out who made the report? You know, ask the cops?"

"Doesn't work that way. Besides, when I call it in, I use one of those pre-paid phones. All the cops can figure from that is somebody called them from the roof of the general store." He pushed aside a couple branches and ducked into the heavy brush.

"Any of this stuff poisonous?" I hesitated, staring at the leaves.

"Nah. It's manzanita."

"Come on, Queenie." I followed Ben along a narrow trail through the bushes, the dog at my heels. I sure hoped he was right about the plants being safe. Nothing itched, but still… I bet all kinds of spiders and bugs lived in here. We continued on in silence for about fifteen minutes, then Ben changed course. We began to climb. "How far we going?"

"As far as we need to." He sounded impatient. "Don't worry. By the look of your legs, you can handle it."

Ben checked out my legs? My face grew warm. I wasn't sure if I was flattered or annoyed. The guy was cute, but knew it. And he hadn't done much to make me like him. He had way too much attitude. If I knew anyone else who wanted to hang out with me or was sure I could find the way back to Grandpa's, I would've turned around and headed home about twenty minutes ago.

The hill climb seemed endless. Up, up, up we went, keeping beneath the cover of trees and shrubs. Other than the fact that Queenie periodically growled at Ben, the dog seemed to enjoy the journey. Though the pine-scented air felt cooler under the trees, my T-shirt soon became soaked with sweat. I wanted to take a drink from my canteen and pour some water into my palm for Queenie, but worried about the etiquette. Would I have to offer Ben a drink? I wasn't sure I wanted to swap germs with the guy. I longed to ask how much farther we had to go, but held off. He sounded pissed enough the last time I asked. Instead, I kept my mouth shut and continued climbing.

Ben stopped, held up his hand. He leaned in, his body heat adding to the day's warmth as he whispered in my ear. "We gotta keep real quiet now. Watch where you step. Try to make as little noise as possible." He moved off, walking in a strange semi-crouch.

I tried to mimic his stance as I followed. He stopped at the hill's crest and knelt behind a tree. I hunkered down in his shadow, my arm around Queenie.

Below us stretched rows and rows of bright green plants. Slender pines edged the field. Two men walked between the rows, the height of the crop almost to their knees. The large buds on the branches of the closest plants were easy to spot. Each man carried a plastic jug, dribbling liquid on the crop rows as they passed. The nearer of the two wore khakis plus a dirt-and sweat-stained undershirt. The distant man looked more pulled together: short-sleeved shirt tucked into his pants, hair tidy.

From what I could see, other people had spent time in the clearing, too. Maybe even lived there. Hammocks hung between half a dozen trees. Empty food cans rusted in a pile. The remains of an old campfire sat surrounded by cooking pans, food wrappers, and discarded cigarette packs. On the far side of the field sat a trash heap. Two men didn't make a mess this size.

Black hoses ran between the rows of plants into the woods beyond. Now that we had settled in our spot for a couple minutes, the odor hit me. The place smelled like an outhouse.

Queenie's body tensed, but she stayed silent. I leaned down and rubbed my cheek against the top of her head.

Gemma once tried growing a couple pot plants behind her garage. A gardening crew took care of their property and her parents never went behind that building. But none of the plants I'd seen before looked like this. Star-shaped clusters rose toward the sky, the glossy leaves reflecting back the sun's rays. I stared at the sheer size of the growing area and tried to calculate the number of trees someone had chopped down. This was no home patch. This was a huge commercial operation. Ben warned me, but I hadn't believed him.

Now I knew. We were in way over our heads.

Chapter Seven

The man farthest from us turned to work the opposite side of the row. I covered my mouth to keep from crying out. Queenie stood. I pulled her close with my other arm, hoping she would keep still. And quiet. I felt Ben turn to me, but didn't look at him. My gaze stayed fixed on the huge gun strapped across the back of the man on the hillside below.

A click sounded like a cannon in the quiet. To my horror, Ben snapped pictures with his cell phone. I wanted to shake him, make him stop, but didn't want to risk drawing the attention of the man with the gun. Finally, after several heart-stopping minutes, Ben shoved the phone into his pocket and tugged my arm. He crawled away from the pot farm. I followed, one hand pulling Queenie's collar, keeping her by my side while I silently cursed Ben for dragging us into this mess.

Ten yards below the crest, Ben unfolded a map. He made a couple marks on the colored sheet with a felt tip pen then started walking again. Queenie and I continued to follow. With each step I grew more furious. Eco Warrior? Like hell. This was stupidity times ten. But I kept my mouth shut. Making noise yelling at Ben wasn't going to get us somewhere safe. Queenie's dark eyes watched me. Her instincts about Ben had been right. I bent down to hug her before catching up with our reckless guide. Frequent checks of the woods behind failed to show anyone on our tail. Yet I still sensed a lurking threat. How far did we need to go before I felt safe? Before we actually were safe?

After we walked in silence for close to an hour, the woods started to look familiar. I didn't trust my eyes at first, but another ten minutes on, I was sure we were on one of the trails Queenie and I had explored together. The dog lifted her nose. I took that as a good sign, but waited. When I spied the windmill and log where I ate my first lunch after coming to Grandpa's, I sped up and grabbed Ben's arm. "Are you crazy? If you want to organize a suicide mission, that's fine. But the whole point of suicide is to kill yourself. Not other people."

Queenie growled her support.

Ben's gaze flicked to the dog. He tore his arm free then climbed over a downed tree, putting the hunk of wood between him and Queenie. "What? You're freaked out over the guns?"

Guns. Plural. There'd been more than one gun? My face burned hotter than before. "Yes. I'm freaked out about the guns. And about the huge pot field. That wasn't some itty-bitty operation. What did you drag me into?"

"First, I didn't drag you. You were bored and tagged along. You don't like what happened, next time you don't gotta come with."

I felt like he'd slapped me. I stepped back.

"Second, I told you what I planned to do. If you thought I was making up some story to impress you, that's your problem, not mine. Third, that's the first time I've seen armed guys in any of the fields. That's out of my control. You can either get over it, or we say goodbye right now."

He was right about warning me. I'd gone with him because I had nothing better to do and thought he was talking big. But his argument still seemed like a huge justification. Plus I didn't believe a single word he said about the guns, though I couldn't say why. I stared at Ben, looking for the truth, but his handsome face revealed no sorrow, no regret. That was answer enough.

"Then I guess it's goodbye." Queenie and I headed down the slope. I felt Ben's gaze on my back. Grandpa got it right: the guy was bad news.

Grandpa. What was I going to say to him? Should I tell him about the pot farm? About the men with the guns? If I didn't warn him, he might stumble across the field and wind up hurt. But Ben and I walked a long way before we found the farm. Grandpa probably wouldn't encounter the place by chance. Besides, if I told him, he would go ape shit. He already told me to stay away from the Wilder boys, and instead I went traipsing through the woods with one of them. Right into an armed encampment.

No way he would leave something like that out of his report to Dad. Probably for the best if I kept this whole afternoon to myself.

When Queenie and I reached the cabin, the dog lifted her muzzle and caught some phantom scent. She circled the perimeter of the clearing before trotting back to my side. I sank to my knees, grabbed her around the neck, and rubbed my face against her dark mask. "You smart, beautiful girl. Next time, I promise to listen."

Chapter Eight

When I woke the next morning, I heard the shower running downstairs. But the homey sound failed to wash away the lingering image of the armed men who stalked through my dreams. Was I a fool not to tell Grandpa about the pot field? After giving me a week off, the grizzly in my gut once again had his claws out.

I sat up, holding my stomach. No matter how I justified things, I'd kept mum about yesterday's adventure to avoid getting in trouble. Trouble that – if reported to Dad – would crush my hopes of going home before the end of my sentence. But, what could Grandpa do about the pot field? Other than call the cops – and maybe land on some drug lord's hit list?

In the kitchen, I checked the list of chores pinned to the wall. The first three items read: feed the chickens, gather eggs, harvest vegetables for breakfast. Grandpa planned to show me how to clean the coop on Thursday, so I didn't need to face that task for another four days. Still fretting, I stepped outside. The air was cool and smelled of pine sap as well as something funky. The strange odor sent my nerves humming. Skunk? I scanned the nearby trees for wild animals. Other than chirping birds, the woods seemed quiet.

I retrieved the feed bucket from the barn and lugged it across the clearing. At the door to the chicken run, I leaned against the wood frame and peered through the wire. No sign of the chickens. Yet. I pulled back the heavy bolt and stepped inside. A layer of pine shavings covered the ground, but mucky areas outnumbered the unsoiled ones. I tiptoed around the gross spots and tossed feed on top of the clean areas. Black, brown, and white birds hustled from the coop, clucking their excitement. I hadn't been sure how they would react to me taking their eggs, but, judging by the way they abandoned their nesting area, this promised to be easy.

One rust-brown hen stopped and stood in my shadow. She tilted her head and turned her beady eye my way. We stared at one another. This bird knew I was up to something. From her belligerent stance, I suspected I was more intimidated by her than she was by me. I gave her a wide berth. When she joined the other hens pecking the ground, I headed for the coop.

The building was a good foot taller than me and looked about the same size as my room at home – eight-feet square. The chickens had it pretty good. Granted, sixteen of them shared the space, where I had a room to myself, but they were a lot smaller than me. The moldy smell of the coop pushed me to breathe through my mouth. Maybe the coop-funk was what I caught a whiff of earlier.

Inside the nesting boxes, I found five eggs and slotted them into the carton Grandpa had left out. None of the chickens paid me any mind when I walked out with their eggs and latched the coop's door behind me. Did the absence of a rooster shut down their maternal instincts? One more question to file away for Grandpa.

For the next task, I collected a trowel and a pair of clippers from the barn. Queenie kept me company while I dug, but my thoughts kept returning to those men with the guns. After I uprooted a green onion and a garlic bulb, I went inside to make breakfast. Two mornings ago, Grandpa showed me how to work the stove, but the hulking piece of cast iron and chrome still looked like something straight out of an old Western.

I shoved a handful of kindling into the fire box, double-checked that the latch caught when I closed it, and made sure the ash pan wasn't overflowing. Once the skillet was heating, I rummaged inside a drawer until I found the tea infuser and filled it with dried mint. Then I set it inside an empty mug. When the kettle whistled, I poured hot water over the dried leaves. After the water turned greenish-brown, I filled a second mug with steaming water and dunked the infuser. Right in the middle of multi-tasking, I lost control of the omelet and it turned into scrambled eggs. "Dammit." I held my breath. The swoosh-thunk sound coming from behind the cabin told me Grandpa was out of earshot, chopping wood.

Stomach knotting like loose fishing line, I scooped all the eggs onto a single plate and called Grandpa to the table. After wiping off his boots and pulling out a chair, he looked at my empty place setting. "You're not eating?"

I shook my head and sat.

"You feeling punky?"

"No. I'm not hungry."

Grandpa looked at me for a moment then dove into his meal. "I'm heading out to Orland after breakfast. Gotta take care of some business. You all right to stay here all day on your own?"

"Sure. Queenie will be here, right?" Grandpa left me alone every afternoon. I didn't see how his being gone a few hours longer than usual made a difference.

"Yep." He chewed another bite before pointing at me with his fork. "Gonna turn you into a real chef by the time summer's over."

I picked at a loose thread on my shirt. "It was supposed to be an omelet."

He shrugged. "So?" Grandpa ran a piece of bread across his plate, wiping up the last traces of egg. "It was still damn tasty."

"Yeah, I bet every fine restaurant will want my recipe for not-an-omelet."

"They will if they got any sense. Next time you might want to add some cheese."

"I hate cheese."

He wiped a napkin across his mouth then sipped his tea. "You're tetchy as a polecat this morning."

"Tetchy as a polecat?" I pushed my chair back from the table.

"It's an expression."

"Uh-huh."

He frowned. "What's eating at you?"

"Nothing." Nothing except whether I should tell him about those armed men.

"Your cooking's better than you think. You're starting to put a little meat on those bones of yours." Grandpa carried the dishes and pans to the sink and started washing.

The grizzly in my gut hadn't roared like this since my first day at Grandpa's. For the last seven days, I'd eaten three meals a day. Something that hadn't happened in years. How had I not noticed?

I glanced at the clock. Not even 8 a.m. and half my chores completed. A weight settled behind my breast bone, but did nothing to squash the bear gnawing at my insides. Maybe I would relax if I burned off some steam. Hell, even Grandpa could tell something was bugging me. "Think I'll go for a run."

"Sounds like a good idea. Don't want to lose your spot on the cross country team."

I climbed to my loft and changed into shorts, a sleeveless T-shirt, and running shoes. Without my hiking boots, my feet felt lighter than they had in days.

When I told her to 'stay,' Queenie moaned, but settled in front of Grandpa's cabin. Even though no other traffic shared the road when Grandpa drove us in, if Queenie wound up hit by a car, I'd hate myself forever. "I'll be back soon, girl. You be good." I hugged her thick neck and breathed in her warm doggy scent before heading down the trail.

Thirty minutes later, I reached the T and turned right, toward the road that brought me to Grandpa's. Normally, I liked to jog the first five to ten minutes before ramping up the pace, but by the time I reached the road my muscles were loose from the walk and I started running. The dirt road had some give, but was less spongy and more uneven than the track at school. As I ran, several small birds flapped away from a roadside bush. I smiled. In spite of how strange this place still felt, something out in the wild actually feared me.

I ran on, waiting for the brain-cloud to set in. Running never failed to erase all worry, guilt, and anger. The familiar rush filled me and my thoughts grew quiet against the backbeat of feet pounding the dirt.

The brain-cloud surrounded me and I breathed in the scent of pine and dried grass. For forty glorious minutes as I ran along the road's edge, the grizzly in my gut hibernated. But all the hiking I had done the last couple days wasn't the same as running. When my muscles started to feel soggy, I didn't push it on the rough road. I turned and began walking back. Almost immediately, the weight resettled in my chest. Guilt, my frequent companion, never left me alone for long.

A rumbling noise came from behind. I shielded my eyes and stared down the road. In the distance, a truck kicked up dust. I started walking again, wiping sweat from my forehead. The engine's roar grew loud. A quick glance over my shoulder showed a rusted blue pickup approaching. I stepped into the roadside brush, covered my mouth and nose with my T-shirt, and then waited for the truck to drive by and the dust to settle. Five yards after it passed, the truck came to a stop. A boy stood up in the truck bed.

"Need a ride?" he called out.

The blond boy. Todd, Ben's brother. I uncovered my mouth. "No. Thanks though."

He climbed down, leaned his head in the passenger window, and spoke to the driver. The truck drove away. Todd turned and trotted over to me. "Mind if I walk with you?" He looked a lot friendlier today.

"No. But what would you've done if I said 'yes'? I mean, your ride did just take off."

"Guess I'd have to walk three steps behind you."

Todd was much taller than my glimpse of him in the woods had led me to believe. Not as tall as Grandpa, but darn close. He fell into step beside me.

After we walked in silence for a couple minutes, Todd cleared his throat. "I heard what happened yesterday. Ben never should've dragged you along."

"No kidding. But, to be fair, he didn't actually drag me. Guess I should've believed him when he told me what he was doing. Did he really call the cops on those guys?"

Todd shrugged and stared off into the shadowy woods. "Think so."

I let out a loud breath. "Okay." The cops knew. I wouldn't need to tell Grandpa. The heaviness lodged in my chest began to melt. I squinted up. The bad feeling wasn't the only thing melting. The sun had already cleared the trees, its rays warming the air on the unshaded road by about ten degrees. Good thing I got out early for my run.

"Yeah. Uh, look…" Todd kicked a pinecone into the brush. "This is kind of awkward, but you should know… It's better if you don't believe most of what my brother says. Don't get me wrong, Ben's a great guy. But not real honest." Todd peered at me from beneath floppy bangs, his cheeks red.

Interesting. Even Todd thought Ben was a liar? "Thanks for the warning, but I don't see me doing much of anything with him in the future. Turns out his idea of fun doesn't match up with mine."

Todd nodded then smiled.

Wow. The smile upped his Cuteness Quotient by a good twenty percent. Ben had some competition in the handsome department.

He turned and walked backwards, facing me. "At least Ben didn't give you the usual story."

For the first time, I noticed how broad the guy's shoulders were. I tried not to stare. Or drool. "What do you mean?"

"You won't believe this, but whenever he meets a girl he likes, Ben tells her he's part-Indian."

Ben liked me? I doubted his attraction outlasted our adventure, but maybe it would rub off on his brother. "He's not?"

"Nah. His mom's no more Indian than mine. He says girls like him better when he tells them that." Todd laughed. "He even has this stupid story about how he went on a vision quest and has a spirit guide. He says girls eat that stuff up." He spun around, walking beside me again.

At least Ben didn't think I was stupid enough to trot out the vision quest story, though he pegged me as dumb enough to buy the spirit guide garbage. Not much to brag about. "He does that a lot?"

"Oh yeah. I think my brother's dated every girl between here and Clovis."

Though I didn't know how far away Clovis was, Todd's derisive tone told me enough. Good thing Queenie warned me off the guy. Okay, not just Queenie. I had to give Ben some of the credit – he was the one who acted like a jerk. I wondered if Todd got around as much as his brother. No good way to ask.

"So, other than your adventure with my jackass brother, how do you like your summer so far?"

Movement above drew my attention. A large bird soared overhead. I watched it roost near the top of a pine. "Better than I expected. Things are different from home. Way different. Even though it's pretty, I think I'd go crazy if I lived here all the time. Trees everywhere. It's like, you can't see past them." Todd looked surprised. Maybe I should cut the city girl stuff and get him talking. "And what about places to hang out? Meet up? I mean, where do you go to school?"

"I don't." Todd smiled. "Graduated in May. But there's a bus that picks up kids and drives them to nearby towns."

"How far do they have to go?"

"The high school's about a ninety minute ride. That's the farthest. But me and Ben didn't do any of that. We got homeschooled by Dad."

"Really? Seems like a lot of work. Especially if your dad's running a farm."

A cloud of gnats descended on the road. Todd waved his arms to drive them away. The tiny black pests scattered. "The farm's why he did it. He wanted us home to help out. Scheduled our studies around the work day. Wasn't a bad deal. We worked a few hours, studied a few hours. Back and forth like that. Nice mix. But still tough. Dad didn't let us slack off."

Long hours working on a farm. That explained the well-defined muscles in Todd's arms. I told myself not to stare. "You never went to public school?"

"Did when I was little. I lived with my mom then. Used to stay with her during the school year and with Dad in the summer. I moved here full time when I was twelve."

Something in his tone kept me from asking why he made that change.

Sweat ran down the bridge of my nose. The day was turning into a scorcher. I wiped my forearm across my face. It would feel good to get back inside the shady woods.

"What happened to you?" Todd's eyes widened.

"What do you mean?"

"Your arm." He pointed at the shiny pink flesh that ran from my wrist to my elbow.

"Got burned." My stomach twisted. My deformity. My Mark of Cain. Dressed in my usual running clothes, I hadn't thought to hide the scar. I clamped my arm against my side.

"When?"

My throat tightened, but I forced out the words. "Long time ago. Almost eight years now."

"How'd it happen?" Todd looked curious and concerned, but not grossed out.

I glanced at my damaged skin. The sight still brought back the smell of burning hair and charred flesh. "I'd rather not talk about it."

"Sure." He picked up a broken branch, swung it in an arc. "So, you said you like this place better than you thought you would. Anything in particular?"

I took a deep breath, locked down the memories of our house on fire, and searched for an answer. The most honest one would be: talking and walking with you. But I had other – less embarrassing – truths I could share. "I caught a fish. A trout. That was pretty cool. And I love Queenie."

"Your gramps has got one smart dog."

"Yeah. She's amazing. I never hung out with a German shepherd before. Or any dogs, really. I know, pretty wimpy. And very city. I had no idea what I was missing. She's so clever. And sweet." For the first time it hit me. Leaving here might not be an easy thing to do. Huh. I gave myself a mental shake. "But, the biggest surprise?"

"Yeah?"

"How much I like working around Grandpa's place. No way I'm going to tell him that. But it feels pretty good learning how to tend the vegetable patch, care for the chickens. Become more self-sufficient. Stuff like that, you know?"

Something rustled in the bushes roadside, reminding me this was my first walk without Queenie. "What's that?"

Todd shrugged. "Might be a squirrel or a bird. Lots of them hunt around in the underbrush. Scrounging for food. Or a lizard or a snake."

I moved toward the center of the road.

"Whatever it is, it's nothing to worry about." Todd smiled again. "Nothing too deadly could hide in a bush that size."

"Right." The plant stood six inches tall, max. "It'll probably take me a while to get used to all the wildlife out here."

He pointed to a narrow footpath through the trees at the side of the road. "Better peel off here. Dad gets pissed if me or Ben cut across your gramps' land. And somehow, he always knows when we do. This trail home is outside the property line."

I halted, looking at his lips and strong jaw before dropping my gaze to his scuffed hiking boots. "Thanks for the company."

"Sure. Fun talking to you. Here." Todd held out the branch he had picked up. "When you're cutting through the brush, tap the ground first with this or bat the leaves and limbs. If any critters are hiding, they'll scatter."

"Thanks." His eyes were the same shade as Queenie's. Eyes a person could trust.

"No problem. Remember, they're more scared of you than you are of them."

"I wouldn't bet on that."

He smiled again then turned and slipped into the deep green shadows of the forest.

Wow. Hidden treasure in the Mendo. Unlike Ben, I got the feeling Todd had no idea what a hottie he was. Plus he was nice. Kind even. Weird that his dad didn't want him crossing Grandpa's land, but no weirder than Dad sending me here for the summer.

Chapter Nine

After I finished my chores the next morning, Grandpa told me to dress in jeans and a long-sleeved shirt. Guess he hadn't noticed long sleeves were my usual attire. When I climbed down the ladder he handed me an orange ball cap and vest. "Put these on. We're going hunting."

Hunting? I looked up at the now-familiar deer heads on the wall. Right. Out here, animals were food. I slipped an icy hand through the vest's sleeve.

Queenie scampered to the door. "Stay," Grandpa said.

The dog whined, staring at him with big, pathetic eyes.

I crouched next to her. "You're a smart girl, aren't you?" Again, the look on her face said she understood. I gave her forehead a kiss then stood.

"You can come next time." Grandpa rubbed the dark saddle of fur along her back. Queenie trotted outside and circled twice before settling in the shade. Grandpa pulled on his own orange hat, picked up the shotgun, and strode toward the tree line.

This was my first hike with Grandpa. It felt strange. His long legs made matching his pace challenging, but that wasn't what bugged me. Something else was off. Something besides the thought of killing Thumper or Bambi. Ten minutes in, the answer came. I missed the sound of Queenie's steady breath along with her paws padding through the pine needles. The woods seemed bigger and more foreign without her by my side.

Grandpa hiked deep into the forest. Soon, branches blocked the sun, keeping the air cool. At a clearing I'd not come across before, he stopped and held out the shotgun. "Now watch carefully." He showed me two shells. "This is how you load her. This here's a side-by-side. I also got an over-under back home, but that's a ten-gauge. This one's a sixteen. Less of a kick. We're gonna use a number six shot shell. We could do seven-and-a-half, but for your first time out, we'll try the larger shot. We don't want to go any bigger than a six or the meat'll get torn to pieces."

"What're we hunting?"

"Rabbit. You can hunt blacktail, whitetail, and jackrabbit year 'round with a shotgun or a pistol. Most everything else – except for fish – is off the table during summer. Unless you're a bow hunter." He handed me the shotgun. "I'm warning you, rabbits move like long-eared rockets. That's why we need a wide and heavy pattern to put one down. They're tough to see, too. Look for the eye. That'll reflect the light. Easier to spot than the rest of the critter. When you see one, you aim and shoot. Okay?"

"Okay." Though I'd eaten at least five meals that featured Thumper over the last ten days, I wondered if I'd have the stomach to actually shoot a rabbit. My arm sagged under the weight of the gun. If rabbits were as fast as Grandpa said, maybe I wouldn't be able to lift the sixteen-gauge in time to get off a shot.

"We're gonna walk ten paces, then stop. We'll wait for at least a minute before we move again. Look in the brush piles, around shrubs, snags, fallen tree tops. Ready?"

"Yeah."

"You got the gun, you're in the lead."

I took ten long strides across the crunchy pine needles, stopped, raised the gun, and stared into the brush. All I saw were leaves, twigs, and dirt. After what felt like a minute, I walked forward again. The next time I stopped, a rustle came from nearby. I strained to see something, anything. Instead I saw more twigs, leaves, and dirt. About forty minutes later, I spotted my first rabbit, took a deep breath, pulled the trigger, and staggered back as the weapon roared. The rabbit raced away, still healthy as a horse. "Holy f—" I snapped my mouth shut and turned in time to catch Grandpa's scowl. "Frijole."

He cocked an eyebrow. "Holy frijole?"

"It's an expression."

"Better be."

Time to change the subject. I pointed to the spot where the rabbit had crouched moments earlier. "We could use that guy on our track team at school."

"Let's keep focused on spotting game."

In spite of what Grandpa said about the sixteen-gauge, the shotgun gave a mean kick. But, after my first shot, I managed to curb the impulse to swear each time the stock slammed against me. When we got back to the cabin, my shoulder felt like one enormous bruise. I hadn't hit a single rabbit, but Grandpa bagged three. Queenie trotted over to us.

"Sunrise and sunset are the best times to scout rabbits." Grandpa handed me the game bag then bent to ruffle the fur behind Queenie's ears. He straightened and opened the front door. "Next time we'll get an earlier start. I thought if we went a little later your first time, the better lighting might help you spot the critters."

"Not so you'd notice."

"You managed to shoot the gun six times and not fall on your keister. Holy frijole." He smirked at me as he took the game bag from my hand. "You'll get better with practice."

After giving Queenie a hug, I washed up then joined Grandpa at the oilcloth-covered table.

He set one of the rabbits on the cutting board in front of him. "You need a sharp blade and a light touch to skin a rabbit."

The smell of blood and meat spread with his first cut. I covered my nose, but stayed put, watching Grandpa's deft hands. Within a couple minutes, I went from grossed out to fascinated. "Weird. They're easier to look at once the skin's peeled away."

"That's 'cause they stop looking like bunnies once the fur's gone. Now they look like food."

I continued to watch while Grandpa cleaned and prepared the rabbits for cooking.

"You're not too squeamish. That's good."

"We having Thumper stew tonight?"

Grandpa chuckled. "Nah. Grilled Thumper." He stood and tucked the cleaned rabbits in the icebox before going to wash up.

Queenie trotted to the cabin door and growled.

I stared at the dog, then at the curtained window. Something outside was bugging Queenie.

Grandpa hurried from the bathroom and peered between the curtains before turning to the dog. "Hush."

Queenie stood at alert, but made no sound.

Huh. "That's how you get her to be quiet?"

Grandpa glanced at me. "Yep. Don't want to tell her 'no' or 'stop that.' You want her to know she's doing the right thing sounding an alarm. I taught her that 'hush' means 'good girl, be quiet now.'"

"Is something out there?"

"Someone." Grandpa opened the door and waved. "Give me a minute," he called out then turned back to me. "I need you to take off for a while."

Weird. Grandpa made sure I got out for some exercise every day, but he never sent me away for any other reason. "Why?"

"Because I said so. Remember, on my land, in my home, you're not living in a democracy."

My shoulder ached from shooting and I didn't feel like another hike. What if I dug in my heels and said 'no'? What would he do? Besides rat me out to Dad? The unyielding expression on Grandpa's face said that, unlike me, he was a fighter. I sighed. "How long?"

"Give me an hour."

I climbed to the loft and grabbed the belt with the canteen and knife. This king and commander rule of Grandpa's sucked. But if I wanted to get sent home early, I needed to swallow my resentment. The canteen felt at least half-full so I didn't stop to top it off after climbing back down. "Come on, Queenie." The dog and I stepped outside.

An older woman sat behind the wheel of a battered Jeep. She nodded, her expression stern.

Queenie and I walked into the woods. At the point where the trees began to grow thick, I turned, hid behind one of the broader trunks, and peered back.

The woman strode across the packed dirt to the cabin door. Grandpa ushered her inside. The kitchen door closed.

I patted Queenie's side. "Did Grandpa just kick us out for a booty call?" The dog looked as put out as I felt. "Come on."

Chapter Ten

Over the next week, Grandpa and I seemed to find our rhythm, settling into a routine. Fishing in the morning every two or three days, with me alternating between forty-five and ninety minute runs on the days we didn't fish. My list of daily chores grew, but I didn't mind – the tasks filled the time. I learned how to clean the chicken run and coop, and became comfortable around the hens. I shot and skinned my first rabbit and took over the daily jobs of draining the drip tray for the icebox and emptying the stove's ash pan. Grandpa showed me how to collect and dry mint for tea, and plant rows of butternut squash, sweet corn, and mustard greens.

Most afternoons, Grandpa disappeared with his truck for an hour or two. Queenie and I used that time to head out for a hike but always kept to the road or Grandpa's land. Since I wasn't exactly sure about the location of the pot farm Ben had led me to, I wanted to stay on safe ground – in case the cops hadn't arrested the armed men yet. In hopes of making my iPod battery last out the summer, I rationed my music to fifteen minutes a day. For entertainment, I focused on the books I'd gotten from the general store's lending library. In the first week-and-a-half, I finished off four mysteries – probably more books than I'd voluntarily read in the previous five months. Reading by the flickering light of a Coleman lantern still sent a chill through my veins, but I figured that would pass in time.

A week after he joined me on the walk back from my run, I came across Todd in the woods. As far as I was concerned, if I never saw Ben again, that was fine. But, I warmed at the sight of this Wilder brother.

Queenie ran up to him, tail wagging. If Queenie thought Todd was okay that was good enough for me. Todd's chocolate brown eyes looked into mine. I gulped, turned away, and pretended my canteen needed adjusting. Once the fire warming my face started to cool, I met his gaze. "Aren't you worried your dad will find out you were in Grandpa's woods?"

"Dad took off early this morning." Todd gave me a broad smile. "And I spotted your gramps driving toward the highway. Figured it was safe to do a little trespassing and come see you." He clambered down the hill to my side.

A flutter ran through my stomach. Todd wasn't here by chance. "Grandpa's used to living alone. I'm guessing he needs some time to himself. It's got to be weird for him always having someone around."

Todd opened his mouth as if he was going to speak. Instead he nodded and pushed his wheat-colored hair off his forehead. We paralleled the slope in silence. Midway to the peak, he stopped and faced me. "Why are you here? Not that I'm complaining. I mean, I think it's great. But, a week or two in the Mendo is the limit for most visitors. This isn't the kind of place city folk usually send their kids for the summer."

Todd thought it 'great' I was here? Double wow. I bent to ruffle Queenie's fur. She gave me an encouraging glance before dashing off to investigate a nearby tree trunk. "Good point."

"So, why are you here?"

"For punishment."

"For the town?" Confusion flashed across his face.

"What? Oh. The town name. No, I mean, I was sent here as a punishment."

"Geez. I know we're rustic, but making you live here's a way to punish you?"

I shook my head. "Dad wanted me away from my friends. He thinks they're a bad influence."

"Don't let him talk to your gramps about me. No way he'll let us hang out."

"Believe me, I'm not saying a word about this to Grandpa. He's already warned me off you and Ben a couple times." I picked up a woody kernel and held it out to him.

"That's an acorn cap."

"Huh." I looked up at the towering tree beside me. "Guess that means this is an oak."

Todd touched his index finger to his nose. "Got it in one."

I revised my opinion: not simply a nice guy, a good guy. "You never said. Why doesn't your Dad want you to come onto Grandpa's land?"

"It's not only me. He doesn't want Ben doing it either." He picked up a pinecone, tossed it in the air twice, and then threw it across the clearing into the trees.

"Why?"

"My dad and your gramps had a big fight. Even though Dad's like twenty years younger, the two of them used to pal around. I think they started hanging out, hunting and fishing, after your dad went off to college."

I grabbed Todd's arm. "What?"

A small crease formed between his eyes. "My dad and your dad were buds."

My mouth dropped open. "Dad lived here?"

"Where'd you think he grew up?"

"In a small town in northern California." I released Todd's arm and rubbed the ache starting along my forehead. "That's what he always says."

"Well." Todd spread his arms wide as if to say 'there you have it.'

"I pictured someplace suburban. Not a cabin with no electricity." How had a computer geek like Dad survived here?

"Well, this is where he grew up. My dad's got a bunch of pictures of them together."

Dad knew exactly what kind of place he had sent me to for the summer. Wow. "He never really talks about his childhood. At least not with me. Guess I didn't give it much thought." I chewed my lower lip. "So, Grandpa and your dad used to be friends?"

"Yeah, but after their fight, things changed." Todd grabbed another pinecone. The veins on the back of his hand bulged.

Queenie flushed a squirrel from the brush and gave chase. "Come back, girl." The dog trotted to my side looking pleased. "Every day's a good day for you, right?" I crouched and gave her a hug then continued walking. I turned to Todd. "What'd they fight about?"

Todd shrugged. "I got a pretty good idea, but don't know anything for sure." He dropped the pinecone, climbed over a large log, and held out his hand. When I safely reached the ground on the other side, he didn't let go. "Why does your dad think your friends are bad news?"

The warmth of Todd's palm against mine held my attention. It took a moment to process his question. "Probably because they are."

He cocked his head. "Not the answer I expected."

"If you'd asked me about them two weeks ago, I might've said something different." Two weeks ago I thought I wanted Scott. Two weeks ago I would've done most anything to earn Gemma's approval. Now things weren't so clear. My heart was hopscotching all over the place at the touch of Todd's hand. "Being here, so far removed from everything … I'm looking at stuff in a different way."

We walked with Queenie for close to an hour before Todd had to head for home. When I reached our cabin, I stared at it with fresh eyes. Dad grew up here, in this building. In this clearing. Why didn't he tell me? Did Dad not want me to know this was his home? Why?

I couldn't come right out and ask Grandpa why nobody had told me. He might ask how I found out. Since I wasn't supposed to talk to Todd, that created a problem. After starting the kettle, I noticed the tea jar was empty. I pushed a section of the kitchen's wood paneling. Invisible from the outside, the drying cupboard door swung open, revealing a tall but shallow gap. The smell of mint, oregano, and thyme drifted into the kitchen. Bouquets hung from the ceiling, but in the dim light it was impossible to tell one bunch from another by sight. At least for me. I stepped into the cabinet and sniffed my way toward the mint, unhooked one bundle's twine loop, and stepped back into the kitchen.

While setting the table, I came up with a way to question Grandpa about Dad growing up here – without making him suspicious. I waited until dinner was nearly over and Grandpa stabbed at one of his few carrot slices left on his plate.

"Did you build this place?" I pointed my fork at the cabin wall.

"Yep."

"How long ago?"

He took a sip of tea before leaning back in his chair. "Well, let's see… Must be forty – no forty-five – years ago now."

"Did Dad grow up here?"

"Of course. Where'd you think he lived?"

I shrugged. "He never mentioned growing up in the woods. In a cabin. Why didn't he tell me?"

"Gotta ask him about that." Grandpa's chair squeaked against the wood floor as he pushed back from the table and stood. "You're on dish detail."

I stared at the lone carrot slice on his plate. Grandpa never left food behind. When he finished eating, it usually looked like his dish had already been washed. Had my prying upset him? Or was he bugged by the fact Dad never told me about his childhood in the Mendo?

Later that night, settled in my loft, it hit me. The loft had been Dad's room as a kid. I studied the wood planks and logs for some sign of him, but found no clues to his past.

* * * *

The next day – and each one after – whenever I ran along the road or tramped through the woods with Queenie, I found myself keeping an eye out for Todd. I knew better than to whisper a word of our growing friendship to Grandpa.

We met again in the woods three days later. My heartbeat zoomed, but it felt natural when Todd wrapped his hand around mine as we walked.

"Ever been to the Knob?" he said.

"Uh-uh. What's that?"

"A bare hilltop. One of the few places you can look down on the forest. It's about a twenty minute walk from here. Want to see?"

Grandpa had taken off after we got back from fishing that morning. He wouldn't expect me home for hours. "Sure."

The slope grew steep and the number of trees started to thin. For being so high up, the dirt path was well-trod. When we reached the crest of the hill I rested my hands on my hips and stared. Green treetops stretched to the horizon.

Todd pointed at the land below. "See that brown squiggle weaving through the woods?"

I followed where his finger directed, only half-listening as his arm brushed against my shoulder. "Yeah."

"That's the road to the highway."

"Looks so small from here."

Todd took my left hand and held it. "That's why I like coming here. Being up above everything, it kind of puts things in perspective." He squeezed my hand then led me to a downed tree.

Queenie trotted up to me and gave me her big-eyed stare. "It's okay, girl. Go play." The dog bolted into the bushes, scattering several small birds. I sat beside Todd, my heartbeat speeding up again. He brushed a strand of hair from my cheek, his fingers seeming to leave an electric trail where they touched. When he raised my hand to his lips and kissed my palm, a tremor ran through me.

He released my hand and cocked his head. "I keep thinking about what you told me the other day. About your friends. Thinking how lucky I am you're here. How happy I am that your friends are bad news. Your gramps warned you off me, so I gotta ask – is that why you're hanging out with me? You always drawn to the bad crowd?"

He leaned down toward me. When his lips touched mine, their heat surprised me. He smelled of pine and sage, tasted of salt and mint. His arms wrapped around me and I sank against him. It wasn't my first kiss

– not by a long shot – but I was still glad I was sitting down for it; my legs felt as mushy as my brain. After a few minutes we broke apart, my heart drumming like a woodpecker on pine. I stared at his now-flushed face and smiled. "My summer in Punishment is going to be a lot better than I thought."

"Mine, too," he said. "But that's not an answer."

I remembered how Gemma dared me to say "Hi" to the cutest guy getting high under the school bleachers. How Scott and I dated off and on for the next few months. And how I'd scrambled for his – and Gemma's – approval. Todd's strong hand wrapped around mine, bringing me back to his question. I chewed my lower lip. Even though his tone had been teasing, his eyes looked serious. "I wasn't until I turned fifteen."

"You're only fifteen?" His eyes widened and he leaned back.

"No, sixteen. Almost seventeen. My birthday's in six weeks." I shook my head. "I turned fifteen the summer before I started high school."

"Oh."

A huge sigh escaped me. "My sister, MJ, died when she was fifteen. I was nine. When I turned fifteen, I kind of weirded out. Knowing I'd soon be older than my older sister ever lived to be."

"I'm sorry. I didn't mean to make you talk about…" Todd's brow creased. "I mean, if you don't want…"

I shook my head again. "It's okay. Well, no. It's far from okay. But I like talking about her. I don't get to very often. My new friends never knew MJ. Dad gets upset whenever I talk about her. At least he used to. The last time I tried to talk to him about her was a year ago – when he decided we needed to move again."

Todd's hand squeezed mine. "You can tell me."

A boulder grew inside my throat. I tried to swallow it away. "She was pretty." My voice came out sounding half-strangled. I closed my eyes. "And funny. She used to make me laugh so hard my stomach muscles cramped. I wanted to be just like her. But… after Mom left, MJ changed." I sat up straight, met Todd's gaze. "When I turned fifteen, I began staying out late. Getting in trouble. Started hanging with a new group. Kind of like MJ did before she died.

"That's when Dad moved us again." I shook my head. "New town, new school. I managed to make some new friends. The ones Dad doesn't like."

"How'd MJ die?"

"Our house burned down."

Todd lifted my right arm and pushed my sleeve to my elbow so the long pink scar showed. "Is that when you got burned?"

"Yeah."

He traced his fingertip along my ruined skin. "Does it hurt?"

"No. I can't actually feel what you're doing."

"You can't?" He pulled his hand away.

"Third degree burn. Destroyed the nerve cells. The doctor said the feeling might return in time. Hasn't so far. If you push down on the scar, I'll feel the pressure. But nothing on the surface."

"I'm sorry."

"Me too." But not about the burn.

Chapter Eleven

When Queenie and I returned from our midday hike, Grandpa's truck was still gone. I stood in the middle of the cabin, making a slow circle, eyeing the dead deer heads. So this was what free time felt like in the Mendo. No TV, no internet, no music, no phone. Sheesh. Creepy to the max.

I checked the chore list posted in the kitchen then went out to weed the garden and harvest greens for dinner. Though the cabin's fireplace wasn't used during the summer, wood smoke from the stove lingered in the air of the clearing, along with pine and the tang of tomato vine. After fifteen minutes of pulling out the deep-rooted goose grass, I lugged my supplies to the second row of vegetables. A memory tugged at me: Mom bent over the row of rosebushes in our backyard, deadheading the spent blooms. Browning rose petals drifted to the ground as she reached between branches and snipped. For weeks after she left us, I'd stared out my window at those bushes, expecting her to come out of the garage at any moment, wearing her gardening hat and gloves. One afternoon, Dad stormed into my bedroom, grabbed my arm, and pulled me away from the window. Tears filled my eyes, but I bit back a yelp of pain. Face red, he shook me and yelled, "Stop staring out the damn window."

He let go. Feeling like I might throw up, I'd stepped back. Maybe if I explained he'd understand how important this was. I wiped my nose and said, "I'm waiting for Mom."

"Get it through your head, she's never coming back." He stalked out of my room and slammed the door.

The next morning when I looked out my window, the rose bushes had been cut down to stumps.

* * * *

By the time the old gray truck bumped across the clearing, I'd dried my face and moved on to the next row of plants. When Grandpa climbed down, Queenie ran to him. He rubbed her coat then strode toward the cabin. His long shadow darkened the ground around me. "Too bad Queenie can't help you weed. But if you want a tunnel dug to China, she's the girl for the job." The dog swished her tail as if in agreement. He ruffled her fur and turned away.

The front door bounced shut behind him. Queenie trotted to the door, sniffed the air, and returned to me. "That's right, girl. You keep on helping me." She settled in a strip of shade cast by one of the pines edging the clearing.

Forty minutes later, I straightened, grimy and tired. Half the bed was weed-free; I'd tackle the rest another day. I harvested greens for dinner and dug up a half dozen carrots. Then I led Queenie inside.

Grandpa sat at the kitchen table, an open tackle box in front of him. A length of monofilament line plus bits of hair and fur, and an array of feathers and hooks lay atop the oilcloth.

Queenie circled before settling at his feet, her tail thumping the floorboards. At the sink, I rinsed my face and hands then washed dirt from the Swiss chard. "What's all that stuff?" I turned and nodded at the odds and ends covering the kitchen table.

Grandpa peered over the silver frames of his glasses. "I make a little extra money selling lures in town and over in Orland and Elk Creek." His knobby fingers moved with surprising speed, connecting the transparent line with a few folded over hairs. The end result looked like a bug.

"Wow. Can you show me how to do that?"

"Sure thing. Not today though. I promised Dennis two dozen flies by tomorrow. When I get these done, want to run to town with me?"

"Yeah." I set the dripping chard in the dish drainer then climbed to my loft, grabbed clean clothes, and headed for the shower. This late in the day, the water from the overhead tank was on the plus side of warm. Once under the spray, I scrubbed at the dirt until the rest of me turned as pink as my burn scar. I stared at the damaged skin, the sound of crackling flames dancing in my head. That night had changed everything. I tilted my face toward the showerhead, but the drumming water didn't wash away the vision of MJ's face as she yelled into the phone.

"I've got plans. I can't stay home and babysit." Her mouth had twisted in a frown while Dad said something on the other end of the call. "You can't make me." MJ yanked her hair, listening again. "This is so unfair." She slammed down the receiver, glared at me. "His flight got held up. Dad won't get home until midnight."

After our mom left us the year before, MJ's temper and mood swings had grown. Always volatile, seeing her funny side had become rare. Not wanting to make her angrier, I nodded.

MJ stormed to her room. At the doorway, she turned and yelled, "You can make your own damn dinner, Nicki. I don't want you bothering me." The door slammed behind her.

Those were the last words my sister spoke to me.

* * * *

85

When I stepped out of the bathroom, dressed in clean shorts and a long-sleeve T-shirt, Grandpa looked ready to head to town. I climbed up to the loft to collect my cell phone, the borrowed books I'd finished, and a sweatshirt. Though I felt no strong urge to talk to Gemma, after I called Dad, I might text her.

Queenie settled between us in the cab, tongue lolling, ready to roll. By now, the ride into Punishment was familiar. "How many miles is it from your place to town?"

"About eight. The rough road makes the drive seem longer."

"Still think you should consider paving it."

"The pits and bumps keep out the riffraff. You get to be my age, you'll start to value your privacy a bit more."

I rolled my eyes and wrapped one arm around Queenie. Adults always thought you were going to turn into copies of them when you got old. Like that was going to happen. Besides, from what I saw in the forest with Ben, the riffraff had already arrived.

When we got to town, Grandpa told Queenie to stay in the truck bed. Inside the general store, he headed toward the back counter where the owner stood. After putting my books in the cardboard box labeled 'book return', I climbed the rickety stairs to the roof.

I settled cross-legged in the red square and turned on my phone. Four rings then Dad's work line shunted me to voicemail. This was becoming a pattern; I hadn't reached Dad once since coming to Punishment. Not that we talked much when I was home. Was he avoiding my calls? My stomach twisted, but I did my best to sound upbeat. "Hey. It's me. Thought you'd want to know I survived my first two-and-a-half weeks with Grandpa.

Not only did I muck out the chicken coop, I gutted a bunny and a couple fish, too. Guess it's a good thing I didn't get a manicure before I came. I know you can't call back, so I'll try again the next time we're in town." I disconnected then chewed my lower lip. I'd been going for flip, but suspected I came off sounding whiney. "Great. He'll love that."

I scrolled to Gemma's number. After our crappy phone call two weeks ago, what did I want to say to her? Something casual. Maybe ask what she was up to?

The door to the roof creaked open. A huge slab of a man squinted in the sunlight before walking my way. "Get up." He loomed over me.

"What?"

"I need to make a call. Get a move on."

The man's deep voice sounded like one of Queenie's growls, and his blue eyes stared cold as river water. He was not someone to sass. I got up and stepped out of the painted square.

"What're you doing still standing there? You stupid?" He leaned in close, his hot breath touching my ear. "Get off the Goddamn roof before I throw you off."

Heart racing, I ran to the door and banged my way down the two flights of metal stairs. When I reached solid ground, I realized I had my cell clasped in a death grip. I tried to jam the phone into my pocket, but my hand shook too hard.

"You're pale as goose down. What's wrong?" Grandpa stood a couple feet away.

I wrapped my arms across my chest, trying to stop the shaking. "Some guy told me to get off the roof. Or he'd throw me off."

Grandpa grimaced as he rushed past me and charged up the stairs. The metal rattled and shook under his weight, but he didn't stop. I chewed my lip then trotted after him. At the first landing, the vibration of more feet behind me started the whole structure trembling. I turned. Todd ran up to me.

"What're you doing? Grandpa's on the roof. You want him to see you with me?"

"No. But I think my dad's up there, too. I don't know what he'll do when he sees your gramps."

"Oh." The scary man was Todd's dad? "Right." I jogged up the last section of stairs, pushed the door open, and dashed onto the flat roof. Grandpa and Mr. Wilder stood a foot apart. They reminded me of the bull elephant seals Dad once took me to the coast to see – rearing back, ready to attack. Both men stood over six feet, but Mr. Wilder was at least twenty years younger than Grandpa. If they fought, Grandpa wasn't going to win.

"You ever threaten my granddaughter again, I'll skin you alive." Grandpa's voice roared across the rooftop.

"You and your little girls. If you're so damn worried about them, you might want to stop pissing folks off."

Todd closed the gap between us and gripped my hand.

Grandpa's fists stayed at his side, but he stepped forward. Only an inch separated the two men's chests. "The world don't revolve around you, Bill. Other people matter, too. Why you can't take your head outta your ass and see that—"

"I got a business to run. I don't need your brand of trouble."

"Right. Too busy greasing the wheels to lend anyone else a hand." Grandpa seemed to realize they weren't alone. He turned and stared. "What the hell do you think you're doing?"

"Uh…" I looked at Todd. His face showed the surprise I felt at Grandpa aiming his rage our way.

"Take your hands off my granddaughter." Grandpa's face went from pink to red.

Todd let go of my hand.

"What's wrong with you, boy? We don't mix with this nut job or anyone dumb enough to be related to him." Four quick strides and Mr. Wilder grabbed Todd's shoulder, yanking him away from my side.

Grandpa shook his head at me before returning his glare to Mr. Wilder. "You need to reconsider your position on the matter."

"You want me to let your girl spend time with my son?"

"Hell no. That's not the position I'm talking about."

"Just remember, Mr. High-and-Mighty, with one phone call I could bring your whole world crashing down. Think about that. Come on." Mr. Wilder dragged Todd through the rooftop door.

Todd managed to shoot me a sheepish glance before his dad blocked him from sight.

Grandpa turned on me. "Didn't I tell you to stay away from that boy?"

"I… Yeah. He saw you run up the stairs. He knew his dad was up here. That's all."

"Then why were you holding that punk's hand?"

My face felt on fire. "I don't know. You guys looked kind of scary."

"Don't do it again. I'm not kidding around. You stay away from those Wilders."

I bit back a retort. I'd done everything he asked – learned to hunt, fish, and cook. Hell, I took care of the chickens and the garden. Why couldn't I have one friend? One person to hang out with this summer? I stomped down the metal stairs, but kept my mouth shut. Whatever I said to Grandpa would get back to Dad.

When we reached the street, there was no sign of Todd or Mr. Wilder. Only Grandpa's truck and a sheriff's department SUV sat alongside the road. The dark-haired deputy I met my first time in town stood in the doorway of the gas station office, staring at Grandpa. Even from a distance, the look in his eyes creeped me out.

"Get in the truck."

Queenie jumped from the bed and ran around to the passenger side. I opened the door and she hopped in. We pulled onto the road, the breeze sanding the windshield with loose grains of dirt. Above, the pines rustled. Did the noise of their shuddering boughs mask the sound of the Wilders driving away?

Grandpa gave an occasional huff as he drove and, beneath Queenie's happy panting, a thick silence filled the truck's cab. When we pulled into the barn, I jumped out. Queenie made a pit stop at one of the pine trees and I strode to the cabin's front door. But once Grandpa joined me inside the wood-paneled kitchen, I faced the prospect of more angry silence. How different life was without a room to march off to, without a door to slam.

While I burned up some of my bad mood by scrubbing dirt from the carrots and chopping them for dinner, I replayed the argument between Grandpa and Mr. Wilder. What did Mr. Wilder mean when he said he could bring Grandpa's world down with one phone call? And what was that crack about Grandpa and his little girls?

Chapter Twelve

When I climbed from the loft the next morning, Grandpa no longer huffed each time he looked at me. My anger had fizzled sometime during the night, and I realized I could keep meeting Todd – as long as Grandpa didn't find out.

After breakfast, we loaded our gear. Grandpa pulled on his stinky vest and drove us to Rattlesnake River. Queenie wedged herself against me, getting her snout as close to the open window as possible without climbing into my lap. The trip seemed faster this time, maybe because, with six visits to the river under my belt, I now recognized landmarks like Half-burnt Tree and Cracked Boulder.

Grandpa parked, and while I wrestled on my hip boots, Queenie explored the riverbank. By the time I carried my fishing pole to the river's edge, Queenie had settled in the shade a few feet from the rushing water. A sweet trill mixed with the sound of splashing the water, then a chunky gray bird winged by. Queenie lifted her head, but stayed put under the trees.

Walking into the river wearing boots felt worlds better than trying it barefoot. The lug soles gave decent traction and, without the icy current burning my skin, I managed to wade thigh-deep. Down river from Grandpa, I positioned my feet the way he'd taught me, my right foot back, braced against the muddy river bottom. I started casting. With each try, the fly landed closer to my target.

"Looking good. You're no longer thrashing around like a badger in a bag."

I smiled then faced the water again. My next cast flew true, landing upriver, dead center. As soon as the fly began traveling with the current, a fish struck. Remembering Grandpa's lesson, I raised the rod tip. The fish ran, taking up the excess line. Between his runs, I reeled him closer.

"Keep the tension steady."

"Right." The fish gave a strong pull and danced to the left. I lifted the tip of the rod higher and let him run. If I tried to muscle him in, the line would likely snap – a lesson I learned the hard way the week before. After a ten-minute battle, I got him in my net and hoisted the speckled trout from the river.

"Caught yourself a beaut."

Warmth spread through my chest. "He's heavy, too." The fish would feed us for several days. I waded back to shore and opened Grandpa's creel. "Holy frijole."

Grandpa turned. "Something wrong?"

"No. I caught one before you." I closed the creel.

"Good job." He grinned and cast his line again.

* * * *

Two hours later, we sat at the kitchen table, cleaning and gutting our fish. As far as I could tell, Grandpa's anger from the day before had blown away like a spent storm cloud. I sure wished Dad handled his moods the same way. A stone landed inside my belly.

Dad. I still couldn't picture him living here. "Why didn't Dad bring us up here to visit?"

Grandpa leaned back, as if my question crowded him. He cleared his throat. "You'd have to ask him. But, I think if your gramma hadn't died, he might've. Eventually. He wasn't gonna do that just for me."

"Why not?"

"He blamed me for having to grow up here." Grandpa pointed out the window. "For living where there wasn't any TV. For having to walk a mile to the highway to catch the school bus. Lots of stuff. He couldn't wait to get out of here. But after your sister was born, he got in touch. And we started getting to know each other again. If your gramma'd still been alive, he probably would've brought both you girls up here at some point."

"How'd Grandma die?"

"Cancer." Grandpa shook his head.

I set my knife on the table and stared at Grandpa, unsure what I should say.

He cleared his throat. "She was a mind-over-matter kind of person. Always up and at 'em. All the years we were together, I don't think she ever caught so much as a cold. One day, she tells me she's too tired to get out of bed. Wasn't like her. I got her dressed and hauled her straight to the doctor." He rubbed a mitt-sized hand across his face. "But by then the cancer'd spread throughout her body. Prognosis wasn't good. She decided to come home with some pills for the pain and that was that."

"She died here?"

"In her own bed. She would've liked to see your dad graduate." He turned to face me. "Your dad tell you she's the one who put him through college?"

"No."

"Can't believe he didn't tell you that."

I shrugged.

He shook his head again. "Your gramma was a real smarty pants. Made the Dean's List at school. Studied engineering. Would've gone on to do who knows what… When I told her I wanted to move to the woods, she gave up her studies and came along. It was selfish of me, but I let her. Not that I could ever really stop her when she set her mind on something."

"Why'd you want to move up here?"

The crease deepened between Grandpa's eyes and he looked away.

"I mean, it's beautiful, but kind of remote." I glanced out the window. "Did you grow up around here?"

Grandpa stared down at his fish. "Nah. Guess you could say it was a Thoreau-Walden kind of deal. Wanted to get back to nature. Your gramma was real plucky. She told me she'd live in the forest, but not like an animal. She came up with the idea of the drying cupboard and the mounting system for the water tank over the shower."

"So, how'd she pay for Dad's college?"

"Besides being smart, your gramma had a soft spot for critters. Mind you, she didn't want any wild ones in the house and we didn't have screens on the doors and windows back then. First five or six years, all kinds of lizards, snakes, and rodents found their way inside. Your gramma didn't want to use poison or any of the traps they sold at the general store. So she invented a trap of her own. Probably one of the first humane traps. Caught the critter, but didn't hurt it. She patented it and from there, Steele Trap Designs was born."

"She started a company?"

"Yep. Put ads in newspapers and magazines and ran a nice little mail order business. Kept the money in a separate account. I had no idea how good she was doing until your dad said he wanted to go out of state for college. What little I'd managed to save wasn't gonna stretch that far. That's when your gramma showed me her bank book. Thought I'd have a heart attack. So many zeroes.

"Anyway, your gramma paid for your dad's education. And when MJ was born, I put a chunk of money in a college fund for her. Did the same for you, too."

"You still run the company?" Was that why he took off each afternoon?

"Nah. When your gramma realized how sick she was, she sold the business."

"You have a picture of her?"

"Yep." He wiped the fish guts from his hands and pulled a wallet from his back pocket. "Always keep this with me." He flipped the billfold open to a faded photo of a woman crouched behind a young boy. Her hair looked the same shade of blonde as mine, but I couldn't tell if her eyes were brown like mine, too. One of her arms was wrapped around the boy. Both wore huge grins.

"That's Dad?"

"Must've been about three years old there."

"They look happy."

"We were. Your dad didn't start hating it here until around fifth or sixth grade. That's when he started to figure out how different he had it from other kids. Saw the stuff he didn't have and the ways he wasn't gonna fit in."

"You never thought about moving?"

"Nah." Grandpa tucked the wallet into his pocket and picked up the boning knife.

This was the most I'd ever heard about Dad's childhood. But something seemed off about the story. Or maybe the uneasiness rattling through my gut was because Grandpa stopped making eye contact with me the moment I asked why he'd moved here.

Chapter Thirteen

Todd didn't meet me in the woods the next day or the one after that. I wondered if he was in trouble. Did his dad figure out about us meeting and order him to stay away from Grandpa's woods? On the third day of no contact, I sat on the downed log where Todd and I usually met and waited. Queenie ran off to explore the underbrush. Maybe I should hike over the hill to the Wilders' farm. It didn't seem right that Todd took all the trespassing risks.

Queenie trotted back to my side. "You up for a trip to the Wilders?" I rubbed her head. She swished her tail. "I'll take that as a 'yes'." I stood and stretched, then threaded my way through the trees with Queenie at my heels. When I reached the clearing where Grandpa's windmill stood, I gave the dog a moment to scout around before we headed for the ridge top. She disappeared into the shrubs.

The whir of the windmill's blades filled the air, but didn't completely mask the sound of boots crunching across the ground. I wished I hadn't let Queenie run off. "Who's there?"

"Nicki?" Todd stepped into view and started climbing down the trail toward me.

His broad smile warmed me. I ran to meet him. "I missed you yesterday."

"Only yesterday? I missed you the day before that, too." He hugged me, one hand traveling along my spine until it cradled the back of my head.

"I missed you every day, okay?"

"Okay." He breathed the word into my neck. A shiver ran down my spine.

The scent of wood smoke plus a whiff of skunk and something sharp like cider lingered on his skin. "You scare up some wildlife on the way in?"

"Nothing I couldn't handle. Sorry I couldn't get away until today. Dad's been on a tear, bossing me around. Mad as hell about me holding your hand. He knows there's something going on." He stroked a few loose strands of hair away from my face.

His touch made my skin hum. "Grandpa acted huffy for a few hours, but seems to have let it go."

"Lucky you." Todd kissed me on the lips.

"Lucky me indeed." I leaned in for another kiss.

We hiked back to the downed tree. I told Queenie to have fun checking out the wildlife, then Todd and I kissed for several minutes. My heart sprinted as his hands travelled along my neck, back, and waist. My shirt was up to my chest when I pulled away, shaking my head. "I'm not getting naked in the woods. No way."

"Not even a little?" His lips touched my throat.

I thought I might melt. "No." I pushed him back a couple inches. "I'm still too much of a city girl to feel comfortable out here. Like that."

"Too bad. Maybe we can figure something else out."

"Maybe. But for now, let's walk."

After another lingering kiss, we stood. "Queenie. Where are you, girl?" She ran from between two brush piles, startling a jumbo size jack rabbit into the open. Too bad I hadn't brought the sixteen-gauge along. The dog barked and gave chase.

The last couple days when Todd didn't show had set my worrying into overdrive. Now I hoped he wouldn't think me a coward after I said what I needed to. I squeezed his hand. "Remember that day we met on the road? The first time we talked?"

"Sure."

"You said I shouldn't believe everything Ben told me."

"Uh-huh." Todd lifted my hand to his mouth and kissed my palm.

"You're not listening are you?"

"I am. Kind of."

"Ben said you both scouted pot farms and called in their locations to the cops. Was that true?"

"Why?"

"Isn't that dangerous?"

He met my gaze and gave a small lopsided smile. "You don't need to worry about that."

"You can still get caught. Still get hurt."

Todd placed his hands on my shoulders. He looked down for a moment then nodded like he'd decided something. His gaze met mine. "Here's the thing. My dad's kind of a big wheel in these parts. Nobody's going to hurt me. Or Ben. Really." He gave my shoulders a squeeze.

"How can you be so sure?"

"Years of experience." He grabbed my hand again and continued walking. "You caught any more fish?"

"Reeled in a sixteen-inch trout yesterday." I gave him a blow-by-blow of my battle with the fish. It was only after I watched him head back along the ridge trail to his family's land that I realized he had successfully distracted me from my questions about the pot farms.

When Queenie and I arrived back at the cabin, Grandpa sat at the kitchen table, organizing his lure-making supplies. I plunked myself onto one of the chairs. "Okay if I watch?"

"Sure."

Queenie sighed and settled under the table, leaning her furry weight against my shins.

Once again the feeling flashed through me that leaving here wasn't going to be easy. Maybe it was a good thing I hadn't reached Dad the other day. I was starting to settle in here – the sound of his voice might've made me miss my real life.

"Still want to learn about lures?" As he spoke, Grandpa's hands did something with a bit of line and hair.

"Yeah." I pointed at the water bug he set on the table. "That's so cool."

He harrumphed, but looked pleased. "First thing you gotta know is that different fish go for different bait. Some fish are drawn to shiny objects. Others like contrasts in color. You gotta have the right bait or the fish swim on by. Of course, weather and water gotta get factored in, too."

Grandpa pointed at the small metal spool on the table. "This here's my bobbin holder. I use it to keep the line tension tight when I'm tying a lure. There are a lot of different knots you can use. Me, I like the Domhof. Now, watch this." He walked me through the process then looked up. I nodded my understanding. "Next you take the free end of the line and wrap it around the hook and the upper part of the loop. Like this. Next you pull the knot tight. Now, you try it." Grandpa pushed the line and a hook across the table to me.

When I mastered the Domhof knot, Grandpa grinned. "Good job. Now you're ready to make a San Juan worm." He spent the next twenty minutes showing me a variety of wet flies and tying techniques. My efforts weren't bad, but Grandpa could take odd bits of fluff and feather and turn them into something that looked ready to take wing. He sat back and pushed his glasses up onto his forehead. "You got a future as a lure maker."

I held out my attempt at a Wooly Bugger. "Think so?"

"I know it."

Warmth spread through my chest. "Thanks."

While Grandpa stowed his lure-making supplies, I started chopping carrots and potatoes for tonight's stew. I was down to my last spud when Queenie started to growl.

"Hush." Grandpa went to the kitchen door, peered out between the curtains, and then gave a low whistle. He opened the door and waved at someone before turning to face me. "I need you to take a hike again."

"Kind of late isn't it?"

"Still got at least an hour of daylight left. I need the place for about that long." The easy laughter had fled Grandpa's face.

"Okay." I climbed to the loft and grabbed my sweatshirt. Queenie greeted me at the bottom on the ladder like I'd been gone for days instead of minutes. "Let's go, girl."

"Queenie, stay." The dog froze.

"Huh?"

"I want her to stay with me."

The warmth from my fly-making lesson burned to ash. "You expect me to go wandering in the woods, right before dark? All by myself? That's nuts." I would never understand Grandpa. Never feel at home here. Home. Right. Even the place where Dad and I lived wasn't home. Home was where orange tongues licked and roared like tigers. Home smelled of smoke and melted cheese, and scorched your memories until they tasted of tar and cinder. I pointed at the window. "Wild animals live out there." A look flashed across his face. Maybe I shouldn't have called him nuts? But when he spoke, his voice was calm.

"You're right. Take the dog. Now get going."

Outside, an older woman sat behind the wheel of a Jeep. The same woman Grandpa kicked me out for before. What was their deal? Once again she stayed inside her vehicle until Queenie and I crossed the clearing and stepped into the woods. "Come on, girl." I turned west, walking toward the setting sun. Weary from my earlier hike and chores, my pace wasn't going to set any speed records. The dog bounded ahead. As much as I loved Queenie, Grandpa's quick change in mood stoked both my anger and longing to go back to my real life.

I took a deep breath and stared at the rising tree trunks. The air smelled damp, like a loamy sachet. I stripped a handful of pine needles from a low branch and inhaled their fresh scent, trying to recapture the happy feeling from my hour in the woods with Todd that afternoon.

At each clearing – no matter how small – I stopped to check the color of the sky. By my best guess, we had another forty minutes before we could go back to the cabin.

Queenie stopped. A low growl rose from her throat, the hackles on her neck and back bristled. I followed the dog's gaze. Ben stood among the trees on the slope above. Queenie's nose and hearing amazed me.

Ben stepped from between the trees, a deep frown twisting his handsome face. "You shouldn't be here." His fierce whisper cut through the quiet.

"What're you talking about?" His tone and his expression got me to whisper, too. "This is Grandpa's land."

He shook his head. "It's not safe." His usually tan face appeared pale. "You need to go home. Right now." Ben moved down the hill toward us without making a sound.

My heart started racing. I pictured the men at the pot field with their automatic weapons. But that was miles from where we stood.

Something thrashed in the underbrush behind Ben. The sound moved closer. I retreated into the cover of shrubs. Queenie growled again. "Hush, girl." She stood quivering, but silent by my side.

Ben hurried to us, pulling me deeper into the bushes. His fear travelled like one of Grandpa's lures on the river, hooking me in. Behind the shelter of a low-growing manzanita, the three of us waited.

Queenie's ears perked and she turned away from the approaching noise. Keeping my voice low, I said, "What is it, Queenie?"

She bolted free of the brush and down the hill.

Ben's hand clamped across my mouth, and he whispered in my ear, "Don't you dare call that dog."

I nodded.

The grip on my mouth loosened.

There was the snap of breaking branches. Dry leaves crackling as if crushed underfoot. Someone or something neared. A figure stumbled into the small clearing. A girl. Not the armed men from the pot field. Dark hair fell across half her face, but the visible side looked dirty or bruised. Maybe both. Ben pulled me to my knees, one arm keeping me down, the other clamping a hand over my mouth. The urge to bite him leached away when I heard more people thrashing through the scrub.

The girl looked around, eyes wild.

Ben's hand mashed my lips, and the smell of earth filled my nostrils.

She turned toward the approaching noise. Blood splotched the back of her T-shirt.

Before I could react, a man charged into the clearing. The girl's scream cut off when he clubbed her across the side of the head with the butt of his gun. Another man ran up beside him and leaned forward, hands on his knees, panting. The first man turned, staring at the brush around us.

Ben's fingertips dug into my jaw. I closed my eyes and held my breath.

A heavy silence filled the forest, pressing down on my shoulders. My lungs began to burn; I had to take a breath. I opened my eyes and peeked between the oval leaves and twisting branches of the manzanita. The first man no longer looked our way. He jerked his head at the second man then they dragged the unconscious girl back into the woods.

I stayed kneeling in the brush. Ben continued to hold me, as if he feared I'd chase after the men. He didn't let go until several minutes had passed. When he released me, I stared at the empty clearing, a sick feeling in my gut. "We could've helped her. Instead of hiding and watching them take her away."

"Listen to me." Ben grabbed my arm, jerking me toward him. "All we could've done was get ourselves killed. Those guys … that's trouble you don't want. They'll end you as soon as look at you."

"You know them? Who they are?"

He shook his head. "I know what they are. You don't want to mess with guys like them."

"Will you call the cops?"

"No."

"You did for the pot field."

"Not for these guys. Not for this." He squeezed both my arms, his fingertips drilling my flesh. "You need to keep quiet about this. You can't tell the cops what we saw. And don't tell your gramps either. He's in enough trouble with—" Ben's face paled more. He scrambled to his feet. "We should get out of here."

"Grandpa's in trouble? With who?"

"Never mind." Ben stared into my eyes. "If they figure out we saw them, we're dead. You got that?"

I nodded again.

"Good. Now go home. And keep your mouth shut."

Chapter Fourteen

I jogged down the hillside, keeping off the path, close to the cover of trees. Afraid to call the dog, I strained for ears and eyes, for any signs of Queenie – or those men. My heart pounded and my legs trembled like I had run the 440. After ten minutes, I crouched at the base of a tall pine, wrapped my arms around my knees, and waited for the shaking to stop. What the hell just happened? Who was that girl? Who were those men? Why did Queenie run away? And what did Ben mean when he said Grandpa was already in enough trouble?

If I could call Dad right now, tell him what I'd seen, he would agree to come get me. He had to. My phone still sat tucked in my pocket. I pulled it free, checked the screen – no signal. Right. Still stuck smack dab in the middle of Grandpa's wilderness.

After several minutes, my breathing started to feel more normal. Eyes and ears on high alert, I stood then continued down the hill at a walk. When I reached the cabin, the Jeep and Grandpa's truck were both gone. There was no sign of Queenie either. Thankfully, Grandpa left the cabin door unlocked. I stuck my head in and called out, "Grandpa? Queenie?" No surprise that Grandpa didn't answer, but a bad feeling pricked the back of my neck when I didn't hear Queenie's nails click across the wood floor. What made her take off like that? Was she okay? I dropped my phone on the table and paced across the kitchen. How long until Grandpa returned? No matter what Ben said, I needed to tell Grandpa about the girl.

Twenty minutes crawled by with no Grandpa and no Queenie. I got the bright idea to fill the dog's bowl. I went outside, shook it, and called her name. Though night had reached the woods, the clearing around the cabin still held a hint of daylight. I called again, but Queenie didn't appear.

The general store in Punishment was eight miles away. Even if I gathered the courage to travel on foot through the woods at night, I doubted the store stayed open much past five. That meant the store roof would already be inaccessible. I looked up at the twilight sky. Until Grandpa got back with his truck, there was no way to alert the cops. Shit. Ben said not to tell the cops. Why? How were we supposed to help that girl without the cops?

How did she wind up in the middle of the forest? Chased by two armed men?

I set Queenie's bowl on the kitchen counter then flung myself on the sofa to wait. The soft tick of the clock got lost under the whir of wind coming through the various chinks in the log walls. Shadows began to form in the room's corners. I scurried into the kitchen in search of the Mason jar full of wooden matches. After lighting the lantern on the kitchen table, I lit two more in the living room. The pungent smell of burning oil still set my nerves on edge, but it felt safer than letting the darkness gather around me. The wind picked up, moaning through the cabin like a choir of ghosts. Beneath the windsong, a new sound pricked my ears. A different kind of howl. Wolf? Injured animal? I opened the door. "Queenie?"

Something rustled in the bushes behind the chicken run. "Queenie?" The dog didn't appear. I slammed the door, fumbling with the bolt. Grandpa told me he kept his guns in the bedroom closet. I'd never gone into his room before. But I would feel way more secure holding some kind of weapon. I stood outside his room, gathering my nerve. If he dared to get pissy about it, I'd give him what-for for leaving me here all alone at night. Right. I turned the knob and went in.

A half-burned American flag hung over the bed. For a moment, the charred edges took me back to the night MJ died. Maybe I shouldn't have fanned those memories by talking about the fire with Todd the other day. I stared at the flag. It was a weird kind of room decoration. No other ornaments hung on the wall. Not even a mirror. Feeling like a snoop, I pulled the closet door open. As I stared inside, memory gut-punched me.

After Mom left, how many times had I snuck into their room to check the closet? To see if her clothes had magically reappeared? After she'd been gone a month, Dad started hanging his clothes on both sides. After two months, Mom's scent – the lemony-floral fragrance I thought of as hers – had disappeared. Just like Mom.

I took a deep breath and inspected the contents of Grandpa's closet. Several wool and flannel shirts hung along with a couple jackets and one necktie. Each item smelled of pine and wood smoke. After sliding everything to the side, I spied the shotgun I used on our rabbit hunts. I stared at the gun rack set into the back of the closet. Only the sixteen-gauge nested there. Did Grandpa take the ten-gauge with him when he went out?

What the hell was going on?

* * * *

A loud crack sounded. I sat up, confused. Not thunder. Someone was pounding on the door. Light leaked in around the curtains. It was morning. I had dozed off on the sofa with the shotgun in my arms. In between nightmares where a bloody girl ran endlessly through the woods, I'd dreamed of my sister burning to death. Amazing I didn't shoot myself or blast a hole in the cabin in the middle of all that.

The pounding started up again. I crept to the far side of the door, trying to peek through a small gap between the curtains without letting whoever stood on the other side know I was there.

It was the same old woman Grandpa kicked me out of the cabin for.

I slid the bolt free and wrenched the door open. "Where is he?"

She stepped back, eyes wide. The muscles along her narrow jaw bulged for a moment. "Is that any way to greet a person?"

Her accent reminded me of the actress who played Hermione Granger in the Harry Potter movies, but dressed as she was in worn khakis and a faded denim shirt, this old woman looked and sounded tough. "Manners seem kind of unimportant right now. Where's my grandpa?"

"That's not your concern."

Heat crackled up my throat. My fists clenched. "Not my concern? Who the hell are you to tell me what's my concern?"

"Young lady, if your grandfather wanted you to know where he was, he would have told you. Circumstances – being what they are – he chose not to do so. I recommend you respect his decision and move your butt."

The mix of her cultured British tone and slinging the word 'butt' stunned me. "Move my butt where exactly?"

"To my car. I need help moving her." She turned and walked toward the battered Jeep.

Moving her? Moving who? I followed the woman. She was shorter than she appeared when sitting behind the wheel; the top of her head didn't quite reach my shoulder. "Who are you anyway?"

She turned. "My name is Cecilia Bonnard." Her stare started at my feet and ended at my face. "You look strong enough. Grab her arms, I'll take her legs." Cecilia opened the vehicle's back door.

A body was inside. No, not a body. Breath lifted her chest. A girl. Thank God I wasn't being asked to move the dead.

"Go on. Pull her out."

I leaned into the car, tugged my right sleeve down over my wrist, and then grabbed the girl's bony shoulders through the thin fabric of her T-shirt. This wasn't the girl from the woods. She was blonde, not brunette. Her mouth hung slack, but her face and arms showed no bruises, no blood. I lifted her torso and dragged her out. Cecilia pushed up the girl's blue jeans and grabbed her ankles. Small but with stringy-looking arms and hands, the older woman hoisted the girl's legs like she was toting nothing heavier than a load of laundry. We carried the unconscious girl inside the cabin. "Where do you want to take her?" I bit back the impulse to explain the choices. This woman had been inside Grandpa's cabin before.

"We're not dragging her up that ridiculous ladder. But I don't want anyone to see her while she's here. Let's put her in John's room."

I hesitated. Right. John equaled Grandpa. We got the girl settled on top of his bed. After pulling Grandpa's quilt out from beneath her, I draped it across her inert form. "What's wrong with her?"

"A number of things." Several strands had escaped the woman's long gray ponytail. Cecilia swatted the loose hairs away from her face then pulled the curtains across the room's one window. "First off, she suffers from low self-esteem and I suspect body dysmorphia." She checked her watch. "Not to mention a dangerous fondness for alcohol and amphetamines."

"I mean, what's wrong with her right now?"

"Drunk. She ran out of Adderall." Cecilia's sharp gaze met mine. "You need to keep her here until John returns."

"How? What if she wakes up and wants to leave?"

"Give her something alcoholic to drink. That or a sleeping pill. John keeps his whiskey on the top shelf over the kitchen sink. You'll find a vial of sleeping pills in the spice rack. Watch her until John gets back. We need to keep her safe. Can you do that?" She stared at me again.

In this wild wooded world, I had no confidence I could keep myself safe, let alone an unconscious girl. "Strange way to keep her safe."

"Believe me, it's the best option."

In spite of my reservations, I nodded. "Will Grandpa come home soon?"

"I hope so. I need you to give him a message."

"Why should I? It's not like you've explained anything to me."

"Don't try my patience." Cecilia frowned at the unconscious girl. "Tell him our last passenger didn't only miss her stop. She broke the rules. Tell him the Lilith Express has gone off the rails. Again. He'll understand." She left Grandpa's bedroom and walked through the kitchen and out the cabin door.

I trotted after her. "Who's the girl?"

Cecilia climbed into her Jeep.

I rested my hands against the cool metal below the open driver's side window. "A name. Something.

Anything?" Questions clumped like soggy leaves in my throat. Cecilia threw the Jeep into reverse. I jumped back. A quick three-point turn, then she drove away. I kicked a pine cone and watched the dust cloud triggered by her tires move farther down the track.

When I returned to the girl in Grandpa's bedroom, reality slammed against me. I was charged with keeping this unnamed person safe. Safe from who? From what? Grandpa was off God-knew-where. I couldn't count on his help. I stared at her. What if she wasn't just drunk? I had no medical knowledge. No special skills to help. What if this girl was dying and I was too stupid to see it?

Images of MJ flashed before my eyes. Lying on her bed. Gasping for air. My knees buckled and I grabbed the wall for support. Now was a time to keep it together. This girl needed me. Six or seven deep breaths later, I straightened.

A glass of water. If what Cecilia told me was true, the girl would wake up hungover and thirsty. I set a full glass on the bedside table and stared again at my mute companion. Unlike the girl Ben and I'd seen, this one showed no visible injuries. But she still looked lost in the woods. I peeked between the curtains on the bedroom window. The sun haloed the tops of the pines. When would Grandpa come back? I needed to tell him about the girl. The other girl.

Plus Cecilia wanted me to tell Grandpa the Lilith Express had gone off the rails.

One more item to add to the list of things I didn't understand.

Chapter Fifteen

After dragging a kitchen chair into Grandpa's bedroom, I went back for the shotgun. I watched the slow rise and fall of the girl's chest. Seconds turned into minutes then the minutes ganged up into quarter hours. She kept on breathing, but didn't move in any other way. Who was she?

After the first half hour, I overcame my squeamishness and slid a hand into the front pocket of her jeans but came away with nothing except lint. Going through her clothes felt creepy – like something a perv would do. I took a deep breath before checking her other front pocket. A scrap of paper? I tugged until a small square came free. Thin cardstock, folded into quarters. I flattened it out. A bus ticket to Elk Creek. Grandpa sold fishing lures in Elk Creek. The town was at least twenty miles from here. Did knowing that help? Not that I saw. I chewed my lip and reached under her. Fortunately, she was as light as a water bug. I dug into her back pockets but found nothing. No ID. No ideas.

An engine rumbled. My head jerked up. Where was I? Right. Grandpa's bedroom. The girl slept on. I tiptoed into the kitchen and shut the door behind me. When I stepped outside, Grandpa was already latching the barn. He walked toward me across the clearing, shotgun over his shoulder, Queenie at his side. His gaze seemed pointed to the right of my waist. I looked down. The sixteen-gauge was still gripped in my hand. All at once, fear, worry, and anger tumbled from my mouth. "Where've you been? You didn't come home last night. Queenie ran off. Where'd you find her? What happened?"

Grandpa pulled the shotgun from my grip and opened the breach. He removed the two shells, tucked them into his shirt pocket, and returned the gun. "Something came up. I needed Queenie's help so I called her." A silver tube glinted in his open palm. "Handy things, dog whistles."

"What came up? The Lilith Express?"

One of his large hands cupped my shoulder. "Where'd you hear that name?"

"From your friend, Cecilia. She came by earlier. Said to tell you the Lilith Express had gone off the rails again. And that the last passenger broke the rules. What'd she mean by that?"

Grandpa moved past me and opened the screen door. "That's not your concern. I don't want you mixed up in any of it."

For a moment, I put aside my fury, crouched, and threw my arms around Queenie's neck. After releasing the dog, I followed Grandpa into the kitchen ready with my next attack. "Does guarding the girl passed out on your bed count as getting 'mixed up' in things?"

Grandpa stopped, frowned, and then thumped across the kitchen floor to his room. When he returned, he sank into one of the chairs at the kitchen table. I stayed on my feet. "I'm sorry, Nicki. You shouldn't have got stuck watching out for her."

"Who is she? And who's Lilith?"

"Never mind about any of that. I'm home now. I'll take care of things."

Tears stung my eyes. "Yeah, you're home now. But what about yesterday when I needed your help? When that other girl needed your help. Can you take care of her, too?"

"What are you talking about?" His shoulders straightened.

"There was a girl being chased by two men. I saw her. In the woods."

"What?" Grandpa stood, knocking his chair to the floor. His face went white. "When?"

"When you kicked me out yesterday. Queenie and I ran into Ben Wilder." I told him what happened, how the girl ran into the clearing and Ben covered my mouth. How the men dragged off the bleeding girl.

"Did they see you?" Grandpa grabbed my arm. "Did those men see you?"

I thought about the one who turned and stared at the shrubs near Ben and me. "No." The man wouldn't have walked away if he'd seen us. "What kind of place is this? Where stuff like this happens? My phone was useless. It was too late for me to go to town and call the cops. Too late for everything."

"No." Grandpa wrapped his arms around me. "It's not too late."

The sobs came without warning. When I was able to breathe normally, I pulled away, grabbed a paper towel from the roll on the kitchen counter, then wiped my face and blew my nose. "So we'll go into town and call the cops?"

"No. No cops."

"But—"

"I said no." The crease that ran between his eyes deepened.

That deputy who scowled at Grandpa when we were in town – was that why he said 'no cops?' But Ben had said not to tell the cops, too. "So what do we do? How can we help her?"

"Don't worry. You've given me a starting place. First I'm gonna look in on our guest again, then you and me will have a little talk before I scout around in the woods. See what I see. If I need to, I'll bring in some people. Trust me, they can handle this better than the cops."

Chapter Sixteen

Grandpa settled next to me at the end of the kitchen table. "You learned about the Underground Railroad in school, didn't you?"

"Uh…"

Grandpa harrumphed. "What're they teaching you kids? Before the Civil War, the Underground Railroad helped slaves escape to Free States. They had secret routes and safe houses where runaway slaves could hide as they made their way north."

"Right." I nodded. "I remember now. Harriett Tubman. And the abolitionists, right?" I leaned closer to better hear his hushed voice.

"To name a few. Well, the Lilith Express is an underground railway for women and girls. There's stuff I can't tell you, because it's not mine to tell. But since you met Cecilia when she brought that girl here" —he nodded toward the back wall of the kitchen— "I can tell you more than I normally would. Cecilia started the Lilith Express over thirty years ago. To help battered women escape and give them a chance at a new start. I'm not sure how this became her cause. I never asked. And she did me the same favor. Over the years, Cecilia's helped hundreds of women. Most of them have become part of the railway, guiding others here, or helping them on their way to their new town, new job."

"Who's Lilith?"

"That was Cecilia's idea. In case someone was foolish enough to talk about the Express in front of outsiders, the name wouldn't mean anything to them."

"You got that right."

Grandpa rubbed his red-rimmed eyes then smiled at me. "Lilith was Adam's first wife."

"Adam who?"

"Adam. You know, Adam and Eve? From the Bible?"

"Oh."

"There's a story that says Lilith was created at the same time and from the same earth as Adam. Not made from his rib, like Eve. Lilith saw herself as his equal and Adam didn't much care for that. Long story short, Lilith left him and the Garden of Eden. Cecilia thought the name fit for what she was doing.

"That one" —again he nodded toward his bedroom— "never should've been sent to us. When Cecilia came by yesterday, it was because the girl had gone missing. She never showed up at her next stop. No one'd told Cecilia about the girl's habit." He rubbed his forehead. "The ones with drug and alcohol problems, they don't have the spine needed for all the changes they gotta make. Cecilia's giving them a new life. Takes real strength to choose that. To choose the unknown. To leave everything behind – even if what's there is awful. One of the women Cecilia helped start over thought the girl was a good candidate." He lowered his voice further. "Cecilia was afraid someone might've snatched the girl, but it looks like she took a detour to get high."

He pushed his chair back from the table. "I help Cecilia in a number of ways, but when one of the passengers isn't up to the journey, I step in." His voice dropped to a whisper. "I'm the cut-out man."

"What—"

He shook his head.

The question died in my throat.

117

"We do everything possible to protect the women who travel and have travelled on the Lilith Express. We can't rely on cops. Sometimes the girls we help are underage. The young ones get sent to us as a last resort. But also, we got a couple cops up here who are more interested in lining their pockets than upholding the law."

I leaned forward until my lips practically touched Grandpa's ear. "What's going to happen to the girl?"

He gave his head another shake. "We'll talk about that after I take her … to the next stop."

What did that mean? Grandpa looked sad. Whatever the next stop was, it probably didn't come with candy and kittens. "The girl Ben and I saw attacked in the woods – was she one of your passengers?"

"No." He sat back and sighed. "That's a whole other problem we got. We can talk about that later. After I get back. But first I'm gonna take Queenie and hike to where you spotted the girl. See if Queenie can pick up her scent."

If Dad was any example, adults said 'later' when they meant 'never.' I crossed my arms over my chest. "When that girl got grabbed, Ben said something about you already being in enough trouble. He wouldn't tell me anything more. Who are you in trouble with?"

Grandpa gave a mirthless chuckle. "Seems like everybody right now. That boy shouldn't have said that much." He sighed. "We'll talk about that later." His gaze met mine. "I mean that."

* * * *

Too nervous to sit watching the strange girl passed out on Grandpa's bed, I started in on my chores. I pressed the hidden latch for the drying cupboard and leaned in to grab a bunch of mint, brushing several bundles of oregano on my way out. Even after closing the panel door, the kitchen smelled like the pizza parlor near our house in Orange. I hated the reek of that place. But without the cheese stench, the smell of the drying cupboard was okay. I stripped the mint leaves from the stem, bottom-to-top like Grandpa taught me, over the half-empty tea jar. Next, I put away the dishes and pans sitting in the rack by the sink. Inside jobs completed, I checked the girl again. No apparent changes. I went outside.

After cleaning the chicken coop and collecting several eggs, I lugged the rake and the five-gallon bucket full of supplies back to the barn. Eggs hammocked in the front of my T-shirt, I latched the barn door with my free hand.

Grandpa and Queenie had been gone almost an hour. I doubted I walked more than twenty minutes into the woods the other day before I ran across Ben. By now Grandpa must have reached the spot where those men grabbed the girl. I didn't know what he hoped to find, but that was only one thing among many that made no sense.

The cabin door banged open. The skinny girl stood in the doorway, blonde hair matted on one side, the sixteen-gauge in her hands. "Where am I?"

The dark center of the barrel was pointed at my chest. Heart racing like a jack rabbit, I ran my tongue across dry lips. The shotgun wasn't loaded. Right? Unless she found where Grandpa kept his ammunition. Eggs still cradled in my T-shirt, I inched forward, keeping my free hand open and away from my side. Looking harmless, I hoped. "You're at my grandpa's place. Cecilia brought you here."

"The old lady?" The gun vibrated in her trembling hands.

"Yeah. You want something to eat?"

She shook her head. "Got anything to drink?"

"I left water by the bed."

She looked at me like I was an idiot. "Something stronger than water. I got a killer headache."

The gun slipped downward, the muzzle pointing at the ground. With the barrel no longer aimed my way, I felt safe enough to walk around the girl and enter the cabin. She clomped in after me.

"What's your name?"

"Everybody calls me the Snake Dancer."

Sure they did. I resisted the urge to roll my eyes. No point pissing her off – she was still armed. I set the five eggs into a bowl, amazed I hadn't cracked any of them when I first saw her holding my gun. "Why would anyone call you that?"

"'Cause I got a big tat of a snake on my back. And 'cause when the adder calls me, I follow."

The lightbulb went on. "Oh. Cecilia said you ran out of Adderall."

"Yeah. How about that drink?"

I crossed the kitchen and stood on tiptoe to reach the top shelf over the sink. My fingers brushed against cool glass. I checked the label. Whiskey. Cecilia was right. Was her deal with Grandpa limited to the Lilith Express?

Shotgun tucked under her left arm, the Snake Dancer grabbed the bottle, unscrewed the cap, and drank.

All I could do was hope she kept pounding down the booze until she blacked out once more. Then I'd grab the gun and not be stupid enough to leave it where she could get her hands on it again.

Three gulps later, she sighed and waved toward the five-point buck head mounted on the kitchen wall.

"What the hell kind of place is this? You guys a bunch of freaky survivalists?"

Heat flashed across my face. How dare she insult Grandpa's home when he was giving her shelter? "No—"

The sound of a car engine interrupted my retort. The girl's face paled. She clutched the whiskey to her chest.

The guttering roar coming from outside was way louder than the motor on Grandpa's truck. "Give me the gun." I held out my hand. Without a word, she surrendered the sixteen-gauge. I stole to the door, peeked between the curtains. A truck with the Sheriff's Department seal on the side pulled into the clearing. "Get in the bedroom. Close the door. Don't make a sound."

The girl scurried out of the kitchen.

I took a deep breath. Were the cops here about yesterday's bleeding girl? Or today's snake girl? As confused as I was by the weird things going on around me, I trusted Grandpa. And he had told me 'no cops.' I leaned the shotgun against the wall, opened the door, and stepped outside.

Two men dressed in tan and olive uniforms climbed from the vehicle to stand in the dirt. Both frowned at me.

"Can I help you?"

The one with the big belly and red-veined nose spoke. "You live here?" With his white hair, angry eyes, and cherry red lips, he looked like a bizarro version of Santa Claus. The silent officer behind him was the deputy I met in town. The creepy-eyed one. He turned away and gazed at the barn.

"Yeah. What's going on?"

"You live here alone?" Santa seemed to study the cabin's exterior.

I resisted the urge to turn and see what was so fascinating about the building. "No. With my grandpa."

Santa nodded toward the cabin. "He here now?"

"No. What's this about?"

"What's your name?"

Creepy Eyes walked toward the chicken coop, his gear belt creaking with each step.

Why wouldn't they answer my questions? I took another deep breath. "Nicki Steele."

"What's your grandfather's name?"

"John Smith." Across the yard, Creepy Eyes opened the door to the chicken run. "What're you doing? Don't let the birds loose!" Clucking frantically, the chickens charged toward the gate in search of food. The officer retreated, barely managing to slam the door and secure the bolt before any hens got free.

The cross-looking Santa spoke. "We got a report of an injured girl running through the woods near here. We're following up. Your neighbor, Mr. Wilder, told us there was a young girl living here. Thought maybe you were hurt. You all right?" Both his bored tone and the frown weighing down the corners of his mouth showed a lack of concern for my well-being.

"Yeah. I'm okay." Did Ben notify the cops after all?

"Mind if we come in, take a look around?"

I was pretty sure if Grandpa were here he would tell them to go to hell. "Think you better wait for my grandpa to get back. You want him to get in touch with you when he returns?"

"Where is he?"

Out hunting for your injured girl. I swallowed hard before I spoke. "Hiking."

"Hiking where?"

"Up in the hills. I'm sure he'll be back soon."
Though I feared for the bleeding girl's safety, something
more than Grandpa's warning made me doubt the
deputies' desire to help. The creepy-eyed one now stood
at the barn door. Should I tell him to keep out? Could I?
Was a barn like a house? Maybe they didn't need a
search warrant for it.

Santa cleared his throat. "You seen any young
women running through these woods?"

The memory of Ben saying we were dead if
anyone discovered what we witnessed smothered any
urge to truth tell. "No."

The cranky Santa took a step closer and held out a
business card, the smell of stale coffee tagging along like
an invisible shadow. "You or your grandfather hear
anything about this injured girl, you let us know. Come
on, Walt."

Creepy Eyes – Walt – retreated from the barn,
shoulders slumped.

I waited by the cabin door until the dust cloud
from their departing truck settled onto the dirt road. Back
inside, I locked up, grabbed the shotgun, and raced to
Grandpa's bedroom. The Snake Dancer's eyes looked
glazed. She lounged on the bed below the burned flag,
her back supported by the wall. She had already guzzled
a generous amount of Grandpa's whiskey.

She raised the bottle in my direction. "This is
more like it. That old lady had a stick up her butt. I could
tell she didn't like me." The Snake Dancer seemed to
have forgotten her fear from moments earlier and showed
no curiosity about the vehicle now roaring away through
the woods or who had come to the door.

"What?"

"The old lady. Bitchy thing." The Snake Dancer took another swig. "Kept saying 'You weren't supposed to call anyone.' and 'No drugs or alcohol allowed.' How's the old bat expect me to get through all this without ups or alcohol? Or without Stan."

"Who's Stan?"

"My boyfriend." Her words slurred around the edges.

This could be my chance to find out if Grandpa had given me the whole story. "What exactly does Cecilia expect you to get through?" The Snake Dancer did something weird with her eyes. Trying to glare at me? I wasn't sure if she was angry or unable to focus. Maybe both.

"This." She waved the bottle. Whiskey sloshed out the open top. "Oops." She licked the spilled liquid from her arm. "Don't want to waste the good stuff. What was I saying?"

"You were telling me how you ended up here. With Cecilia."

"Right. Had to get gone. Ralph couldn't keep his slimy hands off me."

I ignored the chair and sat on the edge of the bed. "Who's Ralph?"

"Mom's wastoid boyfriend."

Ick. There were worse things than having no mom. "Oh."

"Yeah. Oh. Sicko wouldn't leave me alone. Mom didn't care. At least not enough to tell the perv to shove off."

A hot stone of dread landed in my stomach. "She let him…"

The Snake Dancer swigged from the bottle. "Yeah. So I took off."

I nodded. "Cecilia helped you?"

"Her and the rest."

"The rest?"

A long squeak. I jumped, recognizing the sound. Someone had opened the cabin door.

I grabbed the shotgun, peered into the kitchen. Queenie trotted to greet me. My heartbeat slowed to normal. I set the gun on the counter and crouched to hug the dog. "You're back." The planks creaked under Grandpa's weight. I looked up at him. "Find anything?"

"Found the place where the girl got snatched. Dirt was all churned up. There were traces of blood. Queenie and me followed the trail for a while. Queenie's an amazing air tracker, aren't you, girl?" He ruffled the fur behind her ears. Queenie stared at him with adoring eyes. "Looked like someone put the girl in a truck. We tried to follow their route. Managed to stay on the scent for a few miles." He rubbed the gray stubble along his jaw. "How's our guest doing?"

No good way to tell him. "Uh, she's enjoying your whiskey."

Grandpa frowned, but didn't scold.

"Also, the cops came by."

"What for?" Grandpa massaged his scalp, further disturbing his already messy hair.

"Said they heard a girl was running around in the woods injured. Wanted to know if we'd seen anything."

"What'd you tell them?"

"I told them 'no'. Just like you said to."

"Good girl."

"They wanted to come in, look around, but I said no to that, too."

"Even better." Grandpa nodded then stretched his back. "I'm supposed to take our houseguest to her next stop. But I'm gonna need to hold off on that while I hunt for that girl. From the place we lost her trail, I got a pretty good idea where she's being held. Queenie and me will take the truck and see what we find. Can you keep an eye on our houseguest?"

"Sure."

"When I get back – if I need to – I'll call in the reinforcements. But first I gotta grab some more ammo." Grandpa walked back to his room and ushered out the Snake Dancer. The bedroom door snicked shut.

The Snake Dancer stalked into the living room and flounced onto the sofa, arms crossed, looking out of sorts. Took me a moment, but then I figured out why. Grandpa had relieved her of the whiskey bottle.

Chapter Seventeen

The Snake Dancer spent the rest of the afternoon dozing on the sofa. After thirty minutes of watching over her, I gave up and went outside to finish my chores. While I weeded the vegetable patch, I found myself longing for a walk in the woods. Weird. I hiked to exercise Queenie or to meet Todd. I didn't hike for me. In spite of its strangeness, this place continued to grow on me.

Hours later, as night settled over the forest, the wind picked up. I stood in the doorway staring across the clearing at the empty dirt track below the shimmying tree branches. Still no sign of Grandpa or Queenie.

Awake now, the Snake Dancer sat up on the sofa, face pale, hair mussed and knotted. "The old guy took the whiskey with him, didn't he?" When I didn't answer, she continued to grouse. "Cheap bastard. Like he couldn't spare a little something to help my head. I'm the victim here. I'm the one stuck in the middle of nowhere. No one told me I was gonna wind up dumped in the wilderness."

Though I never voiced those words to Grandpa, I'd sure thought them during my first night here, too. Funny, the place still felt mysterious, but now I also saw the beauty.

After enduring ten minutes of complaints, I decided desperate times called for desperate measures. Up in my loft, I retrieved my iPod, tucked in the earbuds and scrolled through my playlists. The list titled 'Dad's Hard Rock' jumped out at me. Lots of loud music on that one. I cranked up the volume. Drowning out the Snake Dancer's whining with the Ramones was worth using up the iPod's battery.

When I climbed back down, her mouth was still flapping. I moved into the kitchen, debating whether to start dinner. Might as well – it would make it easier to ignore our 'guest.' I got the fire going inside the stove then opened the icebox and pulled out one of the rabbits Grandpa had butchered, along with carrots, onions, and potatoes. I started chopping. Once everything was bubbling away in the big pot, I peeked into the living room. Looked like the Snake Dancer was still bitching. No way did I want to sit on the sofa and listen.

Lights flickered across the kitchen window. I turned off the music, heard Grandpa's truck, and ran to the door.

"What's your malfunction?" The Snake Dancer frowned and gave me a bleary-eyed glare.

"Grandpa's back."

"Who gives a rat's ass?" The Snake Dancer slumped lower on the sofa.

Outside, the air was cool but not cold. Grandpa surprised me by parking in the clearing instead of the barn. Was he heading out again tonight? Queenie bounded from the truck bed. Another surprise. She usually rode inside the cab with Grandpa. "Hey." The dog ran to me, nosed my leg. I crouched beside her. "You're such a good girl." I rubbed behind her velvety ears.

The truck door slammed. Grandpa walked around to the passenger side.

I straightened. "You found her?"

"Yep."

With Queenie at my heels, I raced to the far side of the truck. The cab light came on when Grandpa opened the door. I peered around his shoulder and gasped.

Grandpa scooped up the bruised and bloody girl. "Get the doors."

After shutting the truck door, I trotted ahead to the cabin and held the screen while Grandpa carried in the girl. He quick stepped through the kitchen and into his room. When he set the girl on his bed, she moaned. He straightened, joints creaking. Hands on his hips, Grandpa arched back then leaned forward and placed a hand on the girl's shoulder. "You're safe here."

Her eyelids fluttered open. The girl's gaze appeared unfocused.

"You're safe," Grandpa repeated. She closed her eyes.

I draped the worn quilt across her, trying not to stare at the necklace of green and purple bruises ringing her throat. Grandpa pointed toward the kitchen. He hesitated outside the bedroom door, then left it open a half-inch.

After adjusting the heat under the big pot on the stove, we huddled at one end of the kitchen table. The Snake Dancer had stopped bitching, but still sat slumped on the sofa. Grandpa spoke, his voice low. "I got a problem, Nicki. I need to get our passenger out of the cabin now. The less she knows about that one" —he nodded toward his room— "the better. You gonna be all right staying with the girl? Queenie'll keep you company."

"Sure, but shouldn't we get her to a doctor?"

Grandpa rubbed his forehead. "Wish we could. If Cecilia wasn't running around warning the others, she could help, but…" He shrugged. His eyes were bloodshot and the wrinkles creasing his brow looked trench-deep.

"Okay."

"There's first aid supplies in the bathroom. Under the sink. If you feel up to helping her."

Always squeamish, I couldn't even dissect a frog in biology class. But in the three weeks since I'd come to the Mendo, I'd skinned and gutted rabbits and filleted fresh fish. I could do this. Besides, who else was going to patch up the girl? "Sure."

For someone who whined about getting stuck in a cabin in the woods, the Snake Dancer sure kicked up a fuss when it came time to get into the truck and leave with Grandpa.

Finally, passenger secured, Grandpa rounded the front of the pickup and spoke, his voice hushed so the Snake Dancer couldn't hear. "I won't get back until noon or so tomorrow." He rested his hand on my shoulder. "Sorry to leave you alone with our new guest."

"I'll be okay."

"Good. Lock the door and keep the shotgun with you. Just to be safe."

"When you get back, you'll explain the rest of what's going on?"

He ran a hand along his jaw. "At this point, I don't see how I can do anything else."

The 'cut-out man.' The name alone made my stomach twist. What did Grandpa do to earn that title? I watched him drive away. It looked like his passenger was already nodding off. It was not going to be a fun drive for Grandpa, but it would probably be a better ride with a sleeping Snake Dancer than a whining one.

Door locked, curtains pulled tight, I investigated the first aid supplies. Then I went to face my patient. Definitely the girl from the woods. Half her face was bruised and swollen, her lip cut, and dried blood caked her mouth and chin. The injuries I could see were already scabbing over. That was a good sign, right? But what about the less obvious wounds? Bile burned the back of my throat. I didn't want to think about what else those men might've done to her.

Shoeless and dressed in a dirty T-shirt and blue jean skirt, the girl looked damaged and exhausted. If she was sleeping deeply enough, this might be my best chance to deal with her cuts and scrapes without causing her more pain.

After filling a bowl with warm, soapy water, I soaked a washcloth. I began cleaning dried blood from her face. She opened her eyes briefly and murmured something undecipherable. Next I washed down her arms and legs. Once the dirt was off, the multitude of scrapes, cuts, and bruises became visible. I blinked away tears. The thought of those men throwing the girl down, raping her… My stomach turned again. I took a deep breath, then spoke, my voice a whisper. "You're safe now."

The soles of her feet were torn and bloody, like someone took a sander to them. How far had she been forced to travel without shoes? While I cleaned the rest of her and covered her cuts with antibiotic ointment and gauze, she moaned a few times, but didn't open her eyes again. The long chain of knots that was her hair didn't look worth the effort of trying to untangle. I settled for pushing back the dark strands from her face. When I'd done all I could, I wrapped her small hand in mine.

She muttered something that sounded like, "Are you May?"

"I'm Nicki. You're safe now. Sleep."

A couple hours later, when my eyelids started to droop, I lay down on the living room sofa, shotgun in my arms. Queenie padded into the room and sprawled on her stomach on the floor nearby. Over and over again, gusting whistles and whines jostled me awake. Each time I woke, I waited, staring into the darkness, straining for any sounds that shouldn't be there. All I heard was Queenie's breathing and the wind.

* * * *

The next morning, my eyes felt burned and grit-scratched. Afraid to go outside and possibly miss hearing it if the girl called out, I hovered nearby, first straightening the kitchen, then the living room, trying to make as little noise as possible while the girl slept. Grandpa said he wouldn't get back until noonish, but when twelve o'clock rolled around with no reappearance, I got antsy. What was taking so long? Had he run into trouble?

From the doorway to Grandpa's room, I watched the girl. Her chest rose and fell, breath coming in hoarse sighs. The bruises on her face had turned bluish-purple, but the uninjured side looked healthier, less washed out. The ring of bruises around her neck must've been older; they were the brown and green of dying pine needles.

It was late enough that when I went outside the sun shone overhead, warming the open space around the cabin. Queenie trotted off to investigate the trees edging the clearing. I fed the chickens. Before starting in on my other daily chores, I checked the girl again. After a half-hearted job of digging in the vegetable patch for newly sprouted weeds, I emptied the icebox drip pan and wound the kitchen clock. When I next checked in on the girl, she lay on her side, her back to the door.

By two o'clock, the wait was driving me crazy. Queenie, too. Every time I neared the cabin door, she thumped her tail, ready for our daily walk. "Sorry." I rubbed her head. "Not today." I opened the door. She gave me a sad-eyed look then trotted past the vegetable garden and flopped down in a sunlit patch by the barn.

The girl in the bedroom still hadn't stirred. My nerves hummed. Should I shake her, make sure she was okay? She was breathing – so at least she was alive. From what I could see, she hadn't bled through any of her bandages. That was something.

The next few hours passed in an exhausted blur. Whenever I took a break from pacing to sit with the girl, I nodded off. But my drum-tight nerves never let me sink into a deep sleep, and every cabin creak jolted me back to wakefulness.

Butt sore from sitting so long on the wood chair, I walked into the kitchen and looked at the clock. Half-past five and still no sign of Grandpa's truck. When I returned to the bedroom, the girl opened her eyes. With a sharp intake of breath, she scuttled to the far side of the bed. The paleness of her undamaged cheek contrasted with her bruised one, making her face look like one of the dramedy masks that decorated the theater at school.

"It's okay. You're safe." The touch of my fingertips on her shoulder seemed to scare rather than reassure her. I withdrew my hand.

"Donde soy yo?"

"What?"

"Quien eres?"

Spanish. Right. "Um, yo soy Nicki. Este es la casa de mi…" Oh hell, what was the word for grandpa? "Abuelo." Right. "Es la casa de mi abuelo."

The girl rattled off a phrase in rapid-fire Spanish.

"Repite por favor. Y lentamente." Thank God I took Spanish instead of French for my foreign language requirement. She apparently understood me, speaking more slowly this time. After a few back and forths, I got her name – Manuela – and her age – seventeen. I wished I had a Spanish-English dictionary to help with translation, but I must have said something right. Her brown eyes grew less alarmed. I did my best to explain she was safe and that, when my grandpa returned, he would take her where she wanted to go. She resettled against the pillow.

After being out of it for at least ten hours, she had to be thirsty. "Queire usted agua?"

"Si." She nodded.

Queenie came along when I brought back a glass of water.

Manuela's eyes widened and she snatched away her hand.

"Lo siento." I led Queenie into the kitchen, petted her, and told her to stay. When I returned without the dog, Manuela let me help her sit up and drink. After a few swallows, she sank back on the bed, wiped out. Time to rest. "Sleep, I mean, sueno ahora, okay?"

She nodded again. "Si." Her eyes closed.

For a while, Queenie followed me as I paced, but soon that game lost its luster and she lay down on the rug in front of the empty fireplace. Hunger almost drove me outside at twilight to investigate the vegetable patch before I remembered the stew from the previous night was in the icebox. After fetching a few split sections of log from the wood pile, I heated up the pot. Queenie leaned against me and whined. I turned down the flame under the pan and filled her bowl.

Where was Grandpa?

When the pot began to bubble, I checked on Manuela. Though I'd gotten an A in Spanish, it seemed like everything I ever learned had leaked out of my brain during the first three weeks of summer. Still, Manuela seemed to understand and acted interested in dinner. I brought in a steaming bowl of rabbit stew then helped her to sit up in bed, propping her against the wall. Though her mouth looked bruised and battered, she ate as if she hadn't tasted food in days. I tried not to stare at the hand-shaped bruises on her arms, but my gaze kept returning to them. How long had those men held her?

After a few minutes, I felt confident she could finish on her own and left to boil water for tea. My own appetite crushed by thoughts of what Manuela must have gone through, I put away my unused bowl and moved the pot from the burner. While the kettle heated, Queenie and I stood outside, eager for signs of Grandpa's return. But, no headlights strafed the tree trunks, no engine roar disturbed the night. Queenie sighed. "I know what you mean, girl." The dog sniffed about until she found a suitable place to pee then trotted back inside.

I followed and pulled a few fragile mint leaves from the Mason jar, crumbled them into the infuser, and dunked the metal ball inside a mug of hot water. The fresh aroma rose with the steam, combining with the scent of cooked rabbit and potato. When I checked on her, Manuela traded her bowl for the mug and drank half the steaming brew before settling down again.

Back in the kitchen, I drank a cup of tea and paced some more. Grandpa had been gone almost twenty-four hours. Did that mean something went wrong? That he was in trouble? What should I do?

Around eight o'clock, my body gave out. Once again I settled on the sofa, afraid I might not hear Manuela if I slept all the way up in the loft. Fully dressed, I collapsed against the nubby fabric, shotgun gripped in my right hand. Queenie took up her position on the floor.

I reached out to pet her thick coat. "I'm glad you're here with me, girl." I closed my burning eyes for a minute.

Chapter Eighteen

I was awoken by the growl of an engine and tires crunching along the rough track. Grandpa. Finally. I sat up, rubbed my eyes, and stretched. Pitch-black night surrounded me. The lantern I'd left burning on the kitchen table continued to glow, a small oasis in the dark. The fuel hadn't run out; I couldn't have been asleep too long.

Thud, thud, thud. The door shook. "Sheriff's Department. Open up."

Something must've happened to Grandpa. Shotgun in one hand, I ran into the kitchen. The clock read 10:30. Did he get in a car accident? I peeked through a slim gap between the curtains on the door's window. Two uniformed men stood in the dirt – bizarro Santa and Walt, the creepy-eyed deputy. Footsteps padded across the hardwood floor. Manuela leaned against the kitchen counter looking like one swish of Queenie's tail could knock her over. Even in the shadows, her wide eyes and taut mouth were plain to see. Grandpa warned me the police couldn't be trusted. Her alarm reinforced the message. I tiptoed to her side, took her hand. She pulled away. "Por favor." I kept my voice low and pleaded with my eyes for her to trust me.

Some of the tension left her face. She nodded.

I led her to the ladder, pointed up. Shit. How did you say 'hide' in Spanish? I settled for 'go.' "Va. Okay?" I pointed at the loft again then pressed my finger against my lips.

Manuela nodded one more time.

"Police. Open up." The shout was followed by more banging.

Manuela grabbed the first rung and started climbing. Obviously in pain, she moved like she was seventy, not seventeen. When she reached the top, I pantomimed for silence again. She moved back until I could no longer see her through the railing.

The cops hammered the door again.

"Coming." I trotted to the kitchen, leaned the shotgun in the corner next to the door, and picked up the lantern from the table. Queenie stood beside me, the weight of her against my leg giving me courage. I wiped the sweat from my palm and turned the knob. "What happened?"

"Where's your grandfather?" Santa said.

"What?" They were searching for Grandpa? Did that mean he was okay?

"Answer the question." Santa moved his bulk closer. Queenie gave a low growl and Santa reversed course.

"He's out. Why're you here?"

The cross-looking Santa spoke. "You know a girl by the name of Samantha Dean?"

I shook my head. "No."

"Trust me. You don't want to lie to me." He moved closer again. Queenie growled. "Control the goddamn dog before I do it for you."

Do it for me? What did he mean by that? "Hush, Queenie." Not a tall man, Santa's chin came level with my shoulder. The scent of coffee and something sour mingled with his breath.

I took a step back.

"Got that picture, Walt?"

"Sure thing." Creepy Eyes handed a three-by-five photo to Santa. He flipped the picture to show off the captured image.

My brain scrambled to make sense of what I saw. After about twenty thumps of my heart, I was able to start cataloging: Blood. Bruises. A swollen eye socket. Dirt-crusted nostrils. Or was that dried blood? "The Snake Dancer." My stomach lurched. I set the lamp on the table and covered my mouth, afraid I might puke right then and there.

"What the hell's that supposed to mean?" Santa's bushy eyebrows slanted down.

Bile burned my throat. I swallowed hard. "What happened to her? Is she... I mean..." Judging by her damaged face, she had to be severely injured. "Is she alive?"

"What'd you call her?"

"The Snake Dancer. That's what she called herself. Is she okay?"

"When did you see her last?"

She looked like someone beat her bloody. Did that mean Grandpa was injured, too? Or was this what the 'cut-out man' did? My stomach rolled again. When the feeling passed, I answered. "Yesterday. I saw her yesterday."

"How come she had your phone?"

"My phone?"

"Modoc County deputies found your phone in Samantha Dean's possession. Traced it through the service provider to your father's account."

"You called Dad?" Oh God, getting a call from the cops – he'd be freaking out. "What did you tell him?"

Santa ignored my question. "In addition to the phone, we got a report that someone witnessed your grandfather driving a young woman out of town last night. The description matches Samantha Dean. Before this." He waved the snapshot. "Why was Samantha Dean with your grandfather?"

I stared at the picture again. "Was there an accident?"

Santa pocketed the photo. "This was no accident. What was she doing with your grandfather?"

"She spent the night here." I needed to be smart and keep the Lilith Express out of this. The tips of my fingers brushed against something rough. I looked down. My left hand moved back and forth across my scar like a windshield wiper. No amount of scrubbing was going to erase that damage. I clenched my fist. "I think she was a friend of a friend and needed a place to stay. Last night Grandpa gave her a lift out of town."

"Mind if we come in and check the place out?"

"You'll need to come back when Grandpa's home and get his permission." If Grandpa was hurt, wouldn't they have to tell me?

Santa turned to the officer behind him. "Walt, you hear a cry of distress coming from inside that cabin?"

Creepy Eyes made a show of cocking his head and raising his dark eyebrows before he drawled, "Yes sir, I do."

The only sound was Queenie's whine and the pine boughs shuddering in the wind. "What're you talking about?"

"Exigent circumstances, Miss. Sounds like someone needs our help. We're coming in."

Heat flooded my face. "You can't do—" The two men plowed past, knocking me against the wall, bringing the smell of coffee and cigarettes with them. Queenie bared her teeth. I grabbed her collar and crouched by her side. "Stay." I pressed my face against Queenie's back. "Good girl."

Each deputy wore a belt with a holster that held a large gun. They also carried powerful flashlights and began training their beams around the downstairs area. I held my breath, hoping Manuela had the good sense to stay low and keep quiet. The kitchen felt several sizes too small with two deputies tramping around inside. How dare they bend the rules to barge in? Queenie's shoulders tensed below my hand. I wrapped my arm around her, afraid they might hurt her if I didn't keep her still. As long as Manuela stayed hidden, there was a good chance the men would leave soon.

Creepy-eyed Walt pointed the beam of his flashlight at the ladder to the loft. "What's up there?"

"My room." My voice sounded funny. I took a deep breath, then tried to sound in control. "I mean, where I sleep."

Walt aimed his light at the door set into the rear wall of the kitchen. "What about back there?"

"Bathroom and my grandpa's bedroom."

He went to explore.

This didn't feel right. The cops showing up at night. Faking a reason to come inside. Were they hunting for Manuela? Why not come out and ask about her? Grandpa would go wild if he came back now and found these guys poking through his stuff. Police or not. "What're you looking for?"

Santa didn't answer. He moved into the kitchen and started opening cupboards. "Where's your grandfather?"

"Not in there."

He turned, frowned. "This isn't the time to be a smart-aleck. Answer the question."

I took another deep breath and patted Queenie's shoulder. "Out."

"Out where?"

"Running a few errands." I wanted to bite my tongue. Errands? In the middle of the night? In an area where everything shut down at sunset? "He'll be back soon." Queenie continued to hold her position, ears pricked forward, eyes trained on Santa. I let go of her and stood.

"Uh-huh." Santa opened the icebox, looked at the contents then slammed the door. He pulled a chair out from the kitchen table and straddled it. "What kind of errands does your grandfather run at…" He aimed his flashlight at his wristwatch. "At 10:45 p.m.? Besides giving rides to young girls?"

This would probably go better if I kept my mouth shut. After repeating the 'stay' command to Queenie, I walked to the sink and filled a glass with water before I answered. "You'll have to ask him."

"Oh, I will. Count on that. But, what kind of grandfather leaves a little girl like you all alone out in the middle of the woods at night?"

I clutched the glass, turned, and stared. Santa tilted his chair back and looked me up. For the first time I understood what it meant when someone said their flesh crawled. Queenie growled again. I returned to her side. "Good girl. Stay."

The legs of Santa's chair thumped against the wood floor.

I jumped. Water sloshed over my wrist and dripped onto Queenie's back. I ran my free hand along her damp fur. Images of the Snake Dancer's damaged face rippled inside my brain. After getting a call from the cops, was Dad picturing me the same way as the Snake Dancer? "What did you say to my dad?"

"Huh?" Santa pulled a toothpick from his shirt pocket and began digging around between his teeth.

"My dad. When you called about finding my phone on the Snake Dancer. What did you tell him?"

In spite of the gloomy lighting, he squinted at me as he crossed his forearms along the chair's back. "All I know is he told a Modoc County deputy that his daughter was staying in the Mendocino Forest with her grandfather." His mouth curved into a humorless smile. "Oh yeah. He also said this wasn't the first phone she'd lost."

So Dad wasn't worried. One problem down. I gulped more water, ignoring the magnet-like pull of the loft. The other deputy rattled around in Grandpa's room, the sounds clear: the creak of the closet door, hangers sliding across the clothes bar, drawers scraping open. Sweat pooled under my arms. The clock ticked at regular intervals, like the cabin's heartbeat, but its hands seemed frozen in place. From her hiding place, could Manuela see what was going on? Did she have to pee as bad as I did?

Santa stood. "Walt, you about done back there?"

Creepy Eyes marched from Grandpa's bedroom. The broad smile on his face didn't make him look any more agreeable. He nodded. "We're good."

Santa raised his bushy eyebrows. "You sure?"

"Yes sir," Walt said.

There was nothing pleasant about Santa's answering grin. The two swaggered out of the cabin.

This was about more than an injured girl, but I didn't know what. I was missing something here. Something big.

Even through the pitch-black night, the dirt cloud raised by their wheels was visible as they drove off. I

143

waited in the open doorway until the dust settled. After I relocked the door, I stared at the lantern on the kitchen table. What had happened to the Snake Dancer? Was she alive? Grandpa couldn't have done that to her. Could he? Though he hadn't been a part of my life until this summer, I'd lived with him for a little over three weeks now. I couldn't picture him doing something violent. Not to a girl. But if Grandpa didn't beat the Snake Dancer, who did? And was Grandpa okay?

  I hurried to the base of the ladder. "Manuela? Ahora estás safe. Um … seguro." Right. I didn't know what was going on, what right did I have to tell the girl she was safe? Her bruised face appeared out of the shadows. She stared down but didn't speak, her eyes huge in the dark. Maybe she should stay up there. Might be safer. I searched my brain for the words. "¿Usted quiere quedarse allí?"

  "Sí," she whispered.

  "Okay." I couldn't blame her. In her shoes, I'd stay hidden, too. "Come on, Queenie." The dog followed me to the kitchen where I leaned against the counter. On this visit, the cops didn't say a word about the injured girl from the woods. My stomach continued to churn. Though they showed me the picture of the Snake Dancer, it seemed like they'd come for some other reason. Creepy-eyed Walt looked like he'd found something in Grandpa's room that made him happy. But what? Nothing made sense. More than anything, I wanted to call Dad and ask him to come get me. Things were way out of hand here. He probably wouldn't hesitate to drive up – especially after getting a call from the cops. But I couldn't leave Manuela alone. Besides, town – along with the closest phone – was eight miles away.

Hopefully, when Grandpa got back, he would come through on his promise and explain everything.

Chapter Nineteen

Midnight came and went. The hours dribbled then darted; time no longer seemed measured. My thoughts wandered from the injured girl in the loft to the Snake Dancer's battered face to the creepy deputy and the smile he gave when he came out of Grandpa's room. Why did Walt look so happy? Whatever sparked his joy, I doubted it meant anything good for Grandpa. Still wide awake at 2:30, I decided to inspect his room.

On top of the dresser sat a jar half-filled with coins, a deck of cards, and another Coleman lantern. I placed the lighted oil lamp from the kitchen next to the unlit one, took a deep breath, and opened the bottom drawer. Plaid flannels and sweatshirts. Nothing earth-shattering. Even so, going through Grandpa's stuff felt icky. Make that way icky. But that didn't stop me from pawing through the contents of his drawers. I opened the next one. A stack of T-shirts nestled against faded blue jeans. Nothing for that cop to smile about. The drawer above that housed socks and a few thermal shirts. The top drawer held underwear. No way was I going to search through his boxer shorts. When I pushed the drawer in, it jammed. Not wanting to wake Manuela by thumping at Grandpa's dresser, I eased the drawer back, then gave it a shove. It stuck in the same spot. I swore. I pulled the drawer out and in, but each time it refused to budge beyond the midway point. I snaked my hand between the top of the drawer and the frame, stretching my fingers until they reached to the back. No clothes stuck up or behind to block the path. Stumped, I chewed my lip. Seemed like a bad idea to leave evidence for Grandpa that I searched his room. Of course, he would probably blame the cops, not me. Still the sticking drawer bugged me.

The dresser looked old. Maybe the drawer bottom hung loose, keeping it from closing. I ran my hand across the rough wood underside. My fingers bumped against a thick piece of paper. The stiff sheet drooped beneath the drawer. I crouched to look: a manila envelope, one end taped to the wood. Either gravity and the passage of time – or someone like Walt – had loosened the strip of tape at the other end. I yanked the envelope free. Tucked inside was a piece of newsprint. When I unfolded it, yellowed flakes of paper crumbled free, drifting to the floor. Was this what the cop found? The thing that made him look happy?

The top part of the news clipping showed a photo framing faces blurred by smoke. Several hands held a burning flag aloft. I studied the flag on Grandpa's wall. No way to tell if it was the same one. Most of the accompanying article was torn away, leaving only the caption and opening lines of the story: Protesters Burn an American Flag. The portion of the first paragraph above the tear read: *Radical leader Thomas Buckley incited the crowd to violence on Saturday during an anti-war demonstration in Washington DC where—*

I flipped the tattered clipping, but found an unrelated story printed on the reverse. If this was what the cop found, why was it important? Maybe I was jumping to conclusions. Just because the envelope had come unstuck from the drawer bottom, that didn't mean the cop pulled it loose. Yeah, right. I checked the date printed in the upper right hand corner of the page. Why had Grandpa hung on to this thing for forty-five years and hidden it under one of his dresser drawers? Did the flag over the bed mean Grandpa was at the protest mentioned in the story? So what? Who cared if some oddball burned a flag nearly half a century ago? I dropped the paper onto the bed and continued my search.

The closet held no surprises other than a lot more ammunition than I would have guessed Grandpa needed for hunting. Under his bed, I found a neatly rolled sleeping bag plus a box of canned goods. Emergency supplies? I returned to the kitchen and dropped the envelope on the table. One more thing to talk about when Grandpa got back.

* * * *

Half the day was gone before Manuela climbed down from the loft. She seemed to move with greater ease today. When I showed her how to operate the shower, she didn't seem fazed by the open sky peeking around the water barrel above the enclosure. I pointed out the soap and shampoo, gave her a towel, and brought her my hairbrush. While the water ran, I climbed the ladder and searched through my duffle for a T-shirt and jeans she could wear. Other than her shorter height, we looked about the same size. She could always roll up the pant legs.

Ten minutes later when Grandpa pounded on the door, I raced to turn the bolt, Queenie by my side. I only remembered one other time I'd been so happy to see someone. I hugged him hard while Queenie leaned against our legs.

When we broke apart, Grandpa bent down and patted the dog. "How's our guest doing?" He sagged onto a kitchen chair, rubbing his eyes.

"She's in the shower." I pulled a chair close and sat. "The cops came by last night."

"What?" At his agitated tone, Queenie sat up. "It's all right, girl." He leaned forward to stroke her flank.

I told him how they showed up late at night with a photo of the Snake Dancer, broken and bloody. "What happened?"

"You sure it was the same girl?"

"Yeah. Even though she was all… Yeah, it was her. Samantha Dean."

"Dammit." He sat back and ran his hands through his already wild hair. "I took her up to Altura." His gaze met mine. "That's Modoc County's only city. The Greyhound Bus doesn't go anywhere else up there. I told her she had a choice to make. She could take a bus home, take a bus to someplace new, or stay put and get a job. I'd also got in touch with a special halfway house in Deep Creek to see if they had space available. It's off the radar, but they do good work. The girl wanted nothing to do with that. Said she didn't need any help." He sighed and shook his head. "I gave her enough money to last a while. When you got an addict like that, you can't expose the other people in your network to her. You can't trust that she'll protect them."

"So that's what the 'cut-out man' does?"

"Yep. I separate the passenger from the network. Take her someplace where we don't have anybody who was ever on the Lilith Express. It's always a long ride and while I'm driving the girl, that gives Cecilia time to warn anyone the passenger came in contact with." He rubbed his eyes again. "So I left her in Altura. She must've made the wrong choice. Called the wrong person. Or tried to score something from the wrong dealer."

My initial relief that Grandpa hadn't caused the Snake Dancer's injuries sputtered out. "The cops wouldn't tell me if she was alive."

"Sorry I got you messed up in all this."

"You really think one bad decision caused whatever happened to her?"

Grandpa placed a hand on my shoulder. "If that girl did make a bad choice, believe me, it was one in a long string of them." He shook his head. "But, no matter what she may have done, what happened wasn't her fault. We all screw up. Nothing she could've done gave someone the right to beat her bloody."

"What about the other girl? Manuela. You said she wasn't part of the Lilith Express."

He faced the window, shook his head. "Far as I'm concerned, this is the most beautiful place on God's green earth. But, nothing's perfect." He turned back to look at me. "We got a helluva problem up here with cartels running pot farms in the forest. That's why I wanted you to stay on my land or the road when you went running or hiking. And, if having pot fields with armed guards out there isn't bad enough, every now and then the cartels kidnap a girl or two and bring them up to the farms – to keep the men happy. They usually grab someone who's in the US illegally, knowing no one's gonna go to the cops when the girl goes missing. But we got a couple deputies who aren't above grabbing runaways. That's why Cecilia gets worked up if one of her passengers misses a stop in these parts."

"Oh."

"Cecilia does what she can to fight back. And I've helped what girls I can, helped them to get away. Cecilia's always ready to put them on the Lilith Express. As for the girl from the woods"— he nodded toward his bedroom— "she was the latest one to get kidnapped and dragged up here. She had more spunk than a lot of the others. Got away on her own. Before they grabbed her again. Queenie and I tracked her to the camp where they were holding her."

"You took her from them?"

"Don't look so amazed. The men were drunk. Made taking her pretty easy. It's keeping her that'll be tough. Those bad seeds in the sheriff's department, they help the cartel keep the girls under control. And those two aren't gonna stop looking until they find her. We need to get her out of here fast."

The sound of running water stopped. "Manuela must be done showering." I picked up the buff-colored envelope. "When the cops were here, I think they found this."

Grandpa took it from my hand and ran his finger along the loose flap. "What happened?"

I recounted how the cop named Walt rummaged around in Grandpa's room for several minutes and came out smiling. Next I confessed how, once they'd gone, I looked around his room, trying to figure out what made the deputy look that way. "The top dresser drawer jammed. When I checked underneath it, this was hanging down. The tape had come loose from one end."

Grandpa stalked into his bedroom and I trailed behind him. He wrenched open the second dresser drawer, kneeled, and tore an envelope from the underside. After slamming the drawer, he repeated the process with the other two drawers.

Apparently I had a lot to learn about searching someone's room.

Grandpa's knees creaked when he straightened. He tossed the sealed envelopes onto the bed then went to his closet and ran his hand along the bottom of the lone shelf inside. "Dammit. They got one." He turned and looked at me. "Ego." He shook his head. "Ego'll bite you in the butt every time." He grabbed a satchel from the closet and began stuffing clothes inside. "I'm sorry to do this you to, Nicki. But I gotta get going. I'll be gone for a while. Don't know how long." He pulled the sleeping bag from underneath the bed then looked at me.

"What?" My stomach wobbled.

"Don't worry, you'll be all right. I can't go through town on this trip, but the first payphone I come to, I'll call Cecilia. She'll come get you and Manuela. When you get to her place, you can call your dad." He hefted his carryall, picked up the envelopes, and walked to the kitchen.

I trotted after him. "You're leaving?"

"Got to." Grandpa tossed the envelopes on the table. He crouched by the dog and rubbed her ears. "I want you to take care of Queenie for me. Take her with you when you go back home. I'll come get her when I can." He stood, fished around in the pocket of his jeans, and then handed me her dog whistle. "In the meantime, give her a good home."

"Where're you going?"

"It's better if you don't know. Those deputies used Manuela as an excuse to come knocking. Don't get me wrong – if they'd have found her, they would've hauled her back to the cartel." Grandpa pointed at the news clipping on the table. "But they were really looking for stuff like that." He shook his head. "Didn't find everything, but they got enough." He rested his free hand on my shoulder. "Listen. A long time ago I made a mistake. A big one. A girl got … hurt. If those cops come back and I'm here, I'm going to jail. You probably think

I'm coward and maybe I am. But there's something else, too. If I'm locked up, I can't help Cecilia with her work. Can't help those poor women. And girls. I made a commitment here. To pay for my past."

He cleared his throat. "There's still the fish and one rabbit in the icebox. And you can always shoot another rabbit if you need to."

I nodded, staring at the scattered envelopes on the table.

"If Cecilia hasn't shown up here by noon tomorrow, that means she's gone to ground. You go in to town. The walk will take a few hours. But you can handle it. It's time to call your dad and have him come get you."

"What about Manuela?" The lump in my throat strangled my voice.

"Whatever you do, don't take her to town. And don't call the cops. It's not safe. If Cecilia doesn't show, take the girl to the Wilders."

"The Wilders?"

"Just don't let the dad know. Either Ben or Todd'll help you out."

"But..."

He grabbed the ten-gauge and thrust the sixteen-gauge into my hand. "You hang on to that."

"You're really leaving?"

"You treat Queenie good, and I'll collect her when this blows over."

"How long will you be gone?"

"Depends. I don't know if those deputies only want some leverage to use against me, or if they want me gone entirely. Time will tell."

"What does that mean?"

"Those two get paid to turn a blind eye to the pot fields. I pissed off some folks freeing the cartel girls.

They came digging for a reason." He pointed again at the clipping on the table. "And I'm betting that after our argument on the roof of the general store, Wilder told them about my weak spot. I never should've trusted him." He shook his head. "The dad's a greedy bastard, but his boys are all right."

"But you told me to stay away from them."

"I know what I said. I was trying to keep you from getting mixed up in all this. Those boys scout pot farms for me and watch out for signs of kidnapped girls. If they see anything suspicious, they give me the locations." He pointed to the sealed envelopes. "Those are yours now. Do what you want with them." He kissed the top of my head. "I really enjoyed getting to know you this summer, Nicki. You're a great girl. You impressed the hell out of me with how quick you took to hunting and fishing, to living here in the middle of the woods. I'm real proud of you." He walked to the door. "If the cops come back, keep the place locked. Here's the cabin key. You lock it up whenever you go out."

I took the key and nodded.

He drew me in for a hug. "You take care now."

I breathed in wood smoke and pine and hugged him back. He gave me one last squeeze then strode across the clearing.

Queenie and I ran after him, watching as he climbed into his truck. A part of me didn't believe he would really go – until he drove away.

Chapter Twenty

He was gone. Really gone. I sank to my knees on the pine needles, feeling like I was eight years old again. Abandoned. MJ and I staring into Mom's empty side of the closet. But unlike Mom, Grandpa at least said goodbye. Queenie whined. Was this one my fault, too? Mom leaving – that was my fault. MJ never said as much, but she always gave me a weird closed-off look when I asked. And, even if Mom didn't actually leave because of me, she didn't stay because of me either.

I stroked Queenie's head. The dog leaned against me. "I don't think I could've stopped those deputies from going through Grandpa's stuff. Do you?" Queenie's dark eyes looked at me with love. "Okay, that one's not my fault. But he's still gone." I hugged her and breathed in her doggy scent.

Manuela. I couldn't let her find me on my knees and crying. I had to act strong for her. "Come on, girl." I clambered up and led Queenie into the kitchen. The envelopes on the table top drew my eyes. Sounds still came from the back of the cabin. Manuela getting dressed. While I had the kitchen to myself, I pulled open the flap of one of the sealed envelopes. Out spilled three ID cards: Social Security, Selective Service, and driver's license. All in the name of Thomas J. Buckley. I studied the license. Thomas Buckley stood six-foot-four inches and weighed two hundred ten pounds. He had brown eyes and brown hair. I stared at the photo. A lot of years had gone by, but the man in the picture was Grandpa.

So much for boring old John Smith.

The next envelope contained pages cut from a glossy magazine. Mouth dry, I read how during an anti-war protest, Thomas Buckley's Radical Regiment set fire to a college administration building. A student died from smoke inhalation. She was eighteen years old, a freshman. "Omigod." The girl died the same way as MJ.

I stared at the final envelope, no longer hungry to know the truth. Soft footsteps padded across the wood floor, pulling my attention.

Manuela held out the hem of the T-shirt she wore. "Gracias."

"Por nada." How to tell her Grandpa was gone, that we were on our own? I struggled with the Spanish. Fortunately, Manuela was quick on the uptake and grasped the meaning behind my insufficient words. If my Spanish teacher, Senora Hurley, heard me butchering the language like this, I bet she would've dropped my grade from an A to a D.

I told Manuela I wanted her to become friends with Queenie. That once the dog thought of her as part of the family, Queenie would protect her. The girl's hand shook as she held it out for Queenie's inspection. The dog sniffed Manuela's fingers, palm, and wrist then sat back on her haunches.

"Good girl." I pantomimed for Manuela to kneel on the floor like I did. Not as much white showed around the brown of her eyes, making her look less alarmed. Sometime in her past, Manuela must have had a bad experience with a dog. But, slowly, Queenie won her over. When the girl rested her cheek against Queenie's forehead, I knew Queenie had accepted her as part of our pack and that Manuela trusted the dog.

I encouraged Manuela to rest again in Grandpa's room, but first opened the window and demonstrated how to quietly pop out the screen – something I'd done many a time to my bedroom window back home before getting sent to Grandpa's. This way, if the deputies returned, she had a way to escape. Though we still had people food, Queenie's dog chow was running low. We would need more meat to keep the three of us fed. "Yo estoy miranda..." The word escaped me. I held my hands alongside my head like ears and hopped.

"Conejo?" Manuela made ears of her hands and twitched her nose like a rabbit.

"Si. Conejo. Por la comida. Regresso en uno o dos horas. Okay?"

The girl nodded.

I led her to the door and showed her how to work the bolt. "Quando yo regreso, no abre la puerta hasta yo digo 'Nicki esta aqui.' Tres veces. Okay?"

She nodded again.

Seemed like she understood. I collected the shotgun and ammunition, then donned the orange hat and vest. "No abre la porta hasta yo diga 'Nicki esta aqui.'"

"Si. Tres veces."

"Si." Though I didn't like the idea of hiking through the woods without Queenie, leaving Manuela with some protection was more important.

Ten feet inside the tree line the feeling hit me – the same one I got when hunting for the first time with Grandpa. Without Queenie by my side, the woods seemed endless. Strange. Menacing. Every twig crack made me jump. A lizard darted across the path, and I nearly peed myself. Sweat dripped down my sides. I had to get a grip. To take my mind off the woods, I focused on what happened with Grandpa.

Seemed pretty clear Deputy Walt found something in the closet linking Grandpa with Thomas Buckley. The way the cops acted made me think that though they were happy about what they found, they weren't surprised. If Grandpa was right and the cops were coming for him, how long did Manuela and I have before they returned to the cabin? On TV, cops got search warrants before the next commercial break. How long did it take in real life? One day? Two? Grandpa said that deputy Walt couldn't be trusted.

The earliest Cecilia might show was noon tomorrow. If she didn't come for Manuela, I would run to town and call Dad. If the cops showed up again tonight, I needed to find a better way to protect the girl – besides telling her to climb out the window and hide in the woods with the wild animals. If they came back with a search warrant, lurking in the loft wouldn't work.

Every ten paces, I stopped and stared at the surrounding brush, like Grandpa taught me, looking for the reflection of an eye or any sudden movement. After a half hour with no success, I spotted him. Dusty brown and long-eared, frozen beside a rotted log. I sighted down the sixteen-gauge's barrel.

I heard a new sound. I lifted my finger from the trigger and listened. Twig-crunching steps. The rabbit bolted. Still on Grandpa's land, no one else should be here but me. I lowered the gun and wiped my damp palms against my jeans, staring into the surrounding brush. Nothing nearby moved, though the sounds grew louder. I darted into the scrub and crouched. A few minutes later, a man's head became visible between a gap in the trees, then disappeared. A second man appeared then dissolved into the forest. The men from the pot field? Or the ones who grabbed Manuela? Or some new threat? The thick-growing trees made it hard to see their faces as they walked between the trunks. One man wore a strap across his chest like the guard in the field. Did that mean he also carried an automatic weapon? Armed as I was, I still felt like a rabbit at the wrong end of a shotgun. I pulled off my orange hat and vest and tucked them behind me. The brush was thick, but not dense enough to hide that color. I remembered Grandpa saying the hunter spots the prey's eye first. I closed my eyes and pointed my face at the ground hoping my blonde hair didn't give me away if anyone spotted it.

The crunching footsteps drew near. I held my breath. More branches snapped then the sound began to fade. I lifted my head, peeked through the branches, and stood. About eight yards to the east, two men walked away from me. A huge gun was strapped across the second man's retreating back. Definitely the men from the pot field. Same clothes as when Ben and I spied on them. Same hardware, too. Armed and dangerous. Men to avoid. I ducked down again and waited until my heartbeat returned to something approaching normal. Then I waited some more. Finally, I straightened. The woods looked empty.

My legs were rubbery and my right hand had gone numb from clutching the sixteen-gauge. I gathered my hat and vest and started down the hill, away from the men. The grizzly in my gut roared. I doubled over and took a deep breath. Oh God. The men were heading for the crest, straight toward the Wilders' farm. Did they plan to hurt Todd or Ben because of their part in alerting Grandpa about Manuela or some other girl?

I chewed my lip as I reversed course, keeping behind a screen of trees. Without Queenie's paws and panting, the woods seemed bigger than ever. I hoped they were big enough to keep me from running into the men I was following. At least I was armed, though I doubted I had what it took to shoot at a person – even a dangerous-looking one. A few yards shy of the crest, I tucked the orange hat and vest beneath a rotting log. At the ridge, I hid behind a pine, eyes straining to catch sight of the men between the trees. Nothing. I edged my way forward, moving tree-to-tree, keeping out of sight. Because of Grandpa's warnings against the Wilders, I'd never hiked so far in this direction before and didn't know the lay of the land. Up ahead, the sun looked bright. Some kind of break in the tree line maybe? I tiptoed through the pine needles until I reached the edge of the woods and stared down at a bowl-like clearing.

My mouth dropped open. The Wilders' farm was huge. Eight greenhouses and several small sheds dotted the cleared slopes surrounding the flat area where the house sat. The Wilders' home was constructed from logs like Grandpa's, but that's where the comparison ended. Instead of the age-darkened wood exterior of Grandpa's cabin, the logs here practically glowed gold in the sunlight. Tall windows glinted and a wide porch ran along the front. The whole place made Grandpa's cabin look like a shack. A small dark shack. The satellite dish on the roof meant Todd and Ben didn't spend their nights reading the latest offering from the general store's lending library by lantern light.

Twenty-five yards below the tree line, the two men strode between the plant rows in a wide tilled area near the bottom of the slope. They were headed for the Wilders' house. Should I fire a warning shot? Let the Wilders know danger was coming their way? I crawled from the safety of the trees to the nearest glass house. The panes were coated with something white. I couldn't see in but that meant if someone was inside, they couldn't see me hiding behind the building – and neither could the men below.

The smell of skunk wafted by. I froze, scanning beneath the closest group of shrubs for a black and white stink bomb. The area seemed clear. Maybe the critter had already turned tail. Gun barrel pointed at the dirt, I crept to the building's front corner to see what the men were up to. If they had come for some kind of revenge against Ben or Todd, I wanted to be ready to help. Though I didn't know how.

The angry man I met on the roof of the general store stepped out of the house and onto the porch. Mr. Wilder. He climbed down the steps, waved at the two men. As far as I could tell, he wasn't carrying a gun. He also didn't look worried that the two men heading his way were armed. Mr. Wilder shook their hands then led them inside. They acted like old friends. Not like they were here for payback.

So the men from the pot field knew Mr. Wilder? I pressed my cheek against the cool glass wall. This place and its people baffled me. I retreated a couple steps and faced the greenhouse. Feeling foolish over my sad attempt at playing hero, I gave the wood door a kick. It shuddered and bounced open a few inches. I froze. Nobody yelled in alarm. I peeked back around the side of the glass building. Mr. Wilder and his pals were still inside the house. I cracked the door open another inch and peered in.

"Oh." The air left my lungs. I sagged against the door frame and blinked twice. The scene didn't change: rows and rows of pot plants filled the greenhouse. After double-checking that no one lurked nearby, I stepped inside, closing the door behind me. After a few deep breaths, a new thought formed: that skunky smell on Todd the other day didn't come from an animal. It came from the pot plants. Weed was what the Wilders farmed.

Weed was the family business. And Todd hadn't said a word about it.

The urge to get out of there set my nerves humming.

I heard deep voices. I leaned against the door, chewed my lower lip, and waited. Men were talking, their words indistinct. I pressed my ear against the glass. After what felt like an eternity, but was probably five minutes, the sounds faded. I inched the door open. It was still quiet. No footsteps, no conversation. I pushed the door farther and peered out. No one was in sight. I slipped from the greenhouse, then crept to the rear of the building. A door slammed. I peeked around the corner. Halfway down the slope to my left, Todd stood in front of one of the wooden sheds. I darted back behind the greenhouse and dropped to my knees. Sixteen-gauge clutched in both hands, I tried to make myself as small as possible. Keeping my face close to the ground, I peeked around the building again. The two men stood in front of the Wilders' house along with Ben and his father. Todd jogged down the hill to join them.

While the five men below talked, I crawled up the hill to the tree line, keeping the greenhouse between me and everyone else. Once out of sight among the pines, I started to run. Careful to keep my hand away from the shotgun's trigger, I ignored the trail, crashing through the underbrush. A cut on my arm stung, but I kept going. When I was halfway down the other side of the hill, I finally stopped and peered through the trees behind me. No one seemed to be following. I leaned against a tree to catch my breath. The rough bark against my skin told me this was no nightmare. This was real.

All my friends smoked weed. Maybe not every day, but at parties. It was healthier than drinking – though

we did that, too. But smoking a joint or sharing a pipe –
or even growing a couple plants at home – seemed way
different than what the Wilders did. Wasn't it? Didn't
people who stumbled across hidden pot fields wind up
dead? Did that make the Wilders killers?

I started walking again, glancing over my
shoulder every few steps. When I reached the cabin, a
new thought hit. Grandpa knew what the Wilders grew.
He had to. Was that the reason he and Mr. Wilder fought?
Was that why he called Mr. Wilder a 'greedy bastard?'

Todd lied to me. And he hung out with armed
men. If that wasn't bad enough, Grandpa was gone.
Would I ever see him again?

When I reached the clearing in front of the cabin,
I realized I had forgotten all about scoring a rabbit.
Before calling Manuela to the door, I unlatched the gate
to the chicken run, fed the birds, and collected four eggs.
Plenty for our meal. Queenie could have the one rabbit
left in the icebox.

Manuela had understood my garbled Spanish
instructions and waited for me to announce myself for the
third time before she unbolted the door. I didn't tell her
about the armed men. That was probably wrong of me,
but I didn't want to scare her. Besides, if Cecilia showed
up tomorrow to take Manuela to safety, there was no
reason for her to ever know.

In case the deputies returned, I stayed outside
until night surrounded me, wanting as much advance
warning of their approach as possible. Queenie and I
circled the cabin and scouted possible hiding spots for
Manuela in the nearby trees and scrub, the dog dancing
along, enjoying our forays into the brush. When the last
traces of light left the sky, I went inside, pulled the
curtains, then locked and bolted the kitchen door.

Manuela offered to cook. I added wood to the stove's fire box and showed her where the matches were stored. Popping open the panel to the drying cupboard, I grabbed a bunch of oregano to add to the eggs. When Manuela started dishing up the food, I told her to take my share. The sight of those men with the Wilders had killed my appetite.

Manuela ate almost twice as much as she had the day before, and I took that as a good sign. I poured the last of the dog food into Queenie's dish. Though my hunting trip hadn't worked out as planned, we still had enough food in the icebox for tomorrow – if we needed it. And, if Grandpa's plan worked out, Cecilia would be here by noon to take us to safety.

Chapter Twenty-One

A buttery light filtered through the curtains. I rubbed my eyes and sat up. Except for the whoosh of Queenie's breath, the cabin was quiet. The night before, Manuela went back to sleeping in Grandpa's room. Not as hidden, but, with her bruised legs and arms, it was much easier than climbing the ladder. Me and the shotgun spent another night on the sofa. I petted Queenie before walking into the kitchen to check the time. Had Grandpa managed to find a phone last night and call Cecilia? Pay phones were scarce as hens' teeth. Scarce as hens' teeth? Where the hell did that expression come from? Nice work, Grandpa. I was going to sound like a complete weirdo by the time I went home.

Even if Grandpa found a phone, Cecilia could've 'gone to ground' as he put it. Probably best to plan for the worst. If Cecilia didn't show, I'd head to town and try to call her. I needed to get Manuela somewhere safe and wasn't going to park her at the Wilders. Not after what I'd seen yesterday – no matter what Grandpa had told me.

In case we wound up being on our own for a while, Manuela needed to get comfortable using the shotgun. Seeing the armed men in Grandpa's woods yesterday felt like a warning. If those guys wanted to find the cabin, they wouldn't have far to look. No way would I give them another chance to take the girl.

By the time Manuela rose, I'd fed Queenie and the chickens, and boiled water for tea. Manuela dressed in a pair of my jeans and one of Grandpa's flannel shirts – with both the sleeves and pant legs rolled up. I climbed to the loft and grabbed a pair of sneakers and brought them down to her. Manuela put the right shoe on and chuckled, a warm sound I'd never heard her make before. I looked at her foot swimming around in my boat of a shoe and smiled. "Un momento." Up in the loft, I grabbed two pairs of socks. When I returned, I pantomimed pulling on the socks and Manuela nodded. While she slipped them on, I stuffed a sock into the toe of each shoe. This time, when she tied them, the sneakers didn't look like they would fall off.

Manuela's laugh wasn't the only new thing: the bluish-purple of the bruises on her face had shifted to greenish-blue. She still moved like her legs were made from dry mint stalks, but she seemed to feel better. With a mix of English and Spanish, I managed to explain what I wanted. She nodded, patted Queenie, and followed me outside.

Queenie pranced back and forth between us as I led the way into the woods. Once we reached the second clearing, I got Queenie situated out of the line of fire and told her to stay. I beckoned Manuela to the east end of the clearing and demonstrated how to work the sixteen-gauge. It turned out she already knew the basics. I handed her the gun and supervised while she loaded the shells. In her weak state, I worried the gun's kick might knock her over. While Manuela shot, I stood behind her with a hand on each of her shoulders.

After she reloaded, I took the gun. "Look. Um, mira." I pointed at a downed tree on the far side of the clearing then lifted the sixteen-gauge and aimed. At the shot's roar, birds erupted from the brush. "Mira," I repeated. The downed tree now had one less branch stabbing skyward. I gave her the gun. Her next shot burst through a leaf cluster, but missed the log. Two shots later, Manuela drilled the dead tree.

I kept her practicing for thirty more minutes before heading back. Manuela's face looked pale and her feet scuffed up pine needles with each step. When we reached the cabin, she tottered into Grandpa's room to rest.

Queenie's gaze bobbed from me to the bedroom. "Go on. You keep our guest company." Queenie trotted through the opening before the door snicked shut. I shouldered the gun and walked outside to wait for Cecilia's arrival.

After two hours with only birds and squirrels approaching the cabin, I climbed to the loft, changed into running shoes and shorts, and pulled my hair into a ponytail. I climbed back down the ladder, crossed into the kitchen, and stared at the smoke-stained planks of the bedroom door. Manuela didn't have much stamina yet, but she wouldn't be helpless – as long as she was armed. I knocked.

"Si?" The wood floor creaked and Manuela opened the door. Queenie nosed her way out and leaned against my leg.

"Yo vengo por…" Oh jeez, I should've thought this through before I started talking. "For help. I mean, uh…por ayuda. Okay?"

She nodded.

"Yo regreso en…" For eight miles on the rough terrain, a ten-minute mile was doable. When I reached town, I'd get Cecilia's number. I'd also give Dad a call. The weirdness of this world made me miss him. Though our house was haunted and sad, at least it was familiar. So far my luck reaching him had sucked. I might need to call a few times before I caught him. But I couldn't spend too much time trying; I didn't want to run back through the woods after sunset. To avoid worrying Manuela, I padded my estimate. "Seis horas." That would still get me home before the pitch dark of night.

"Okay." She smiled then crouched beside Queenie and rubbed the dog's thick coat.

For the first time, I got a peek at what Manuela must've looked like before she got kidnapped. A happy, pretty teenage girl. I gave her the cabin key and pantomimed keeping everything locked until I got back.

"Hasta la vista." I waited outside the threshold until the lock clicked.

After all the stress of the last three days, running gave me a feeling of freedom. Freedom times ten. The tension left my jaw and the brain cloud settled around me, muffling my worries, fear, and guilt. Birdsong and the whuff of my shoes against the dirt trail was my soundtrack and warmth filled my chest.

Before leaving the cabin, I'd stowed a sweatshirt and another pair of socks inside my knapsack along with the canteen and knife. On my way out, I spied the manila envelopes Grandpa entrusted me with and tucked them into my pack, too. Leaving them in plain sight didn't seem like a good idea. I also dumped the contents of Grandpa's change jar into the zipper pocket of my pack, making me four bucks and ninety-two cents richer. As I ran, the added weight knocked against my lower back, but I would need the coins for the general store's payphone.

The tree canopy grew thick, the occasional downed tree letting in a pocket of sunshine. My brain cloud fizzled as a hollowness crept through my chest. For some reason, I felt like I was abandoning Grandpa, the cabin, and Manuela. Even though Grandpa was the one who left first.

Stop it. As long as those deputies didn't come by the cabin while I was gone, everything would be fine.

Somewhere in mile six, I slowed to a walk. Running on the lumpy, pitted trail to town was taking longer than I'd calculated. A rustle came from the underbrush. I scurried forward, putting a few yards between me and the sound before pulling out the canteen and drinking. Water dribbled down my jaw and onto my chest, cooling my skin. The rustling started again. I sure wished Queenie was with me. Fortunately, the only critters I spotted were two startled rabbits and a gray squirrel. I shoved the canteen back inside the knapsack and continued running.

The looming trees kept the air temperature from climbing, but the long shadows made my nerves hum and I kept speeding up. Now my legs complained that I'd pushed too hard. I started walking again. Off to my right, a branch cracked. I jumped.

"Hello?"

The sound of heavy wings lifting off came as the only answer. Some kind of bird. Nothing to worry about. But my racing heart disagreed. "Screw it." I began to jog.

Forty minutes later when I reached town, I pulled my sweatshirt from the pack and wiped off my face, chest, and armpits. I looked at the pink scar snaking up my arm. In spite of the heat, I pulled on the sweatshirt, tugging both cuffs down over my wrists before crossing the road to the general store.

Inside, Dennis stood a few feet away talking to a customer.

While I waited, I studied the feed bins. As soon as he wrapped up his sale, I approached.

"Nicki. Hi. Where's John?"

Good question, but none of his business. I put on what I hoped was a bright smile. "Back at the cabin. I felt like a run, and Grandpa wanted me to give Cecilia a call for him. But I forgot to bring her phone number. Do you know her? Cecilia Bonnard?"

He ran a hand along one of his bushy sideburns. "Don't think so."

I tried again. "Short lady. English accent. Long gray hair she wears in a ponytail?"

"'Fraid not. Must do her shopping elsewhere."

Strike one. "Too bad. Thanks anyway."

The payphone hung on the wall behind the tack display. I breathed in the smell of leather as I plunked my coins into the slot then pressed 4-1-1. After telling the mechanical voice what I wanted, it informed me there was no listing for Cecilia Bonnard. Dammit. Why have a phone if you didn't want people calling you? Strike two. I dropped more coins into the slot and keyed in Dad's cell. An automated voice told me the number was unavailable. I leaned my forehead against the cool metal of the phone's faceplate and took a deep breath.

No need to panic. Right. I tried Dad's work number. The call went to voicemail. I opened my mouth, but no sounds came out. The situation was too big to explain in a message. I hung up. Was Dad out of town? I chewed my lower lip and went outside to sit on the store's porch. I'd give it fifteen minutes before trying again.

When the sun moved a quarter hour lower in the sky, I made my way to the payphone. The same message played on Dad's cell. This time when his work line shunted me to voicemail, I was ready, but I kept things vague. That was one thing about Single-Surviving-Child Syndrome – it was way too easy to accidentally freak out a parent. Leaving a message that Grandpa took off and charged me with watching over the battered victim of a kidnapping would definitely fall in the 'freak him out' category. Instead I asked him to call the general store and gave him the number taped to the front of the payphone then went back out on the porch and stared at the empty road.

Four o'clock came with no return call. I went in and gave it one more try. By this point, my butt was sore from sitting on the wood step and I didn't feel quite as concerned about worrying Dad. This time I told him I needed him to come get me.

After I hung up, I stared at the phone. Had I sounded scared or just upset? Mad was okay, but if Dad thought I was scared, he might wind up asking the local cops to check on us. From all Grandpa's warnings, I didn't think that would go well for Manuela.

The prospect of another night at the cabin without Grandpa was spooky, but I didn't see any other choice. I stood in front of the store and stretched. My legs felt as spongy as the pine needle-covered trail I'd run in on. Not a good sign. I checked the sun's progress. Even at a fast pace, walking back would take three hours, and I'd be stuck travelling through the woods after dark. Once more I wished Queenie was at my side.

The rusted white pickup parked at the gas station across the road caught my attention. Something about it seemed familiar. So did the blond head I spied on the far side of the cab. Though what I'd recently learned about the Wilders troubled me, Todd had no idea I knew. He wouldn't see me as a threat to him or his family. Why not ask for a ride? I trotted across the road. "Hey."

Todd turned, smiled.

My heartbeat quickened. As alarmed as I was about the gunmen at his house and the lies he'd told, when I saw that smile and the heat in his eyes, I raced to his side. Todd would get me home safely.

He scanned the street behind me. "You alone?"

"Yeah."

"Good." His smile broadened. "I wasn't looking forward to another run-in with your gramps."

Even though I knew Grandpa's hostility toward Todd was another lie, I managed to smile in return. "Can you give me a lift?"

"Sure." He leaned down and kissed me. Logic melted away and I wrapped my arms around his neck. When we broke apart, he did a quick street scan. "How'd you get here?"

"Ran." I wrinkled my nose. Something nearby reeked.

"Damn. More power to you." He walked me around to the passenger side of the truck. "Climb on in." He closed the door for me, then sauntered to the driver's side and settled behind the wheel. When he pulled away from the pump, the stench didn't lessen.

"Is that your truck?"

"Is what my truck?"

"That stink. Something smells like dog poop."

"That's the manure. I didn't have time to hose out the back after the last load. Manure's a great fertilizer."

I turned. The back of the truck was empty, but the truck bed floor was striped with brown along the ridges. "Oh." One of the last things I wanted to talk about was the Wilders' farm.

"You run into town for the hell of it? Or did you need something?" He took one hand from the wheel and brushed the hair back from my forehead.

What to say? "I wanted to call my dad."

We thumped off the paved road into the woods. Todd slowed, ran his index finger along my jaw.

Wow. The guy could still make my heart do somersaults.

He returned his hand to the wheel. "How's he doing?"

"No idea. He didn't pick up."

"You know, you can always use the phone at our place." Four quails hustled across the dirt track. Todd braked. A dozen baby birds followed the adults like a fuzzy kite tail. "Dad has a satellite phone."

"Won't he get pissed if he sees me?"

Todd's head swung from side to side, checking for more crossing critters before he accelerated. "Yeah. But Dad's schedule is pretty fixed. Most days, he's gone for an hour or two. If you want to use the phone tomorrow, the coast will be clear all afternoon. He's got some business out of town. You can come by whenever your gramps isn't looking."

Huh. Just when I thought I couldn't trust the guy, he invites me to his farm? Maybe I should ask him for Cecilia's phone number. Todd knew about the Lilith Express, so he had to know Cecilia. But if I opened up about that, would I be able to stop? Or would the story of Grandpa taking off pour out, too? How far could I really trust Todd? "Thanks." I swallowed the rest of my thoughts.

When we were still one bend away from the cabin's clearing, Todd stopped the truck. "Should I drop you here?"

"Nah. Grandpa had to run an errand. He won't be back for an hour or so." Pretending Grandpa was out would save me walking the final half-mile. My stomach knotted. It wasn't pretend. Grandpa was out. Who knew if he was ever coming back?

"Door-to-door service it is." The truck lurched forward across the soft ground. "Everything all right?"

"What do you mean?" My voice sounded hoarse. I cleared my throat.

"You don't seem like yourself."

"I'm fine. Got some stuff on my mind."

"Anything you want to talk about?"

I shook my head. "Not right now."

Todd slowed to negotiate the dip in the trail that marked the beginning of Grandpa's clearing. "What the…"

My mouth dropped open. I fumbled for the door handle while the truck rolled forward.

"Wait." Todd stomped on the brake. "What happened here?"

I jumped down from the cab and ran toward the cabin's smashed front door.

Chapter Twenty-Two

"Manuela!"

Inside, the kitchen table lay on its side and the contents of the icebox and cabinets were tossed together on the floor like a strange sort of salad. "Manuela? Queenie?" The smell of lamp oil, spoiled rabbit, and honey filled the kitchen. I covered my nose as I stepped around a sticky-looking pile of paper, food, and clothes and hurried into Grandpa's room. Someone had ripped the flag from the wall and it lay puddled by the dresser. I peeked under the bed, inside the closet. All were empty.

When I raced from the room, I smacked into Todd. He grabbed my shoulders and held me upright.

"What the hell's going on here?"

"I have to find Manuela."

"Who?"

"The girl from the woods."

"What?" His face paled.

"She was here, okay? Oh God." I pushed past Todd, waded through the debris pile, and ran to the ladder. Something crunchy stuck to the bottom of my sneaker and a crackling noise accompanied each step up the rungs. At the crest, I peered into the gloomy loft. "Manuela?" No answer. Two more steps and I was inside the loft. Manuela wasn't behind or under the bed. That was it for hiding places. On trembling legs, I made the trip down to the main room.

Todd stood, hands on hips, staring at the disaster area of our kitchen. "Who did this?"

"Some deputies? Or your dad's buddies from the pot farm?" Heat traveled down my face to my neck and my voice grew loud. I pointed at Todd. "They're probably the ones who took Manuela in the first place."

His jaw moved up and down, but no words came out. Todd licked his lips and tried again. "You know about those men?"

"I saw them with your dad. I saw them with you."

"Look—"

"Shhh." I held my hand up for silence. That sound. Was it the wind? Or something else? I skirted Todd and the pile of trashed belongings, then froze. Not the wind. Something humming? "Don't move." I closed my eyes and strained to hear. I noticed the scent of mint mixed with the odor of rot. "Mint. Oh." I took two steps and shoved the wood-panel that fronted the drying cupboard. The door popped open. "Manuela."

The girl tumbled from the shallow cabinet into my arms, shaking like pine needles in a high wind. I walked her to the kitchen counter to give her something more substantial to lean on.

Slumped over the counter, Manuela covered her face and murmured, "Gracias Jesus, Maria y Josef."

"Are you all right? I mean, estás bien? How long, um, cuánto tiempo in there?" I pointed at the dark recess inside the cabinet.

Manuela's back heaved with each noisy breath. She neither turned to look nor answered.

I peeked inside the cupboard, but there was no sign of the dog. With soft hands, I turned the girl toward me. I couldn't wait until she felt better. Whoever did this might come back. "Donde esta Queenie?"

"No se." Tears streaked her face.

"Who did this?" My voice shook. I gestured at the kitchen.

Eyes wide, Manuela retreated against the counter.

"Shit. Lo siento. Quein…"

"What're you trying to ask her?" Todd stepped toward us.

"You speak Spanish?"

"Yeah. Comes in handy on the farm."

The farm. I didn't want to think about the Wilders' farm. I took a deep breath. "I'm blanking out here. I want to ask her who did this."

He nodded. "¿Quien hizo esto a usted?"

Manuela crossed her arms over her chest then looked down. "Dos hombres." Her dark hair tumbled forward, screening her face.

Had Santa and Walt come back with a search warrant? How long had she been stuck in that dark narrow space? "¿La policía?" At least I remembered that phrase.

"No se."

I turned to Todd. "Ask if they wore uniforms."

"¿Los hombres llevaban uniformes?"

"No se." Manuela lifted her face. Her voice grew stronger as the words poured out.

I couldn't follow their rapid-fire conversation and went to the kitchen window. I stared at Queenie's favorite shady spot by the vegetable patch. Through the jumble of back and forths between Todd and Manuela, one word froze my heart. I rushed to Todd's side and grabbed his arm. "She said something about Queenie. Where is she? What happened?"

"I don't know yet." Todd layered his hand over mine.

I pulled my hand free and balled my fists in front of my mouth as Manuela and Todd continued talking.

Todd turned to me. "She says she hid in the loft when she heard a car approaching. But then someone started banging on the door. When an axe head splintered part of the wood, she climbed down. She was able to lift Queenie out the window in your gramps' bedroom, but wasn't wearing shoes and couldn't follow the dog. Instead, she hid in the cupboard."

Queenie was a smart dog. She'd be okay. She had to be. "How does Manuela know there were two of them?"

Todd translated my question. When the girl finished talking, he said, "She heard their voices. While she hid."

"Grandpa said the deputies would be back." I looked at the mess on the floor. "Would deputies break down the door and tear the place apart?"

"Which deputies? What's going on?" he said.

I faced the girl. "Yo debo … find el perro. Después…" I turned to Todd again. "Tell Manuela that once I find Queenie, I'll take her someplace safe. That I'll keep her safe."

"You don't know what you're getting into."

I pictured the man clubbing Manuela with the butt of his gun. I knew damn well what I was getting into. "Tell her."

When he finished talking to Manuela, he looked at me. "This is a mistake."

"Manuela." I grasped her small hand in mine. "I promise. Prometo. Okay?"

She nodded. Todd righted one of the kitchen chairs and the girl sank onto it.

Outside, the smell of spoiled food and lamp oil mixed with the scent of pine. I raced to the truck and retrieved my knapsack from the front seat. After rummaging in the zipper pocket, my fingers wrapped around a cool metal cylinder. I brought the dog whistle to my lips and blew. An urgent hiss came from the tube. Grandpa had explained that the whistle's frequency was too high for human ears. The sound didn't seem to disturb the nearby birds either. I hoped the thing wasn't broken. I strained for the sound of Queenie's paws charging through the duff, the chug-chug of her breath as she raced to my side, but only heard chirps and rustling branches. "Queenie!" I blew the whistle again.

Todd joined me by the truck. He took my free hand without speaking.

"There. You hear that?" I looked at him.

He shook his head. "No. Wait. Yes. Something's coming."

Queenie burst into the clearing like a black and tan missile. When she reached me, she reared up on her hind legs, her front paws thumping onto my shoulders. I wrapped my arms around her and blinked away tears as she licked my face.

"Oh, Queenie. You're okay."

When we both calmed down, I led her into the cabin. Some of the fear left Manuela's face as she crouched to greet the dog. While Manuela petted and praised Queenie, I searched through the mess for a bowl. After tossing aside two broken ones, I spied a lone survivor. I rinsed off the bits of smashed food and dirt then filled the bowl with water and set it beside the dog. Queenie turned from Manuela and lapped. I crouched, rubbing the ridge of Queenie's shoulders. "You scared me, girl." Queenie lifted her dripping muzzle and gave my face another lick before she continued drinking.

I stood and surveyed the downstairs. Manuela sat next to the upturned table petting Queenie while Todd pawed through the mess on the kitchen floor. I didn't know much – like what was going on here – but I did know staying at the cabin was no longer safe.

Todd held up a large blue cylinder. "They poured out all the salt. What's the point of doing that?" He waved his arm. "Of doing any of this?"

"Todd." I waited until his gaze met mine. "We need to borrow your truck."

"Why?" He dropped the empty container of Morton's Salt.

"We can't stay here. If the guys from the pot field didn't do this, those deputies did. They might come back. Looking for Grandpa. Or Manuela."

"Why would they come here?"

"Maybe you should ask your dad."

"What's that mean?"

No way was I going to tell him about Grandpa's past. Though, for all I knew, Mr. Wilder blabbed about it to both his boys and the cops. "Remember that day on the roof of the general store. Your dad threatened Grandpa."

"That was just talk."

I snorted and waved at the mess. "Does this look like talk?"

"Where's your gramps?"

"He took off. With the truck." Once again I looked at the tangle of broken things on the kitchen floor. "I can't reach my dad. And I can't hang out at the general store waiting for him to call. Not after this. If those deputies didn't tear the place up, I'm betting the men who snatched Manuela did. But whichever ones did this, we've got to get out of here." I held my empty palm out to him. "Please."

"What?"

"Your keys. I need to borrow your truck."

"If I go home without that truck, Dad'll kill me."

"Yeah, but that's an expression. Whoever did this may really kill Manuela. Or me." I took a deep breath, preparing to dive into the rough water I hated. "Besides, I think you owe me."

Creases ridged his forehead. "I owe you? Why?"

"Because you lied to me."

"I never—"

"Yeah, you did. You said your dad was a farmer. But you never said what he farmed." I took another deep breath, hoping the tremor in my voice wasn't noticeable. "You said your dad was a big wheel in these parts, but you never said why. Grandpa said you and Ben helped him watch out for the girls brought here by the cartels. You never told me that either. You let me think you guys and Grandpa didn't get along."

Todd spread both hands wide. "Look, I had no choice. My dad's business … I never talk about that. That's part of my life. It's illegal and I don't talk about it to anyone outside the family. That's how I was raised. As for the girls… Your gramps told me to keep my mouth shut. He wanted to keep you safe. And so do I. You and Manuela should come home with me. We can protect you there."

"Bull. Those men were at your house. They're friends of your dad's. Friends of yours for all I know."

"Nicki…" Todd shook his head then gusted out a sigh and fished in his pocket. He handed me the keys. "I still say this is a mistake."

"Maybe. But it's not like that's a first for me."

I walked to the loft's ladder and climbed again. Whoever tore the place apart hadn't bothered with this portion of the cabin. Manuela's soft voice said something in Spanish and Todd answered. Their voices overlapped as I grabbed my duffle and shoved in clothes. I untangled the quilt on my bed and found the shotgun. Manuela must've carried it up here, but left it behind when she rushed down to get Queenie out of the cabin. I picked it up. As a not-fully-licensed driver, was traveling with a shotgun really a good idea? I returned the sixteen-gauge to the bed.

When I returned to the kitchen, Todd crouched by Manuela's chair. Words tumbled from her lips, too fast for me to translate. I picked my way through the mess, avoiding the stickiest looking portions of the floor.

In Grandpa's room, one flannel shirt had survived the attack, along with a couple thermal tops. I grabbed the thin plaid cloth. The combined scent of wood smoke and pinesap made it almost seem like Grandpa was in the room. Almost. I slipped the shirt on over my T-shirt, rolling up the sleeves as I walked back to the kitchen.

The first cupboard I checked was bare. Manuela and Todd watched me for a moment then joined in. Between the three of us we found two apples, a package of jerky, and a can of tomato juice. I jammed the food inside the knapsack, topped off the canteen, and handed both to Manuela before hoisting the duffle.

"Where you gonna go?" Todd's brown eyes filled with worry.

"Cecilia's. If you can give me directions."

"I don't think she's there."

"Maybe not, but she's got to come home some time."

Todd sifted through the mess on the floor and found a sheet of paper. He tore off the clean top half and started writing. "Here's her number, along with directions to her place. But I know Cecilia. After what happened with the last passenger…" He handed me the route information. "She'll be out tracking down everyone who came in contact with her. Cecilia won't take a chance with anyone's safety. She might not be back for days. And her place is a damn fortress. Unless she's there to let you in, you won't get inside. Trust me on that." He rumpled his hair and stared at the jumble at his feet. "I shouldn't tell you this, but there's another place you can go. A halfway house. Kind of an underground thing on the outskirts of Deep Creek. They've helped a lot of women. I bet they'll take care of Manuela."

"Grandpa mentioned a place like that. For the Snake Dancer. Where is it?"

"About five hundred miles northeast of here." He reached for the piece of paper. "I'll write down those directions, too." He looked at me then shrugged. "I rode along a couple times with your gramps. We took turns driving. It's a long haul. He always made me stay in the truck when we got to Deep Creek, so they don't know me from Adam. But they know your gramps. If you end up going there, head straight to the mini-mart and ask for Tanya. Tell her who you are and who your gramps is. She'll hook you up with the shelter. They can keep Manuela safe until Cecilia comes back."

Todd explained to Manuela in Spanish that she and I were leaving. She looked at me, fear weighting her gaze.

"We'll be okay." I tried on a smile, but my face didn't cooperate. "We'll be seguro."

Manuela nodded.

We carried our supplies outside. Clucking came from the chicken run. The rust-brown hen cocked her head and glared at me between the wire fencing. "Wait a sec." I dashed to the barn and lugged the feed pail to the enclosure. "Shoo." I waved the bird away as I opened the gate. When Grandpa first started me feeding the hens, he told me they would gorge themselves to the point of sickness if I put out too much food. Unsure how long I'd be gone, I scattered the usual amount of scratch grain, then threw down an extra two handfuls. Chickens scurried from the hen house. While I carted the bucket back to the barn, Todd hoisted the duffle and tossed it into the truck bed.

"Queenie. Come here." Todd crouched and the dog ran to his side, tongue lolling. Todd rubbed behind her ears. "You be a good girl. Keep Nicki and Manuela safe."

"Come on, Queenie." I opened the driver's side door and the dog bounded in, settling next to Manuela. Todd stood. We stared at each other. I wanted him to hug me, but worried if I leaned on him, I might collapse. I tried to swallow away the lump blocking my throat. "We better get going."

Todd nodded. "Stay safe."

"You too."

My nose started to run almost as soon as we took off. Probably from all the tears I was choking back. This was ridiculous. I barely knew the guy. And I wasn't someone who got attached fast. I knew better than that. People disappeared on you. That was life. Besides, I needed to be tough for Manuela.

After a thirty minute drive on the two-lane highway, I found a payphone at a roadside gas station. I let the phone ring and ring, but got no answer at Cecilia's. I called Dad. His voicemail picked up. Again. "Dammit." No way was I leaving him a message. Not about this.

I studied Todd's instructions. Deep Creek looked like at least a nine-hour drive. Compared to that, backtracking to take a run by Cecilia's first seemed worth a shot.

Todd's directions took us off-road. I hunched forward looking for the 'fallen oak by the split-trunk pine.' After I made the turn, we bumped along the next bit of road while I tried to avoid the dips and ruts. When I pulled up in front of Cecilia's, I swore. Todd wasn't kidding about the place being a fortress. I never expected to find a solid metal gate and a six-foot-high perimeter fence topped with razor wire tucked deep inside the woods. I climbed out and pushed the button for the intercom. A brief vibration ran beneath my index finger, but no answering buzz or voice came back.

I glanced at the truck. Queenie leaned across Manuela, her snout stuck out the window. I turned. The fence didn't get any less dangerous-looking when I studied it again.

"Well, hell."

Looked like we were heading to Deep Creek.

Chapter Twenty-Three

I shuffled back to the truck. In the late afternoon light, Manuela's face looked washed out. Pale as goose down, Grandpa would say. She leaned into Queenie, both arms wrapped around the dog. But even Queenie's reassuring warmth didn't stop Manuela's hands from trembling. I needed to take her somewhere she could feel safe.

According to Todd's instructions, if we took Route 162 to FH7, we wouldn't need to skirt the southern hem of the Mendocino National Forest. Twenty miles later, we thunked onto FH7. Turned out the 'FH' stood for Forest Highway – which, in these parts, meant unpaved. We cut through the woods, dust billowing behind. Deep green shadows masked the road, and the thin shafts of sunshine that managed to pierce the gloom did little to light the way. After bouncing over dozens of roots and ruts, I fumbled with knobs and levers until I figured out how to turn on the headlights. Near the Mendocino Pass, a swathe of sky opened up and a crossroad came into sight. Somehow it seemed right that a place as strange as the Mendo would have an intersection in the middle of the woods. But the cleared area gave us the chance to see the slope below along with the next ridge over. While the truck idled in the sunshine, Manuela and I both looked out at the pine and oak-covered mountains. If Todd's directions were accurate, the town of Willows and the Interstate were another forty miles ahead.

When we rejoined Route 162, I pressed the accelerator until the speedometer read fifty-five, but didn't dare go any faster. My only other experience driving on the freeway had been under Dad's supervision. If I got pulled over now, who knew what kind of trouble that could lead to? Traffic was light, but I kept scanning the road for the telltale black and white of the Highway Patrol. By the time we reached Willows, my hands were cramping from my death grip on the steering wheel. But we'd reached the eastern edge of the forest. I figured we were far enough from the cabin – and whoever tore it up – to make a stop.

Manuela hit the restroom while I started filling the tank. The thirty dollars I'd collected in allowance since coming to Grandpa's did the job with a couple bucks left over. I walked Queenie then I gathered what was left of Grandpa's change for the payphone. After plunking in coins and tapping the keys for Dad's number, I leaned against the stucco wall. Voicemail again. Where was he? Dad traveled a lot for work. Was he on another trip?

I pictured him pacing the kitchen, the way he did before each trip since I turned fifteen and refused to have Mrs. Horst 'babysit' me. "It's not enough to lock the doors and windows. You need to be on your guard. Even with people you think you know. You can never be too careful."

How many times had I gotten that fun lecture? Maybe he'd saved up all his conferences and out-of-town meetings for this summer while I was away?

Thanks to the sheriff's department, Dad already knew I didn't have my cell, so he wouldn't be trying to reach me – or getting worried when he couldn't. I left a message saying I needed to talk to him and would call again later.

After passing a small airport, I spotted signs for I-5 and we finally joined the northbound traffic. Until the evening deepened to night, I wore my sunglasses, hoping they helped me look older. My learner's permit didn't allow me to drive anybody under age eighteen. A part of me was tempted to take off the glasses and start speeding. If I got stopped by the Highway Patrol, at least someone would get a hold of Dad and tell him where I was. But I shook off the impulse.

Halfway between midnight and 1 a.m., I pulled into a rest stop and rubbed my bleary eyes. After giving Queenie another break and finding a spigot where she could drink, Manuela and I both used the restroom. Back inside the truck cab, I handed Manuela one of the packs of nuts I bought at the gas station and fed Queenie some jerky.

After making sure both doors were locked, I closed my burning eyes.

* * * *

Sunlight warmed my face. I opened my eyes and unscrunched my legs. When I hopped down from the truck cab, the smell of exhaust and burning oil tagged along on the light breeze.

Queenie bounded from the seat and ran to the closest tree, then circled, sniffed, and peed. In spite of Queenie's gallumphing out of the cab, Manuela continued to doze, her head supported by the passenger window.

While Queenie explored, I stretched out the kinks in my neck, shoulders, and legs. When the dog rejoined me, we headed to the restrooms. As I washed up, Queenie investigated the cubicles. The water soothed my tired eyes.

Outside, I found a spigot and gave Queenie a good long drink. By the time I returned to the truck, Manuela was sitting up, staring wide-eyed through the windshield. She visibly relaxed when her gaze met mine and she climbed down from the cab. Queenie turned her big eyes my way.

"Go on. Keep Manuela company."

The dog trotted to the girl's side. Manuela looked like she was walking easier today. While they were gone, I rummaged in my knapsack for the rest of the snacks I bought during our stop in Willow.

Once Manuela and Queenie returned, I cranked the engine and nosed out onto the interstate. As we drove north, Manuela fed Queenie jerky, and she and I munched on peanuts and pretzels. Not many cars were out and the drive was less stressful than yesterday. By the time we reached Deep Creek, the temperature had crested eighty degrees and it was closing in on noon. Todd hadn't been fooling – the place could hardly be called a city, but it was still a bigger deal than Punishment. Deep Creek actually had an intersection with a stop sign. In addition to the mini-mart, there was a gas station, Laundromat, a feed and tack store, some kind of farm equipment place, a coffee shop, and a hair and nail salon. It was almost like being back in civilization. From my glimpse at the handful of pedestrians, snap-front shirts were the rage in fashion. So civilization, just not the type of civilization where I'd fit in.

I told Queenie to stay with Manuela in the truck. Though the girl looked better than yesterday, her bruises would still draw unwanted attention. I pulled Grandpa's flannel shirt on over my tank top and tugged the sleeves down to cover my arms. The door to the mini-mart stood propped open with a cinderblock. When I stepped inside, I knew why: no air conditioning. The place smelled like Hawaiian Punch – probably because of the pink pool spreading from beneath the Icee machine.

189

"Watch where you step." The throaty voice sounded more Deep South than California Country. The woman manning the cash register waved toward the mess. "We had a minor disaster. Pete's getting the mop right now."

I sidestepped the puddle and headed for the counter. The store clerk wore wire-rimmed glasses and looked to be in her forties, her dark hair cut short and gelled into spikes. She didn't wear a name tag, but Todd had told me to go to the counter and ask. I took a deep breath. "Hi. I'm looking for Tanya."

She peered at me over her glasses. "I'm Tanya. Who're you?"

"Nicki. I think you know my grandpa. John Smith?"

Tanya frowned and took a step back, creating space between her and the counter. "Pretty common name."

"Yeah." I wasn't sure what to do. Should I blurt out the name Lilith Express or would that only increase the amount of stink eye I was getting from Tanya? "Um, my grandpa said you know some folks who could maybe help a friend of mine?"

The woman looked past me. "Watch your step, sugar," she called out.

A boy carrying a skateboard under his arm skidded to a stop then walked around the Icee mess. He grabbed a soda from the refrigerated section and headed toward the counter.

I moved to the side. "Go ahead. I'm not ready to buy anything yet." Though he looked about twelve and probably had zero interest in our conversation, I held my tongue until he and Tanya completed their transaction.

Once the boy sloped out of the store, I tried again. "Grandpa said you could help my friend."

"Sounds like your grampa's pretty free with offers of other folks' help. If he's so all-fired concerned, why isn't he helping out this friend of yours?" She leaned against the back counter, arms crossed over her chest.

"He's out of town right now." As I scrambled for something that might get this woman to help, it hit me. Tanya hadn't said, 'Who the hell is John Smith.' "You do know him, right?"

She shrugged. "I know a lot of folks. And, like I said before, that's a real common name."

This was like when Gemma and I worked on a school project together – I always wound up doing all the heavy lifting. "He's got gray hair. Stands about six-foot-four?"

"Sounds like a lot of guys 'round here."

"Jesus." I leaned my elbows on the counter, trying to bridge the distance between us. Keeping my voice a hair above a whisper, I said, "He's part of the Lilith Express."

Tanya shrugged again. "Never heard of it. That one of those new indie bands?"

Heat crossed my face like a wildfire. I clenched my jaw and turned to face the window, my trapped words tasting like ash. Todd and I had both survived my telling him off. But anger always felt dangerous. And rarely helped. Giving in to the impulse to run out of the store and away from this stubborn woman wouldn't help either.

I stared at the quiet street. I couldn't go out there and tell Manuela I'd dragged her all this way for nothing.

Manuela. That was it. "I'll be right back."

"I can't wait." Tanya's tone didn't match her words.

I hustled across the sidewalk and pulled open the truck's passenger door. Queenie barreled across Manuela's lap to pant in my face. "Good girl." I rubbed behind her ears before turning my attention to Manuela. "Venga." I waved her toward me. "Por favor." Manuela pushed Queenie aside and climbed down. Queenie bounded out after her. "Sorry, girl, you can't come along." After I got the dog resettled and told her to stay, I led Manuela inside the store.

At the sight of the girl's bruised face, Tanya's mouth dropped open.

We walked up to the counter. "Should've seen her a couple days ago. She's halfway to healed now. But she needs help." I crossed my arms over my chest, willing her to say 'yes' to my next question. "Is that something you can do for us?"

Tanya nodded. "Sorry I was a little… We don't usually work with strangers. Got to be real careful."

"Sure." I blinked and took a ragged breath.

"You want something to drink?" The question was aimed at Manuela not me.

"She doesn't speak English."

"No problemo. Quiere una bebida?"

"Si." Manuela smiled, a bright white crescent amid the bruises.

Tanya pointed at the refrigerated case. "Help yourself." Manuela got the message and went to pick out a soda. "My Spanish is so-so, but we got plenty of Spanish speakers out at the ranch." She ripped a sheet of paper from a notepad and started writing. "Follow these directions. There's not a whole lot of roads out here, so you'd have to work pretty hard to get lost. I'll call ahead and let Jane know you're coming."

"Thanks."

"What's your name again?"

"Nicki. Nicki Steele."

"I'll tell Jane to expect you and your friend." She held out the piece of paper.

"Thank you." When Manuela and I walked back to the truck, I clutched that piece of paper like a lifeline.

Chapter Twenty-Four

The white clapboard house gleamed in the sunlight, the shutters and doors a cheery robin's egg blue. A wide verandah ran along the facade with five steps leading to the front door.

I picked up the flannel shirt, but it was too damn hot to put it on. I dropped it on the bench seat, then walked around to the passenger side of the truck and opened the door. Manuela lingered in the cab. "Don't want to leave the familiar, huh?"

She stared at me with wide eyes.

"Venga. Por favor. Esta casa es safe. La…" Oh for pity's sake, how could I forget the word for women? "Ah. Las mujeres viven in este casa. Women and girls like you. La casa es segura. Okay?"

Queenie bounded out and circled the truck, flushing a towhee from a clump of grass growing alongside the packed dirt of the driveway. The girl climbed down from the cab, but stayed to the rear of me and the dog as we walked up the path, trailing us like a thin shadow.

The front door opened when I stepped onto the porch.

A tall red-headed woman in jeans and a sleeveless blouse stood in the doorway. "I'm Jane. Tanya called to tell us someone was coming for a visit. Who're you?"

"I'm Nicki." I stepped to the side, revealing the girl behind me. "This is Manuela. And that's Queenie." Queenie nosed past me, ready to meet her new friend.

At the sight of the battered girl, Jane's brow creased and her mouth pulled down at the corners. "Come on in." She crouched and offered her hand to Queenie to smell, then patted her flank. "You can come in, too." Jane ushered us into a cool entryway and closed the front door. "Have a seat in here."

'In here' was a high-ceilinged room off to the left with large windows that flooded the space with light. The furniture was a mix of old and new in a variety of colored fabrics and patterns. I sat on a purple loveseat and patted the cushion. Manuela joined me.

"Want some lemonade?"

"Sure."

"Coming right up." Jane strode out the door, the wood floor creaking beneath her.

"Que diga la mujer?" Manuela said, her voice soft as pine needles on the breeze.

"Um, she said…" I shook my head. "La mujer diga … bebir la limon?" No way was I coming up with an explanation in Spanish for an offer of lemonade. I pantomimed drinking. Manuela nodded.

Footsteps clopped across the wood floor outside. A round-faced woman peeked in. "Jane wanted me to see if you're hungry." She stepped inside the room. Her short black hair tufted like a crest. With her indigo overalls, she looked like a blue jay.

"Yeah. Some food would be nice."

"We're kind of between meals right now, but there's some leftover cornbread. That sound all right?"

"Sure."

"I'll be back in a flash." She smiled and her face went from plain to beautiful. "I'm Tess, by the way." She ducked back out of the room.

Manuela gripped my hand in hers. I wished I could explain what was going on. I squeezed her hand and nodded in what I hoped was a reassuring fashion. Queenie sighed and settled on the floor by my feet.

Jane returned with a tray holding two glasses of lemonade, a bowl of water, and a plate of sliced cornbread. She set the tray on a small table then scooted the table over to the love seat. She placed the water bowl in front of Queenie. The dog sat up and started slurping. Jane settled opposite us on the orange armchair and nodded. "Go ahead and eat. Dinner's not for a few more hours."

I picked up the plate and held it out to Manuela. "La comida. Comer."

Manuela picked up a slice of bread and took a bite.

I felt Jane's gaze and turned to catch her staring at the burn mark on my arm.

Jane cleared her throat before handing us each a paper napkin. "She doesn't speak English?"

"No. And my Spanish keeps drying up."

"No worries. Tess lived in Mexico for years. She speaks Spanish like a native. What happened to your friend here?"

"I'm not exactly sure. I know she was kidnapped. My grandpa rescued her. But I don't know where she's from or how long she was held. Or where. I can ask her how she is, if she's hungry, but my Spanish isn't up to much else."

"The person who took her – did he do this to her?" Jane pointed at Manuela's bruised face.

"Yeah. She looks a lot better than she did."

"And you brought her here because…?"

"My grandpa's John Smith."

The smile left Jane's face. "He told you to come here?"

Uh-oh. Was that something I shouldn't have said? "No. He had to..." I shook my head. "He took off. And I don't know when he's coming back. I... It wasn't safe for Manuela to stay at his cabin. A friend of Grandpa's told me about this place."

Jane leaned back, looking more relaxed. "That I believe. John would never—" Her cheeks reddened. She cleared her throat. "He wouldn't tell an outsider how to find us." She looked out the window and tapped her index finger against her lips. "What do you want us to do? Take her in? Take her home?"

"Can you do that? Get her home?" My chest suddenly seemed ten pounds lighter. "That'd be great. That's what Grandpa was going to do. Before he had to leave. But, I think she may live in Mexico. I don't have much money left, but maybe my dad could pay for her ticket home?"

"We have people who can transport her. That's not an issue. But what about you? You're here and your father's where?"

"In Orange. It's south of L.A. Near Anaheim. He sent me up to Grandpa's for the summer."

"And now John's gone. I'm guessing you'd like to call your father?"

"Yes. Thank you." I didn't realize how tight my shoulders still were until they released at the offer of a phone.

"Looks like your friend's done eating." Jane turned toward the open doorway. "Tess? Is that you hovering out there?"

The dark-haired woman clomped inside again. For such a small person, she sure had a loud tread.

"What's up?"

Jane gestured at Manuela. "I'd like you to meet our new guest. She speaks Spanish."

"Hola. Yo soy Tess. Me gustaría encontrarte. ¿Como está usted?" Tess crossed the room and held out her hand to Manuela. The girl smiled and stood, then started talking, too. Their two voices overlapped and blended, the syllables too fast for me to dissect the words or their meaning. At one point I thought they were discussing a dog, but that made no sense. I tuned out and picked up another slice of cornbread.

After a good five minutes of chatter, Tess put her arm around Manuela's narrow shoulders. "We're going to go upstairs and get her cleaned up and find some clothes that fit a bit better. I'll make a few calls. Turns out Manuela's from Chihuahua. She lives right outside of Lucer. My friend Josefina lives in Villa Ahumada. They're practically neighbors. I've explained to Manuela that she can stay here while we make arrangements for a ride home."

Chihuahua. That explained why I thought they were talking about a dog. "That's great." My eyes started to sting. I blinked several times. Manuela launched herself at me and I found myself in a cobra-like hug.

Manuela released me and took both my hands. "Un millon de gracias." She smiled. Tess started to lead her away, but Manuela pulled her arm free and crouched in front of Queenie. Queenie leaned into the girl and Manuela hugged her, too. With one last pat to Queenie's flank, Manuela straightened, wiped her eyes, and followed Tess out of the room.

I sat, flopping back like a fish that'd broken its line. I'd done it. Manuela was safe.

Jane cleared her throat. "Phone's in the kitchen. If you want to call your dad."

The rotary dial on the bright yellow phone took forever to tick-tick-tick around with each number. Finally, the line for Dad's cell started to ring. Once, twice, three times. No, not voicemail again.

"Hello?" The voice sounded hoarse.

"Dad?"

"Nicki? Is that—"

"Dad?" Static crackled. The line wasn't dead.

"—you?"

"What? I can't hear you." I pressed the phone against my ear.

"What time is it?"

I squeezed the receiver, like I was holding Dad's arm. I could stop worrying. He could take over, take that job out of my hands. "Um…" I glanced at the wall clock. "Almost 2:30."

The sound of a second muffled voice came down the line, then Dad spoke again. "It's almost—"

"What?"

"I said it's almost midnight here."

"What do you mean? Where are you?"

He cleared his throat. "Paris."

Dad was in France? How was he going to come get me? "What're you doing in Paris?"

More muffled talking.

"What?" I spoke louder, hoping increased volume would conquer the bad connection.

"Is something wrong?"

"I need you to come get me. Grandpa—"

"Nicki, stop. I picked up—"

It sounded like Dad's words were being broken into tiny bits by the phone service. Words popped through, but I couldn't follow. "I can't understand what you're saying."

"… work messages… heard your complaints. About the cabin … your grandfather."

Dad's voice cut out.

"Are you there?" I shouted down the line. "I can't hear you."

"…need to stop this. I'm not changing my mind … for the summer. Besides … halfway around the world…You'll survive … without your friends. And they'll survive without you."

"But Grandpa's gone."

"Are you there, Nicki? I can barely hear you."

"Yes, I said—"

"I know your Grandpa … tough ... for your own good. Try and … best of the situation … hanging up … love you."

The line went dead. My pulse rocketed. I stared at the hand piece. He never let me tell him what was wrong. "The hell with that." I dialed the number again. An automated message came on telling me the number was not available. Dad turned off his phone? I sank onto the kitchen floor, the curlicue cord linking the hand piece to the phone's base stretched taut. My stomach rolled, cornbread threatening to make a reappearance. I closed my eyes and took a deep breath. First Mom, then MJ, then Grandpa. People left you. That was life. But now Dad was abandoning me, too? Tears wet my cheeks. I wiped my forearm across my damp cheeks. What was I supposed to do?

Dad sounded like I'd woken him up. So who did that second voice belong to? At 'almost midnight' in Paris?

Oh. Yuck.

A distant beep repeated from inside the handset. I stood and hung up the phone, then leaned against the cool tile of the kitchen counter. My stomach still felt uneasy, but no longer rolled. I needed to figure out what to do next. It wasn't like I had a ton of options. I'd burned through almost all of my cash gassing up the truck on the way here. I didn't have enough money to make it to Orange County. Not that anything waited there for me.

Through the kitchen window above the sink, the tree line of the Modoc National Forest rose dark against the blue sky, a green-gold field spreading across the land in between. A beautiful place, but I hadn't gotten a 'stay awhile' vibe from Jane. Which meant I had to get going. But where?

A stoop-shouldered woman limped across the field. Something about her face seemed familiar. I watched until she disappeared around the corner of the house then wandered back to the entryway. The room where Manuela and I had our lemonade and cornbread was empty except for Queenie sleeping by the loveseat. She raised her head. "It's okay, girl. Stretch out while you can." A murmur of voices came from upstairs, but I didn't feel like I could roam around up there looking for people. I slouched out to the front porch and sat on the top step.

What was I going to do now?

The front door creaked open behind me. I turned. Jane stepped onto the porch. "Your dad coming here or are you going to him?"

A lump formed in my throat and my eyes started to burn. I turned away to stare at the field. "He's out of town."

"So what's your plan?"

I shrugged.

"Got enough money to get back home? If not, we can scrape a few bucks together to help."

I did my best to swallow away the lump. "Thanks." I didn't know what I was going to do, but one thing was clear. I wasn't getting an invite to stay here. "I have a couple bucks, but not enough to get to Grandpa's, let alone all the way to Orange."

"I'll see what we can spare." The door clicked shut behind me.

The woman with the hunched shoulders came into view again. She lugged a bucket with one hand and gripped a trowel in the other. Once again I was struck by how familiar she looked. My heart started to race, but I didn't know why. I stood, knees shaking. I wrapped my arms across my chest before walking down the four stairs between the porch and the ground.

The creak from my weight on the steps must have drawn her attention. The woman turned and for the first time, I got a full look at her face.

"Mom?"

Chapter Twenty-Five

When Jane returned to the porch with two twenty dollar bills in her hand, she found me staring open-mouthed at my mother.

"I see you've met Roslyn."

"Huh?"

"Roslyn, aren't you supposed to be weeding the side garden?"

Mom bobbed her head. "Had to come back for the trowel. I was headed that way when..." She waved the empty bucket in my direction.

"Why's she calling you Roslyn? Your name's Marilyn. Marilyn Steele."

Jane's large hand pressed against my right shoulder. "Some of our guests need to make a clean break from their former lives. Including their names." The line sounded well-rehearsed, but when I turned, Jane's expression looked wary.

"That true, Mom?" I faced her again. "Or should I call you Roz?"

Mom's mouth opened and closed, like a fish stuck on dry land.

Jane cleared her throat. "Roslyn, would you like to talk to your daughter?"

"What?" I glared at Jane. "I'm standing right here. Talking to her. You're not going to stop me."

"I will if that's what Roslyn wants. This is a place of refuge and healing for our guests." Jane's face lost all traces of warmth. With her gaze still drilling into me, she said, "It's your decision, Roslyn. What do you want to do?"

"I ... I'd like to talk to Nicki."

"That's fine." A plastic-looking smile spread across Jane's face and she nodded at me. "You have fifteen minutes. Then Roslyn needs to get back to her chores." She tucked the two twenties into my hand. "After that, I think it's time you head on home, Nicki." With a parting nod to my mother, Jane went inside.

The long drive had blown away the lingering manure smell from the truck bed. We sat on the tailgate, keeping a good three feet of empty metal between us. In spite of the sun's heat on my shoulders, a chill traveled down my spine. I hadn't seen Mom in almost nine years. She looked used up and worn out, but showed no surprise at seeing me. "Did Grandpa tell you I was living in the Mendo?" My voice came out sounding thin and frightened.

"He thought I should know."

My cheeks burned. "He thought you should know? But not me? How's that fair? Because, believe me, he didn't say squat about you. Ever."

Mom shifted away, putting another couple inches between us. "He asked if he could tell you, but I said no."

"Why?"

She pursed her lips and stared at the field.

"Do you know how long I... How much…" A fiery ball seemed to have lodged itself where my stomach used to be. "You could've called. Written. Said goodbye." I swallowed hard and stared at her. In profile, she didn't look so tired. She looked like MJ. Same honey-colored hair, upturned nose, and graceful neck.

"I… There wasn't time when I left. And afterwards…" She spread her arms and faced me. "I didn't want you to see me like this. I wanted to be more pulled together when that happened."

"I don't care how you look." Not exactly true, but what else was I going to say?

"I don't mean my clothes or makeup."

"What do you mean?" A lava wave of nausea rolled through. Did I really want an answer to my question?

"This is my fifth time here at the ranch. Each time I thought I was ready to leave..." Mom shook her head. "I never seem to last long out in the world and keep ending up back here. The last time I left, I got a good job doing the books for a builder. Everything went great for close to a year. I even thought about getting in touch with you. But then..." She shrugged.

"What?" It felt like bile was burning its way through my throat.

"Everything fell apart again." She ran a bony hand up and down the top of her thigh, her palm sanding the denim. "I have a problem. An addiction. Over the years, it's caused a lot of trouble. Hurt people I cared about. Hurt me, too." She lifted her hand and started rubbing her bare forearms as if she couldn't feel the ninety degree heat.

I thought about MJ's drinking and how wild Dad acted whenever he talked about me drinking or smoking pot. Was this the reason? I took a deep breath. "Are you like an alcoholic?"

"In some ways, that would be easier." Mom shook her head. "No. Not easier. More socially acceptable, I guess."

"Drugs?"

"This isn't something I ever wanted to talk to you about." She fisted her hands, drumming them against her thighs. "But, I owe you some kind of explanation for leaving."

My shoulders hunched, the anger in her voice driving me to make myself small.

"I…" She cleared her throat. "I made a lot of bad decisions when I was high. Including cheating on your father."

I stared at this stringy woman who, once upon a time, had sung me to sleep. My mouth opened and closed twice before I managed to say, "What?"

"That's all I'm willing to say about it."

"Jesus! I don't want to know more."

Mom stared off at the field again before speaking. "That's what started the trouble between me and your father."

The silence stretched between us until I wasn't sure my voice would reach all the way across the void. I took another deep breath. "I don't get it."

Mom shifted, looking toward the empty road. "Get what?"

"Dad has a good job. You had a good job. You guys had money. You could've got some kind of treatment. Gone to rehab. And if it cost too much, Dad would've sold the house. I'm sure of it. We could've moved to an apartment. If you told him about your problem ... we could've all stayed together."

Mom stood, walked five paces, and then turned back. "You don't understand."

Heat raced up my neck. "What? That you were a big 'ho'? Is that what I don't get?"

Her face turned red, but Mom didn't contradict me. "Your father knew I had a problem. But he had a problem, too. I put up with him hitting me, because I felt like I deserved it." She shook her head. "But when he broke my jaw … that was the end. After I got out of the hospital, I started making plans to leave."

I wanted to shout 'liar,' but the image of Dad yelling, pushing his way through the crowd toward our smoldering house filled my head. When he reached the wreckage, he'd torn at a smoking piece of window frame, not seeming to care about burning his hands as he tried to get inside. Raging and red-faced, he looked crazy enough to throw away what little we had left. It had taken two firefighters to subdue him. As much as I didn't want to believe my mom, the fury sounded real. "Dad hit you?"

"Yes."

"And you wound up in the hospital?" I rubbed my hands over the goose bumps dotting my arms.

"Your father told you I was visiting friends. He didn't want to upset you girls."

An image of MJ huddled on her bed grew bright inside my head. The Santa Anas had been blowing, making it too hot to play outside. I was eight years old and bored. I had opened the door to her room without knocking, breaking the rule MJ made the year before when she turned thirteen. Tears streaked her face and she cradled one arm. Even against her tan skin, the red mark above her elbow had been visible. When she saw me, she screamed at me to get out.

"Did Dad ever hurt MJ?"

"I... He wouldn't hurt you girls. It wasn't like that. It was me. I drove him over the edge. Even brought men home while he was on his business trips. And when MJ walked in on me that time... She didn't understand. She didn't know what would happen when she told your father."

"So he did. He hurt her."

Mom wiped her hands across her face. "Everything I touch turns to shit." She took a deep breath. "You two were better off with your father. As long as I

207

wasn't there to upset him. And you were safer than if I'd taken you with me."

I felt like someone had punched my heart. "We were safer? Like when MJ died in that fire because we were home alone?"

Mom spun and strode to the tamped down dirt of the path, then turned to face me. "I did what I thought was best. For everyone. Grownups don't have all the answers. I didn't have a crystal ball. If I'd known MJ would start drinking..." She wiped her nose with the back of her hand. "Pass out with those candles burning in her room—"

"What?" My skin sizzled like an electrical current ran through my limbs. "What're you talking about?"

"I thought I was doing the smart—"

"Not about that." I forced my body to work and pushed to my feet. "About the fire. MJ had candles burning in her room?"

"Yes. That's what started the fire."

"It was?"

"Nicki? Maybe you should sit down. You don't look so good."

"Oh God." I leaned against the tailgate.

"You need water or something?"

"No." Tears filled my eyes, softening the sharp angles of Mom's face. "Dad never said anything about how the fire started." I wiped my eyes. "I don't believe this. I always thought..."

"Nicki?" Mom reached out her hand toward me, but stopped a couple inches shy of making contact. "Thought what?"

"MJ was so mad at me. She didn't want to stay home and babysit." I pictured MJ's face, a frown twisting her mouth. "She told me to make my own dinner and stormed off to her room. She never wanted to spend time with me anymore. I was sure she was sneaking out of the house while I made my grilled cheese." I shook my head. "All these years, I thought I left the stove on. I thought I was the one who started that fire."

"Oh Nicki." Mom moved closer.

"I never asked what started it because I didn't want to hear Dad say I killed her. That I killed MJ." I fisted my hands and took a deep breath. "It was bad enough I didn't pull her out of the fire."

That night, by the time Dad made it home from the airport, only a charred shell of our home still stood. The smell of burnt paint and wood smoke had clung to me. Our cat, Whiskers, kept trying to wriggle free from my grip, but I'd held on, ignoring the screams of pain from my right arm. Just as a firefighter took the cat away from me, Dad started to howl. He pushed through the gawkers and grabbed my shoulders. "What did you do? Where's MJ? Where's your sister?" In the revolving light of the ambulance, fear and anger twisted his face into a ghoulish mask. Until then it hadn't occurred to me MJ might still be inside the house.

Mom touched my shoulder, bringing me back to the present. "The fire marshal said MJ's bed was where the fire started. By the time you woke up and smelled the smoke, it was probably too late to help her. Even if you could've reached her through the flames, you wouldn't have been able to carry her outside."

I wiped my face with both hands. "Dad told me MJ was passed out in her room. That she never woke up, didn't feel a thing. He never mentioned the candles." Black dots skittered in front of my eyes. I leaned forward, grabbed my knees, and tried to breathe. When the dizziness passed, I opened my eyes but stayed hunched over. A lizard ran past the toes of my boots. "How do you know all this?"

"Your grandfather told me. I'd found a job in Bishop and wasn't at the ranch when the fire happened. I didn't find out about MJ's death until ten months later."

Mom ran her hand along the length of my burn scar. This was the first physical contact I'd had with her since I was eight years old—and she'd chosen to touch the one part of me that couldn't feel anything. I straightened. Her hand fell away.

"I'm so sorry things turned out the way they did." Mom traced the outer seam of her jeans with her thumbnail. "You've had to deal with a lot of stuff. And I know I don't have any right to tell you what to do. But your grandpa told me you're angry with your father for sending you here."

"I was. But, that's not the big issue anymore."

"Good. He did it to help you."

I wanted her to shut up; I needed quiet to absorb everything. But, who knew when I'd get to talk to Mom again? "So, now you're defending Dad?"

"He was scared."

"Of what?"

"Of you ending up like MJ."

"How was me hanging out with my friends this summer going to get me killed in a house fire?"

Mom gusted out a breath. "You were drinking, doing drugs. Like MJ."

"I drank too much at a party. That doesn't mean I'm going to set the house on fire."

"Nicki. He's not worried about fire. He's worried about you. About you overdoing things the way your sister did. He's scared he'll lose you, too."

"Right. Single-Surviving-Child Syndrome."

"What?"

"Nothing." Since MJ's death, I'd learned to be extra careful around Dad – editing what I told him about my life to avoid accidentally freaking him out. But I'd never really thought through to the heart of his fear.

Mom shifted her weight from side to side as if riding an unseen wave. When I was little, she wore pastel blouses, tailored jackets, and matching skirts. Every morning as she got ready to leave for work, Dad would say, "I sure married a looker." Now, in her too big jeans and faded T-shirt, she looked as stringy as the old tan chicken Grandpa kept threatening to turn into soup. Strands of gray hair mixed with the blonde. She'd aged more than nine years' worth. And she'd chosen to live this hard life rather than return to Dad. That I understood. But she also chose not to return to me. Tears blurred my vision. "I get it." I wiped my eyes again. "Now I get it."

Mom leaned against the truck's open tailgate. "What do you get?"

"Why you never came back. Why you live like this." I waved at the empty land, the distant trees, the dried grass in the fields.

"I left to keep you safe."

"Maybe. But that's not why you stayed away. This place is supposed to be temporary, right? One of those places you go when you hit rock bottom. They take you in. But sooner or later, you're supposed to start living again. Get back to real life. But not you. Getting high and screwing up – is that your real life?"

Mom's face stayed pointed at the dirt. She didn't speak.

I stretched my hand toward her then snatched it back. "I need to get going. Got a long drive ahead."

"Sure." Mom stayed seated on the truck's tailgate.

I walked up the path. This was unreal. I hauled Manuela up here – out to the ass-end of civilization — and ran into my mother. In what sort of freaky universe did that happen? "Oh shit." A sick feeling washed through my gut. I turned and looked back at her. "This isn't some weird coincidence, is it?"

Mom stared down at her palms, but didn't speak. Reading her future?

"Grandpa took you away, didn't he? Put you on the Lilith Express. You managed to get hold of him somehow. Maybe while you were in the hospital? And you told him Dad hit you."

She didn't answer or look up.

I climbed the stairs and went inside. Queenie ran to me. I crouched and threw my arms around her. "At least I can trust you, right, girl?" I inhaled her doggy scent like I was starved for oxygen.

When Queenie and I came out of the bathroom, Jane stood waiting in the hall, chewing her lower lip, forehead furrowed. "You were trying to get me out of here before I ran into my mom, weren't you?"

Jane's mouth thinned as she nodded. "How'd it go?"

I shrugged.

"She's trying."

"Not hard enough."

"Probably not. From your perspective. But she's trying as hard as she can."

"She said my dad's afraid I'll turn out like my sister." I shoved my clenched fists inside the front pockets of my jeans. "But MJ started drinking because Mom left. Everything's Mom's fault. And I can't tell her because I'm afraid she'll fall apart." To my surprise, Jane wrapped her arms around me. And I let her.

Mom no longer leaned against the truck when Queenie and I walked down the front steps. The dog leaped onto the front seat and I scooted in after her. I turned the key in the ignition and scanned the surrounding field and gardens. There was no sign of my mother. The tires kicked up dirt as I drove away. In the rearview mirror, I thought I saw the figure of a slender woman, but the dust cloud made it hard to be sure.

Two miles down the road, my eyes filled and sobs erupted. I pulled onto the shoulder and cut the engine. Queenie sat up, ears forward. "I didn't kill MJ," I said between sobs. "I didn't kill my sister." I wrapped my arms around the dog and cried. When my tears slowed, I rubbed Queenie behind her ears. "Thanks, girl." I straightened. Queenie leaned against me, panting. I continued to stroke her fur as I stared out at the empty road.

Mom cheated on Dad. Dad punched her. More than once. Grandpa took Mom away and hid her from Dad. Hid her from MJ and me. Dad hurt MJ. At least once. How could I not know that? Had I been so locked in my own little world that I failed to recognize what was going on around me? Being six years younger than MJ was no excuse. What was wrong with me? And why didn't Dad tell me MJ started the house fire that killed her?

Maybe because I never had the guts to ask.

The dog nosed my shoulder. I turned and wrapped my arms around Queenie again, tears landing on her thick coat. "It's okay, girl. It's going to be okay. Somehow." When my nose snotted up to the point where I could only mouth-breathe, I got my tears under control. I gave Queenie a hug, then sat up and ran my hand along her back. "I always thought it was my fault."

Queenie's eyes showed nothing but love.

I wiped my face with Grandpa's flannel shirt. "Guess we should get going." When I pulled back onto the road, I clenched the steering wheel and pressed the accelerator, picking up speed. I didn't give a damn any more about getting pulled over. Queenie stuck her snout out the window, looking ready for whatever came next.

In spite of the forty bucks Jane gave me, I still didn't have enough money to make it all the way home. The added cash would buy gas for a return trip to Grandpa's – with a little left over for a few staples in town.

Before I left the cabin yesterday, Todd had promised to fix the front door, so it should be safe to stay there. I didn't like the idea, but didn't see any other options. Besides, I needed time to think. With everything I'd found out today, even if I had enough money to get there, how could I go home and pretend I belonged? How could I jam myself back into old routines and act like they fit me anymore?

Chapter Twenty-Six

Driving ten to fifteen miles over the speed limit cut my travel time, but did nothing to improve the choices in radio stations. Todd's old pickup didn't come with an iPod dock – not that I'd brought my iPod along. I shook my head. Four weeks ago, I wouldn't have gone across the street without my iPod, let alone across several counties. In spite of the music's general suckiness, I blasted the volume to help me stay alert.

As soon as the sun set, the air temperature dropped as well. Driving one-handed, I pulled Grandpa's flannel shirt on over my tank top. A bright spot on the drive came with an hour-long show featuring a country singer named Haggard. Queenie howled along with each number. From the way the DJ talked, he obviously thought the guy a genius. Couldn't prove it by me, but Queenie seemed to like him.

When I reached the junction of I-5 and Route 162, it was closing in on 10:30 p.m.; I'd shaved over two hours from the journey. So much for playing by the rules. The next forty minutes or so would be on paved road, but then came the forest route. I lifted my foot off the accelerator. "What do you think, girl?" I glanced at the dog. "Feel like driving through the dark woods at night?"

Queenie whined.

"Yeah. Me neither."

A neon 'Truckers Welcome' sign caught my attention. I pulled off the freeway and headed for the well-lit lot. Todd's pickup couldn't match the big rigs in size, but hey, it still qualified as a truck. The place had gas pumps, a mini-mart, and a restaurant. I found an empty space near the restaurant and made sure the passenger door was locked before climbing out. Queenie bounded after me. When the dog finished her business, I returned her to the truck and cracked the window. "Back in a minute."

A restaurant meal would cost too much, so I loaded up on nuts and pretzels at the mini-mart and bought six bottles of water. To my surprise, the place offered a couple choices of dog bowls. I bought a bright red one and took my purchases to the truck. I set the bowl on the asphalt, poured in water, and called Queenie from the cab. She lapped with enthusiasm. I'd bought kibble at an earlier stop and when she finished drinking, I filled the bowl with food. Queenie wolfed it down.

We climbed back inside and the dog settled on the seat, her chin warming my thigh. I petted her thick coat, wishing I could drop off as easily as she did. My anger had seeped away sometime during the second hour of the drive, but the questions hammered on. True, I never asked Dad what started the fire, but why didn't he ever mention MJ's candles? For almost eight years I'd beaten myself up. Been haunted by guilt. For all those years, I believed MJ's death was my fault.

Even if I could let go of that piece of guilt, I still failed to save MJ. Sure, I saved her cat. But not my sister. When Whiskers died three years later, it was like I'd lost my last link to MJ. I pushed up the flannel sleeve and stared at the burn mark running along my right arm. "I thought she went out." Queenie shifted at the sound of my voice, then sighed. I rubbed behind her ears. "I thought she left me home alone. She did it all the time when Dad was out of town. If I'd known she was there…" Tears stung and my pulse started to race. I closed my eyes and focused on Queenie's steady breathing, trying to match mine to hers. "I didn't know."

* * * *

A roar jerked me awake. The front seat shook. No, the ground around us was vibrating. Queenie sat up and barked. The big rigs were leaving. What time was it? Still dark, but a sliver of sky glowed above the tree tops to the east. A huge truck rumbled by, heading out of the lot. "It's okay, girl." I petted Queenie then retrieved her bowl from behind the seat, poured in water, and held it while she drank. When she was done, we stretched our legs. Queenie ran to a nearby tree and barked at a squirrel. I shivered in the chill air, but couldn't help smiling. "Come on, girl." We climbed back inside the pickup. Queenie leaned against me and I kissed her forehead. "Let's get going."

Except for the eighteen-wheelers, the road was empty. Forty-five minutes later, when I turned off the interstate onto Route 162, it was only me. Me and Queenie. The sun turned the sky rosy behind us, disappearing when we drove into the forest, a canopy of branches blocking the sky. The amber tunnel carved from the darkness by the high beams made the world feel narrow yet mysterious. We spotted several deer grazing near the road and Queenie gave each one a thorough barking.

After a slow drive through the woods, we stopped in Punishment at the general store. It didn't surprise me to find the place open at 7:30 in the morning. I picked up a big bag of dog food, a block of ice, and some staples. Dennis put my purchases in a wheelbarrow and rolled them out to the truck.

"Everything all right with John?" Dennis straightened then arched his back. "Haven't seen him for a few days."

"He's fine." Far as I was concerned, the fewer people who knew I was alone in the cabin, the better. "Wanted to get an early start hunting today. Sent me on the supply run." Damn, I was talking too much. I forced a smile.

"Tell him I need some more of those lures." The morning sun glinted off his silver front tooth. "Another two dozen by next Friday ought to do it."

"I'll tell him." Great, now I was promising Dennis inventory Grandpa wasn't here to deliver. As I drove off, I waved at him in the rearview. He stood in the road looking at the truck a beat too long for my taste. Did he recognize it as one of the Wilders' vehicles? I hoped my guilty conscience was just working overtime.

In spite of the way I'd taken off on Wednesday, bumping along the familiar dirt road to Grandpa's cabin felt right. We were at least five minutes from the clearing when Queenie sat up, sticking her muzzle out the window with ears perked forward. "You know where we're going, don't you, girl?"

While I wasn't sure this was the smartest place to go, it wasn't like I had a lot of options. Dad was in France and, even if he had been home, I needed time to work through what Mom told me before I saw him again. If Mr. Wilder didn't scare the bejesus out of me, I might consider going to Todd's. But the mere thought of the man left me bejesus-less. My short list of choices came up, well, short. "Doesn't matter, right?" I rubbed Queenie's flank. "We've got each other."

Queenie snorted and stuck her nose out the open window again.

When we reached the clearing, I saw Todd had kept his word. More than. He hadn't only fixed the front door – he'd installed a brand new door and screen.

"Wow." I parked in the dirt next to the vegetable garden. Queenie trotted straight to the door and sniffed the new screening. She lifted her head, sampled the air, and walked alongside the cabin wall. When I tugged on the screen door, it swung open without the tired squeak of the old one. I grabbed the front door handle. Locked. "Perfect. I give Todd the key so he can fix up the place and now we're locked out."

Hands on hips, I surveyed our surroundings. We were the middle of nowhere, where people didn't usually lock their doors. After what happened here the other day, it made sense Todd locked up the place. But my gut said he would've hidden the key somewhere nearby.

Queenie nudged her way in to sniff the door frame.

"Where do you think he put the key, girl?" The dog continued nosing the wood. "Wait a second." Grandpa had told me Queenie was a great air tracker and, since Todd installed the door, it should carry his scent. Why not try Grandpa's search command? "Follow your nose, girl. Follow your nose."

Queenie lifted her head and trotted toward the chicken coop. She sat at the door to the run, head up, ears forward.

"You smell something, girl?" I joined her and stared through the wire fence. As far as I could tell, the chickens had scarfed down all the extra seed I'd put out. Nothing else looked different from when we left. I pulled back the heavy bolt. Chickens started clucking. A tan hen burst from the nesting area, saw Queenie, squawked and flapped, then squawked again. The dog nosed through the opening. "Follow your nose, girl. But don't scare the birds."

Too late. Chickens cackled and lifted off with an awkwardness that would make a person think they didn't know how to fly. After a lot of commotion and lost feathers, each of Grandpa's sixteen birds roosted on the henhouse roof. Even the mean-tempered rust-brown one who always gave me the evil eye. I trailed inside the henhouse after Queenie. She sat with her back to the nesting boxes, eyes focused on a spot high on the wood wall. "Holy frijole." Hanging from a nail was a shiny brass key. "Are you telling me this is the new door key?" Her gaze fixed on the wall, Queenie didn't move. I lifted the cool metal piece from the nail. "If you got this right, girl, I'm in awe."

The chickens stayed on the roof, even after Queenie and I left the run. The new front door lock was stiff, but the key turned. I crouched and gave Queenie a hug. "Great job."

Inside, the mess was gone. Not merely cleared of debris, the wood floor shone. The smell of Murphy's Oil Soap and Pine Sol hung in the air. "Wow. Todd must've worked on the place the entire time we were gone, huh, girl?" Queenie trotted through the kitchen to Grandpa's room. When she came back out, her tail wasn't wagging. "Sorry, Queenie. It's just us. For now."

After wrestling the block of ice inside and positioning it in the icebox, I hauled in the rest of the stuff from the truck. I tossed the duffle on the floor by the sofa and my knapsack on the kitchen table. The loft didn't look inviting anymore. If the bad guys – whoever the bad guys were – came back, all they had to do was take away the ladder and I'd be trapped. I filled Queenie's food and water dishes, bolted the cabin door, and then flopped onto the sofa. The exhaustion of the last twenty-four hours wrapped around me like a blanket. I closed my eyes.

When I woke, I found Queenie up on the cushions, wedged between me and the sofa back. She'd never climbed up here before. Guess with Grandpa gone, she figured she was top dog. "Queenie. Down." She lifted her head and gave me those big hurt eyes. But I knew Grandpa wouldn't approve of her behavior. "Down. Now." Queenie sighed and jumped to the floor. She circled before settling again. I rubbed my eyes and went into the kitchen. According to the clock – which Todd must've found still ticking in the mess – it was only 1:35. I felt like I'd slept eight hours instead of five.

I washed my face and pulled my hair back into a ponytail. Though Grandpa was gone, chores still awaited. Even so, the first order of business was to return Todd's truck. I grabbed the cabin and truck keys from the table and unbolted the front door. At the sound, Queenie got up and trotted to my side. Together we went out to the truck. We both piled into the front seat and I cranked the engine. Then we sat there, idling. I had no idea how to reach the Wilders' farm by road; I only knew how to get there through the woods.

"Huh." I cut the engine and climbed out. "Feel like a walk, Queenie?"

Queenie jumped down and danced around me. I'd said the magic word. The poor dog hadn't had a walk in two days. I unlocked the cabin and climbed to the loft. The shotgun lay on the bed where I'd left it. After lacing up my hiking boots, I carried the gun downstairs.

Grandpa's fishing vest, with the eight million pockets, hung from a hook near the front door. I grabbed it, pulled it on. The heavy fish scent reminded me of mornings on the Rattlesnake River; the smell didn't seem so bad anymore. I tried to stuff Todd's car keys into a large pocket on the right side, but it was filled with a roll of fishing line. I patted the vest until I found an empty pocket for the car keys and another one for the cabin key. I worried my lower lip as I trotted to Grandpa's room and grabbed some extra rounds. A box marked '00 Buckshot' caught my attention. If I was bothering to take the gun, it made sense to bring some serious ammo, right? I scooped up a handful of shells and stuffed them inside another of the vest's pockets.

As I locked the cabin door, I felt a little foolish bringing the sixteen-gauge along on our walk. But once we stepped into the woods, gripping the smooth stock made me feel in control. I looked at the dog. "If you'd told me a month ago I'd be tooling around in the forest with a shotgun and a big German shepherd, I would've said you were nuts."

Queenie lifted her nose, caught a scent, and sprang forward. A rabbit darted across the path and into the brush. I followed the narrow trail upward, breathing in the rich pine smell. A hawk cried somewhere above the tree canopy while a woodpecker drilled nearby.

After hiking for twenty minutes, the whirr of the windmill told me I was nearing the ridge. I called Queenie to my side and held her collar as we drew close to the tree line marking the boundary between Grandpa's and the Wilders' land. Since two armed men had been here the last time I came to the Wilders' farm, I wasn't taking any chances. I stopped beside a thick pine trunk and stared at the cleared land below. The vegetable garden that filled the lower portion of the slope in front of the large log home was empty, workers gone. The smell of broccoli hung in the air.

Queenie moved, her collar straining against my hand. Her tail thumped against my leg, wagging wildly. I followed her gaze, focusing on the slope to our left. Todd's wheat-color hair and broad shoulders caught my eye. He stood thirty yards away, at the bottom of the northern slope, near one of the greenhouses.

Creepy-eyed Deputy Walt stepped out from behind the glass house, followed by Deputy Santa and Mr. Wilder.

A hand clamped down over my mouth. My pulse rocketed. I let go of Queenie and tore at the fingers gripping my jaw. Queenie started to growl.

"Shhh." Ben pulled me around to face him. "Keep quiet. And shut up that dog. If they figure out you're up here, too…" He shook his head as he uncovered my mouth.

"Hush, Queenie." The dog sat on her haunches and stopped growling. "What's going on?"

"Badness." He pulled me farther into the shadows. "I'm pretty sure Walt spotted me when I ran for the woods."

"What happened? Did those deputies find out what you grow?"

Ben snorted. "Those two work for the cartel. They've always known what we grow."

"What?" I peered between the tree trunks at the slope below. The grizzly in my gut roared. Walt and Santa's guns were both drawn and pointing at Todd and his father. Mr. Wilder was saying something but was too far away for us to hear him. "Oh God. We've got to call the cops."

"Get a grip. Those are the cops."

"They're not the only ones, are they?"

"They're the only ones within shouting distance," Ben said.

The men began walking two-by-two, the deputies bringing up the rear, guns still aimed at Todd and Mr. Wilder. The group stopped in front of a small wooden shack at the base of the hill.

Though I hadn't moved, my heart thumped like I'd run at least a mile.

"Shit," Ben muttered. "If they go inside that drying shed, they'll be trapped."

Santa waved his gun and Mr. Wilder opened the door to the shed. Walt pushed Todd inside then his dad followed. Santa went in behind them while Walt turned and scoured the area with his gaze. He cupped one side of his mouth with his free hand. "Get your butt down here, boy. You don't come out, I'm gonna shoot your brother in the knee. He won't be much help 'round the farm with a blown-out kneecap."

I ducked behind the scrub. "Why are they doing this?"

Ben wiped his forehead. "Instead of skimming their usual percentage from Dad's payment to the cartel, they kept the whole bundle. We didn't know until a couple guys came by last week looking for the money."

"Those armed guys from the pot field?"

"You saw them?"

I nodded.

Ben moved to the right and stared through the manzanita branches, then turned to me and pointed at the sixteen-gauge. "You know how to work that thing?"

Chapter Twenty-Seven

I pulled the stock flat against my chest, barrel pointing toward the sky. "Why?"

Ben placed his hand on my wrist. "What ammo are you using?"

Before I found my voice, my mouth opened and closed like a beached trout. "Number six birdshot."

"That's not good enough."

"I brought some double-ought buckshot, too." My voice sounded far away.

"Good. You shoot from this distance with the birdshot, you'll piss them off rather than hurt them. You need to reload. But don't start shooting until I draw the deputies away from the shed. Otherwise you could hit my dad or Todd."

"What're you talking about?"

"They already know I'm up here. I'll go down and lead them away from the shed. Then you shoot."

"That's nuts. I can't shoot at a deputy." Not even ones who helped the cartel keep Manuela prisoner? My face burned while my fingers turned to icicles.

"Bullshit. Those assholes are gonna kill my dad. Kill my brother. Don't you get it? They're on the take. They're the bad guys."

Walt's voice called out again. "I'm losing patience, boy. You want me to hurt your brother?"

Queenie began to whine. I wrapped my free arm around her flank and whispered, "Hush." She quieted.

Santa joined Walt outside the shed. Walt cupped one hand around his mouth again, the other gripping his gun. "We know you're up there. Come on down, boy.

You haul your ass down here or your brother's gonna get hurt."

Ben grabbed my arm and moved a few yards to the left. I let go of Queenie and she trotted at my heels. We cut across the woods then hid in the shadow of the trees directly upslope from the drying shed.

"I'm not gonna wait much longer." Walt's voice sounded hoarse and angry. "You want your little brother to wind up a cripple?" The deputy used his free hand to pull a long-bladed knife from his belt. "Maybe after I shoot out his knee, I'll blind him, too."

A gasp burst from between my clenched teeth. I covered my mouth. Ben turned to stare at me. "That's Grandpa's knife," I whispered.

Ben leaned forward until his forehead touched mine. "Stay here. Reload and wait until I've gotten them to move away from the shed."

I pulled my head back and looked into Ben's eyes. "No. I might hit you. Besides, you said they're going to kill you. What's to keep them from shooting the minute you step into the open?"

"Because they haven't killed Dad or Todd yet," he said, his voice an urgent whisper. "My guess is they want the combination to our safe before they do anything too final."

"Don't go."

Walt's voice twanged again. "That's it, boy. I'm going in and blowing out his kneecap."

I grabbed his arm. "They'll kill you."

Ben's gaze met mine. "Not if you shoot them first."

I pictured MJ gasping for breath, dying in the fire. I knew what it felt like to not save someone you loved. I nodded.

Ben pressed his index finger to his lips then jumped to his feet. "Wait!" He turned away and thrashed through the brush to the tree line. "I'm coming."

Oh God. What had I agreed to? I was as crazy as Ben. My fingers tightened on the sixteen-gauge. Shooting at a deputy was the kiss of death. If I managed to hit either of them, the buckshot could kill as easily as a bullet. The minute I opened fire, they'd shoot back. And they had experience shooting at people. I peeked over the scrub. Ben was halfway to the drying shed. Shit.

"Raise those hands."

I peered down the slope again, my heart drumming fast as a woodpecker. Walt's gun pointed at Ben's chest as he tromped toward the deputies. How was Ben going to draw them away from the shed with a gun pointing at him? Ben continued walking across the rough ground until he was within a foot of Walt. Santa said something and Ben turned toward him. While Ben looked the other way, Walt smacked him on the side of the head with his gun. Ben crumpled to the dirt.

Oh no. Bad just got worse. Town was too far away to go for help. At least in time to save the Wilders. How could I get those deputies away from Ben, away from the shed? Maybe if I tried to divide and conquer?

What was it Grandpa told me? Different fish went after different bait. Right. So what kind of bait might lure at least one of the deputies away from the shed? I patted the pockets of Grandpa's vest and pulled out the fishing line. Did I have enough time to bait a hook?

I grabbed the loose end and ran the line around a nearby tree trunk. After checking that the knot was secure, I peeked downslope. Ben sat on the ground, leaning against the shed wall, one hand to his head. I scurried to another tree four feet away. As I finished tying the knot at the second tree, a brief cry came, followed by a moan. I hurried to the edge of the woods, used a broad tree for cover, and peered at the scene below. Ben lay on his side. Walt kicked him in the ribs. Another moan reached me.

My hands shook. I gripped the shotgun's stock in a stranglehold as I moved away from the clearing. "Come," I whispered to Queenie. I led her deeper into the brush, rubbed the fur behind her ears, and told her to stay. Then I hurried back to my trap, propped two broken branches by the tree trunk as a marker, hid the shotgun, and stepped over the taut line.

One deep breath. Two. The Wilders needed my help. No more stalling. Heart thundering, I walked forward, out from the shelter of the trees. "Hey there," I called out. "Is Ben okay?"

Both deputies looked up at me. Santa's face paled, but Walt's eyes narrowed.

I waited, doing my best to look puzzled instead of alarmed. "Everything all right down there?"

Walt turned to Santa. His lips moved, but I couldn't hear his words. He holstered his gun and began walking toward me, up the hill.

My face grew hot. I tried to control my breathing as I waited. I needed him to get closer before I made my move. Walt didn't appear to be a runner, but looks could be deceiving. Even so, no way he was faster than me – especially wearing that gear-laden belt of his. My feet itched to turn and make a break for the tree line. I took another deep breath and pasted on a bewildered look. "Is Ben sick?"

Walt nodded. "Yeah. We're helping the boy out." His words sounded ragged. Not even halfway up the slope and already out of breath. Good.

The seconds clicked by in my head like a ticking bomb. I forced myself to wait a couple more minutes before positioning my feet. "I'll get out of your hair." I started backing up.

"Wait. Come on down here. We could use your help." He was only eight feet from me now.

I continued to back away. "I'm not real good with sick people. I better scoot."

Walt's hand settled on the butt of his gun. "You're John Smith's girl, aren't you?"

"Granddaughter. Yeah." I took another step back.

"You lied to me." Walt's mouth bent into a frown as he continued struggling up the hill.

"I don't know what you mean." I scurried back another yard.

"When we came out to your granddad's place you said you never saw that girl we were looking for. The one in the woods. And I know that ain't true. You shouldn't have done that. I don't like liars."

I glanced over my shoulder. Only two-and-a-half yards stood between me and the trees. Facing Walt again, I took one more step then turned and ran. The explosive roar of a bullet came from behind. A pine bough shattered to my right.

Oh God.

I reached the tree line, fell to my knees, and crawled into the forest. I hadn't expected Walt to start shooting. What had I gotten myself into? Behind me Walt's panting grew louder. I pushed to my feet. For this to work, Walt needed to see me, to see where his prey went. I turned in time to see the deputy squinting as he chugged into the woods. I ran, leaping over the line strung between the two trees, heading for the split trunk where I'd stashed the shotgun.

Walt charged forward three steps before giving a yell and crashing to the ground. The deputy had run right into my line. Sprawled on his face, his gun had landed a good six inches away from his hand.

I raced to him and kicked the gun out of reach. Then I placed one foot on his spine and pressed the shotgun against the back of his head. Walt froze. I stood over him, trying to catch my breath. "Pull your handcuffs off your belt. Slowly."

"You don't want to do this, girl." The pine needle-covered ground muffled Walt's voice, but his anger still rang through.

"Do what I said and get the cuffs. Now."

Walt didn't move. What was I supposed to do if he refused to do what I said? After the moment stretched well past its breaking point, Walt did as ordered, dropping his handcuffs on the ground beside him.

"Think about who you're messing with, girl. I'm a goddamn deputy."

I took a shaky breath. Shifting my foot from his spine, I edged to the side, keeping the pressure of the gun barrel against his skull. "Put your hands behind your back."

"I don't know what you think you saw back there, but you're interfering with an officer."

My gaze darted from Walt's gun, to his hands, to the cuffs, and back to the gun again. Using my free hand, I grabbed the cuffs, grateful my trembling fingers managed to grasp the cool metal. I tossed them onto his back. "Cuff yourself."

He made a half-hearted show of moving his hands closer together. "I can't reach."

I drilled the gun barrel into the skin at the base of his neck. "Try harder."

As if by magic, Walt was suddenly able to wrap the cuff around his left wrist. Keeping the pressure on with the gun barrel, I crouched and snapped the empty cuff around his right wrist. I stepped back, hands and legs shaking, my breath coming in funny little wheezes. I moved to the tree line and checked downslope. Santa still stood in front of the drying shed, shifting his weight from foot to foot. Ben lay curled in the dirt. I stumbled back to Walt's side, pulled out the spool of monofilament line, and bound his ankles. Six layers of line seemed more than strong enough to hold him. The tremor in my fingers made for slow going, but I finally managed to tie and test the knot.

"You're in a world of trouble, missy. You let me go right now and I'll forget what you've done. Don't make this worse for yourself."

Yeah right. He'd brought up Manuela because he was prepared to forgive and forget. How stupid did he think I was? I straightened. The vibration from my legs felt like a temblor rolling through. Six-point-five on the Richter scale. At the least.

I'd really done it now. Dirty or not, Walt was a deputy and I'd assaulted him. Maybe I was stupid after all.

He turned his head to the side, an oak leaf sticking to his cheek, one eye glaring at me. "When I get loose, I'm gonna kill you."

I pulled off his right shoe and tossed it into the brush, then tugged the damp black sock from his foot. The smell of sweat mixed with pinesap as I circled Walt. I allowed myself another deep breath before I crouched and grabbed a handful of his hair and pulled his head back.

"What the fu—"

I stuffed the sock into his mouth, shutting him up. For the moment. But I needed something more permanent; I couldn't have him calling out and warning Santa. I wound fishing line around his head and across the makeshift gag. I kept layering the line until I was sure Walt wouldn't be able to spit out the sock. When I tied the final knot, I sat back, panting.

"Walt? Where are you?"

Hands still shaking, I picked up the shotgun. What would Dad think if he knew what I'd done? Sneaking out to drink and smoke at Gemma's was nothing compared to this. I made my way back to the edge of the clearing, leaned my cheek against the rough bark of a pine, and peered down the hill. Santa hadn't budged.

"Walt?" Santa's head swiveled from left to right, face pointed toward the hill's crest.

I looked back at Walt then trotted to his gun lying among the dry needles. Though unable to yell, the deputy was grunting and thrashing about.

As I checked his ammunition clip, Walt rolled onto his back. His face had turned pink and, judging from the look in his eyes, I'd better be long gone before he was set free. I turned away from the deputy, pointed the gun barrel at the ground to my right and pulled the trigger. The noise sent birds squawking and flying, but the recoil lacked the punch of the shotgun. I hated to waste any ammunition, but to lure Santa, I figured he needed to hear both Walt and me shooting. I shouldered the sixteen-gauge, aimed at the ground a yard away, and pulled the trigger.

When I looked back at my prisoner, Walt's eyes had grown wide and sweat streaked his face. I made sure his gag was secure, returned to Queenie, and told her to stay again. The dog let out a high-pitched whine. I backed away, eyes on the dog. When sure she was going to stay put, I turned and moved past Walt to the tree line. Ben no longer lay by the drying shed. Santa must have put him inside with Todd and Mr. Wilder. Below, Santa puffed his way up the incline, gun grasped in both hands. In worse shape than Walt, his face had turned red as a chicken's wattle before he climbed half a dozen yards.

Santa stopped and wiped his face with his sleeve. "Walt? You all right?" Santa's words came out more like a wheeze than a yell. After a moment, he started climbing again.

This guy wasn't going to be moving fast enough for another trip-and-fall trap to work. And once he spied Walt trussed on the ground, he would know I was a threat. Dammit. Did that mean I had to shoot? I opened the shotgun's breech, pulled the shells full of buckshot from my vest and reloaded.

Chapter Twenty-Eight

"Goddammit, Walt. Where are you?" Santa stopped two-thirds of the way up the hill, his gun pointed at the crest but a good three yards to my right.

Leaning against the thick tree trunk, I shouldered the shotgun and sighted down the long barrel. A light wind blew from the west, nothing strong enough to mar my aim. At least ten times bigger than a rabbit, Santa made an easy target. But I didn't pull the trigger. I watched his slow climb. The smell of broccoli drifted up from the recently harvested field. I couldn't wait much longer. If I let him get within thirty feet, the buckshot would turn him into hamburger – if I managed to stop shaking long enough to shoot straight. My stomach lurched. No way was I going to puke. Not now.

MJ's face filled my head, her bright green eyes morphing into the warm brown of Todd's gaze. I took a deep breath, exhaled until I felt empty, then focused on the line of buttons running down Santa's shirt front.

No. This was wrong. Clubbing Ben in the head didn't warrant getting shot. Working with Manuela's kidnappers probably did, but my finger stayed frozen. Dammit. Maybe I could scare Santa. I shifted the barrel, aiming at a clump of coyote bush to the deputy's left.

I squeezed the trigger.

The recoil knocked me backwards, and my trembling legs crumbled. Santa howled like a wounded bear as I landed on my butt in the pine needles. Scrabbling to my knees, one hand clutching the shotgun, I crawled forward and peeked from behind the tree.

Dear God. I shot Santa. He was still standing, but the left side of his uniform shirt was dotted red and black.

One hand shielded the side of his head and his face was speckled with bloody wounds on the left as well.

I'd pulled to right when I fired. That or the buckshot spread wider than I anticipated. Lucky for both of us I didn't hit anything vital. But Santa didn't need to know I shot him by mistake. I ducked behind the tree trunk, licked my lips, and then yelled, "Get on the ground. Now."

Instead, Santa pointed his gun in my direction and shot off several rounds. Blast after blast roared up the hill, bullets smashing into the dirt, kicking up dust and pine needles. I crouched, covering my head as splinters of wood sprayed from the tree trunk.

My ears rang, but Santa had stopped firing. Was he reloading? Sweat ran down my face and sides. Those last rounds were too damn close. I didn't want to shoot again, not from this distance, but what else could I do? If I surrendered, the Wilders and I might all die. Still on my knees, I braced one shoulder against the tree and lifted the gun. Below, Santa slapped another magazine into the butt of his gun. I sighted and fired.

This time, Santa went down.

Walt's muffled cries mixed with the pulse raging in my ears. I kept my focus on Santa. It looked like he still gripped his weapon. "Toss away the gun," I yelled.

Santa didn't move.

With jerking fingers, I reloaded, this time inserting two rounds of number six shot. I wanted Santa down, not dead. I took a deep breath. "Do it!" I hoped my voice didn't sound as scared to Santa as it did to me. "You're a sitting duck out there."

Still no movement from Santa. Was he faking? Another scattershot might kill him. I stood on shaking legs, leaned the shotgun against the tree, and pulled

Walt's gun from my waistband. My arm wavered. I grabbed the gun with both hands and I aimed a few yards to the right of Santa. The bullet tore a channel through the dirt. Santa didn't flinch.

I let out a breath. With the sixteen-gauge in my left hand and Walt's Glock in my right, pointed at Santa's inert form, I headed down the hill. When I drew within eight feet, the stink of blood and piss warned me what was coming, but I continued on. My gag reflex kicked in. Santa was a bloody mess, his chest gouged with shot. "Oh God." I swallowed hard, moved forward, and nudged the gun away from his limp hand with my foot.

He moaned, but his eyes stayed closed.

The world started to go dark along the edges. I leaned forward, head down, a gun in each hand, and breathed until the dizziness passed. I tucked the Glock into my waistband, then snatched up Santa's weapon and half-ran, half-stumbled the rest of the way down the slope to the drying shed. As I caught my breath, I studied the door. A padlock secured a large iron hasp. "I'm here." I sucked in more air. "Outside the door. You guys okay?"

"Nicki?"

The sound of Todd's voice gave me hope. The Wilders could tell the police I'd done what I did to protect them. Maybe I wouldn't spend the rest of my life in jail. "Yeah, it's me. There's a padlock on the door. I can try shooting off the lock, but with the ricochet ... I might hurt one of you."

"Don't shoot," a deeper voice said. "I've got a key."

After a brief wait, the metal tip appeared between the bottom of the door and the dirt, followed by the grooved blade. The waist of my jeans bit into my stomach when I stuffed Santa's gun next to Walt's along the small of my back. I reached for the key. It slipped through my trembling fingers. Twice. I flexed my hand, grabbed the key again, and inserted it in the lock. Once the hasp was free, I wrenched the door open.

Mr. Wilder charged past me. "Where are they?"

Todd and Ben came out of the dark shed, blinking against the light. Blood ran from Ben's bottom lip onto his chin and he kept his right arm tight against his side. Todd grabbed my free hand. "You're all right?"

"No. I mean, I'm not hurt. But I'm not all right. I shot a deputy." I nodded toward Santa, his body spread-eagled on the hillside.

Mr. Wilder put his hand on my shoulder, turning me to face him, his touch surprisingly gentle. "Where's the other one? Where's Walt?" He tugged the shotgun from my hand.

"Up past the tree line. He's tied up."

Mr. Wilder pointed toward Santa. "That one dead?"

I shook my head. "No, but he's hurt pretty bad."

Mr. Wilder nodded and strode away.

Ben stared at me. "I can't believe you got them both."

"I can't either," Todd said. "Thank you. They weren't gonna let us walk, Nicki." He folded his arms around me.

I closed my eyes and waited for the shaking to stop. A shotgun blasted. I jumped, pulled away from Todd, and turned. Mr. Wilder stood over what was left of Santa's head. "Oh God."

"Well, he's dead now," Ben said.

My stomach twisted as I looked away. Unlike his brother, Todd's face went white as goose down.

Mr. Wilder turned and called to us. "You three stay put." He started walking up the slope.

"Oh God." My voice came out a strangled whisper. "He's going to kill Walt, too, isn't he?"

"They were gonna kill us," Ben said. "They jacked our money, put Dad in debt to the cartel. They planned to kill us and make it look like the cartel took us out. You think we're gonna kiss and make up with them after that?"

"But Walt can't hurt you guys now. He's tied up. There's no need to kill him. You can call the cops. I mean, they can't all be bad, right?" I looked at Todd for support. His gaze wouldn't meet mine. "What?"

"We can't call the cops." Todd stared down at his boots.

"Why not?"

"Because we're criminals." His cheeks turned red. "The cops aren't gonna say, 'Oh, you guys are the victims here? We'll just ignore all these pot plants. All this weed.'"

"But pot's legal. Sort of."

"We're way past the maximum number of plants allowed for medical growers."

"He's right," Ben said.

Todd took my hand. "We can't call the cops."

"So you're both going to sit back and let your dad kill a man I left trussed like a turkey?" I wrenched my hand free from Todd's grip. Neither answered me. "To hell with that." I headed toward the slope.

"Nicki, don't." Todd sounded like his throat was lined with gravel.

I faced him and shook my head. "Who are you people?" I turned away. Where was the boy I spent so many afternoons walking and talking with? Had I wanted someone to talk to so badly that I'd imagined Todd into something he wasn't? I climbed the hill, feeling like each step crushed one more bit of my feelings for him. All the way to the ridge, I expected the sound of footsteps to come from behind, but neither Wilder boy followed. When I reached the tree line, I looked back. Todd and Ben still stood next to the drying shed.

I stepped into the woods and took a deep breath. Mr. Wilder was armed and pissed. He had my shotgun and I had Santa and Walt's weapons. My only true advantage was that I knew where I'd left Walt while Mr. Wilder would have to track him down. If I could get to Walt first, I could protect him. Heart racing once more, I crept under the shadowy tree cover.

The dry pine needles on dirt made a quiet carpet as I made my way tree-to-tree, watching for an angry Mr. Wilder. When I reached my trip-and-fall trap without getting shot at, I breathed a little easier. Then I looked at the churned up dirt and swore.

Walt no longer lay bound and gagged where I'd left him.

Chapter Twenty-Nine

I ran into the brush where I'd left Queenie. She was gone, too. "Oh no." The woods seemed to shudder and slide in front of me. I closed my eyes. "Get a grip." This wasn't the time for panic. After two deep breaths, I scanned my surroundings. Where did Queenie go? And how did Walt get free? He couldn't have untied his feet unless he got out of the cuffs first. Dammit. I never checked the one cuff I had him put on by himself. Maybe he didn't ratchet it down all the way.

I returned to where I'd left Walt and studied the ground the way Grandpa had taught me, the signs of the deputy's thrashing around easy to read in the dirt. Uh-oh. A coil of monofilament line twisted around a manzanita branch. I smacked my fist against my thigh. Not only didn't I check that cuff, I didn't take Grandpa's knife from Walt. "Dammit." Walt's shoe still sat where I'd tossed it in the duff under a low-growing sour cherry. That meant he wouldn't be setting any speed records tramping through the forest. I tucked myself behind a wide pine trunk and surveyed the area. There was still no sign of Mr. Wilder. Was it possible he freed Walt for some reason? Led him somewhere else to kill him? No. I headed up the slope soon after Mr. Wilder. There hadn't been enough time for him to move Walt. It was much more likely Walt was free because I screwed up.

Several small branches lay crushed on the top of the pine needles. I strained for the sound of footsteps, but heard nothing. Not even birdsong. Something had spooked the forest critters. Not a good sign.

I edged forward, handgun first, following the trail of broken twigs. Walt – or Mr. Wilder – had trampled a small shrub, crushing half its branches. I crouched and stared at a dark, wet spot. I picked up a twig and poked the damp earth, then lifted the piece of wood to my nose. Blood. I hadn't heard a gunshot. But Walt had the knife.

If Walt hurt Queenie...

I dropped the twig, stood, and continued following the tracks. The unnatural silence set my nerves humming. Using the trees as a screen, I zigzagged through the woods, searching for clues. A shadowy area up ahead caught my eye. Was Walt hiding behind that tree? I crept forward, attention focused on the dark patch. My thigh brushed against a shrub, and something darted from beneath the low branches. I swallowed a scream as a jackrabbit disappeared into safer cover. When my heart rate dropped out of the red zone, I continued toward the shadow.

Not Walt hiding. It was lichen. The mossy growth had turned one side of the oak's trunk darker than the other. But the nearby thicket of manzanita and chamise looked beaten up, like someone crashed their way between the branches. I slipped into a narrow gap, inching my way between tell-tale snapped twigs and bent-tip leaves.

Branches cracked up ahead, followed by a series of grunts. A man's voice. No, two men. Swearing. I crept through the bushes toward the sound. Sweat stung my eyes. I blinked rapidly, as I wiped my forehead with the sleeve of Grandpa's flannel shirt. How I wished he was here. Grandpa would know what to do.

A man yelled. Leaves and branches from the thick-growing bushes blocked my view. I pushed forward, no longer worried about staying quiet. Twigs jabbed my arms and snagged my hair as I shoved my way through to a clearing.

Walt stood behind Mr. Wilder, Grandpa's knife clamped against the big man's throat. Blood trailed down Mr. Wilder's cheek. The shotgun lay on the ground a few feet away. A low growl came from the brush beyond them.

"Queenie." Both men looked my way. Oh no. I didn't have a tree to hide behind. I raised Santa's Beretta and hoped Walt couldn't see how much my hand shook. I didn't have a clear shot at Walt; huge as he was, Mr. Wilder made a perfect shield.

"Get outta here, girl." Mr. Wilder spoke from between clenched teeth.

"She's not going anywhere. Neither of you are." Walt's voice came out weaker than his words.

Mr. Wilder's mitt of a hand circled the deputy's arm a mere five inches from the knife at his throat. "Didn't anybody ever tell you, Walt? You should never bring a knife to a gunfight." Mr. Wilder's green eyes drilled into me. "If you won't leave, make yourself useful and shoot this bastard."

I stepped forward, wrenching my right foot clear from the tangle of branches. Walt turned Mr. Wilder, keeping him between us. Blood trickled from beneath the knife at Mr. Wilder's neck, staining the ribbed edge of his thermal shirt.

A flash of fur rammed Walt. The deputy twisted and screamed, revealing Queenie tearing into the leg of his trousers.

Oh no. "Queenie. Get out of there!"

Mr. Wilder broke the deputy's hold and lunged for the shotgun.

Queenie's hind legs dug into the soft ground, her jaw clamped on Walt's leg while he continued to yell. A shaft of sunlight glinted on the blade as Walt swung the knife toward her.

"No!" I pulled the trigger.

The blast mixed with Walt's scream. Queenie yelped. The two rolled to the ground. Walt flopped onto his back. Queenie jumped up, growled, and retreated. Her leg gave out and she fell to the dirt.

I rushed past Walt to Queenie's side. "Are you okay? Oh Queenie." Tears wet my face. I kneeled beside her. A crimson trail ran from her shoulder down her leg. She looked up at me with her chocolate-brown eyes and thumped her tail once. I ran my fingers along her forehead. "You hang in there. We'll get you to a vet. You're going to be okay. You have to be."

Mr. Wilder grabbed my shoulders. "Come on. I need you to move."

I tried to shake him off. "I'm not leaving her."

"Neither am I. Now step away so I can pick her up. You grab the shotgun."

I stood and shuffled to the side. Mr. Wilder lifted Queenie, cradling her against his chest, like she was no more than a puppy. I looked back at the deputy. Red stained the front of Walt's uniform. His chest rose in rapid puffs, but his eyes looked unfocused as the fingers of one hand curled over the wound on his stomach. A shudder shook me.

I picked up the shotgun Mr. Wilder had dropped, then turned away and followed him through the trees.

When we reached the edge of the woods overlooking the Wilders' farm, Ben and Todd called out. Todd ran up the hill with Ben limping several yards behind.

"Radio the doc, Ben," Mr. Wilder yelled. "Let her know we need her help again."

Ben nodded and turned toward the house.

Todd jogged to his father's side. "You're bleeding, Dad. Let me take the dog."

"Nah, I got her." Mr. Wilder carried Queenie to the bottom of the hill, through the vegetable garden, and into the house where he laid her on the kitchen table.

Queenie whimpered. I stroked the fur between her ears. "You brave, beautiful girl."

Ben joined us. "The doc was in town. Shouldn't take her too long to get here."

In spite of Ben's prediction, the wait felt like forever, marked by the rise and fall of Queenie's chest. Each breath looked like a struggle. While we waited, Mr. Wilder gave his sons the abbreviated version of what happened in the woods.

Finally, tires crunched over gravel. Ben limped outside.

Cecilia Bonnard walked in dressed in her usual khakis, but carrying a large canvas bag marked with a red cross. She looked from Ben to Mr. Wilder to the dog. "You didn't tell me I had three patients." Even though her forehead only came to Mr. Wilder's chest, she managed to look intimidating. She gave him a curt nod. "Sit down before you fall down." Cecilia leaned in to peer at his neck wound. "You'll live." She glanced at Ben and said, "Ribs?"

"Yeah. Right side."

Cecilia nodded then headed to the sink where she washed her hands and pulled on gloves. "I'll take the dog first. I'm going to need to shave her. Any of you have a decent razor?"

Todd darted from the room.

I stared at Cecilia. "You're a doctor?"

She brushed past me and touched Queenie's flank. She glanced over her shoulder. "I know you're a tough young lady, but you crying all over my patient is not going to help. Wait outside."

"But—"

Cecilia cut me off. "No buts. I'm in a hurry." Todd rushed into the room with a straight razor. She pointed at him. "You go with her. Outside. Both of you." She turned to Ben. "I'll need you to sterilize the razor. First, wash your hands."

I gave Queenie one last pat before leaving the room. Todd and I sat on the porch steps. "If anything happens to Queenie ... I don't know what I'll do." Another loss was more than my heart could take.

Todd wrapped his hand around mine. "Cecilia's a great doctor. She doesn't have a practice anymore, but she's patched up a lot of injuries around here – including animals. She'll take good care of Queenie." He squeezed my hand.

I wiped my face with my shirt sleeve. "When she's done with Queenie and your dad and Ben, will you bring her up to the ridge to treat Walt? If he's still alive." Though I shot him to protect Queenie, I hated the idea I might've killed him. The scream of a hawk sent a shiver down my spine.

Todd cleared his throat. "You know, after you took off in my truck, I went home and had it out with Dad. He told me it was those two deputies who broke into your gramps' cabin."

Getting my question ignored didn't seem like a good sign, but I didn't have the stomach to press Todd about Walt's future. I also didn't want to think about what Cecilia was doing to Queenie. "Why'd they do it? Break in, I mean."

"They helped kidnap girls for the cartel. Your gramps was making things tough for them by tracking the girls and setting them free." Todd sighed. "After he and Dad got into it on the roof of the general store, Dad kind of sicced the deputies on him. He told them your gramps was hiding something. According to Dad, those two planned to use your gramps' past as leverage. To get him to stop rescuing girls. I think Dad feels pretty bad about that now."

"He should." I picked at a patch of dirt on my jeans. "Those two kidnapped Manuela?"

"Yeah. When we were at your cabin, I asked her about it. Manuela said she was waiting on a bus bench when two guys in uniform pulled over and asked for ID. Once they knew for sure she was illegal, they stuffed her in the back of their car. She thought they were taking her to jail."

"How…" I shook my head. "I mean, they're deputies."

Todd gave a humorless laugh. "They may have badges, but they stopped being lawmen years ago."

I wrapped my arms across my stomach. "But Walt and Santa got what they wanted when they searched the cabin. I was there. So why come back and trash the place?"

"Santa?"

"The cop with the beard."

"Oh. Right. Not a jolly sort of Santa, but I get it." He nodded. "Deputy Mercer – Santa to you – he and Walt thought their plan didn't work." Todd gave my hand another squeeze then let go. He rubbed his face. "When your gramps didn't bring back the girl, they figured they hadn't scared him off. That nothing had changed."

"Nothing had changed? Grandpa took off. Left me and Queenie on our own."

"Yeah, Dad thinks they missed that fact. Dad thinks Walt and Mercer trashed the cabin to give your gramps a bigger scare. To let him know they could get to you."

I looked up at the tree line. "Grandpa said this was a beautiful place – except for some of the people." Several large birds circled above. "When I saw Walt had Grandpa's knife, I figured he and Santa were the ones who broke in and messed the place up."

Time dripped by. But the passing minutes didn't dull the horror. How was I going to be me anymore? I'd shot two men. My hands started shaking again. I knotted my fingers together. I couldn't think about that right now. I just had to get through Queenie's surgery. After that, I could try to face what I'd done. "Why does Queenie hate Ben?"

"Huh?" Todd turned to me, his gaze unfocused.

"She growls every time your brother comes near."

He pushed a fringe of hair away from his face. "Queenie's got a long memory. When she was a puppy, Ben stepped on her tail and broke the tip. It was an accident, but she hasn't trusted him since."

The silence grew thick again, broken only by the occasional bird cry. I longed to run back inside and check on Queenie, but didn't want to do anything to distract Cecilia. There had to be something else to think about – besides shooting Walt and Santa. Besides worrying about Queenie. "Ben said Walt and Santa stole some of your dad's money."

"Yeah. Dad used those guys to deliver his payments to the cartel. Last time, instead of skimming their usual percentage, they took it all."

"Your family works for the cartel?"

"No. Dad pays the cartel to stay in business. If Dad pays them, they treat him more like a junior partner than a competitor."

"I don't get it. Why would the deputies rob you guys? I mean, if your dad's got a deal with the cartel, wouldn't stealing from him piss them off?"

Todd looked up at the circling birds.

"What? Tell me."

He sighed. "Dad thinks they didn't have enough to pay back the cartel."

"Pay back the cartel for what?"

"For losing Manuela. They didn't only provide girls, they acted as guards. Moved the girls from field to field. After Manuela got away, Dad thinks the cartel demanded their money back, but that those two had already spent it. Stealing from us probably seemed like a good idea at the time."

A soft breeze brought the scent of pine and broccoli. A few of the strands that had slipped from my ponytail tickled my cheek. I pushed them off my face. "So, I tell Grandpa about Manuela. He rescues her. Walt and Santa steal from you to pay the cartel back for Manuela. Then they decide to come back again to get rid of you guys. Erase any evidence of their crime." My insides felt hollowed out, but the grizzly in my gut didn't stir. "Not exactly how I imagined Grandpa's good deed playing out."

I studied Todd's profile. He was still handsome, but no longer the boy I'd started falling for on our walks through the woods. "Since we're being truthful here, what's the real deal between your dad and Grandpa? Why'd they stop being friends?"

Todd cleared his throat then shook his head. "Yeah, us having secrets doesn't make a lot of sense right now." He sat up straight. "Your gramps has been involved with the Lilith Express for like ever. I mean even back when my dad and yours were kids. About five years ago, your gramps asked Dad to join in, too. Dad didn't want to do anything that might call attention to him and risk his business."

"So that's why Grandpa made that crack about him being too busy greasing the wheels to help."

"Yeah. Your gramps thought Dad only cared about the business and making money. But it was about Ben and me, too. About not doing anything that'd make someone notice what he was growing and get him jailed. It was about keeping me and Ben with him."

"Nothing's ever simple, is it?"

"No."

"Oh God." I covered my mouth.

"What?"

I pointed at the slope twenty yards away. Turkey vultures had descended on Santa's body. I closed my eyes. "Walt's dead, isn't he?"

Todd didn't answer.

"Talk to me. You said it doesn't make sense for us to have secrets."

He sighed. "Yeah. If he wasn't dead or dying, Dad would've finished him off before bringing your dog to the house."

An ache started building in my chest. I had killed Walt. I was a killer. "What happens now?"

"What do you mean?"

"You're not going to report any of this to the cops, right?"

"Right."

"So what happens to the two deputies? To their … to their bodies?"

Todd shrugged. "Guess we'll bury them somewhere."

I stood, turning my back on the feasting birds. I'd done a horrible thing. I'd killed a man. But I didn't want to go to jail. "So everyone in the sheriff's department will think Walt and Santa disappeared?"

"I guess." Todd rose to stand beside me.

"But won't they keep looking for them? Until they find them?"

"I don't know." He turned to me, his eyes fierce. "You may find this hard to believe, but this is the first time I've had to think about getting rid of a body. I mean bodies. You got a better idea than burying them?"

I took a step back.

"I'm sorry. I didn't mean to get…" Todd shook his head. "We've had trouble before, but not like this." He placed his hand on my arm. "You did the right thing. The guy had a knife to Dad's throat."

It seemed a bad idea to tell Todd that wasn't why I shot Walt. I pulled my arm free, hugged my stomach, and forced myself to face the vultures. "If Walt and Santa vanish, the other deputies will keep looking for them." I took a deep breath. "But if their bodies are found, the hunt stops, right?" A part of me couldn't believe my brain was trying to work through our situation like it was some kind of logic problem. Or that I was talking about it with Todd.

"Yeah, but if their bodies get found, we all wind up in jail."

"Right." I looked down at my hiking boots.

The wood slats of the porch creaked as Todd paced to the far end then strode back again. "But if the bodies are found somewhere else, the sheriff might still come sniffing around here. Seeing as Dad's not real popular with the sheriff's department."

My heartbeat sped up. "What if those two were found someplace they were even more likely to get killed?"

"Like where?" Todd looked me up and down, like he'd never seen me before.

"That pot farm of the cartel's. The one Ben took me to in the forest."

Todd stared past me toward the hill. I tried not to imagine what the vultures were doing. He nodded. "That'd be some good payback."

The front door clicked open. Ben stepped gingerly onto the porch then grinned. "Cecilia says your dog's gonna be fine."

I rushed toward the door.

Ben blocked the opening with one arm. "Uh-uh. She said for you to stay out here. She's working on Dad now. He wouldn't let her numb him, so expect to hear some swearing."

"Queenie's okay." I wanted to jump up and down. Instead I hugged Ben. He groaned. "Sorry." I let go. "How're your ribs doing?"

"Cecilia'll tape them up when she's done with Dad."

Todd joined us and I hugged him, too. The tightness in my chest eased.

"Dad's all right?" Todd asked.

"Yeah. The doc said it'd take more than a knife wound to take him out."

Chapter Thirty

Dennis paid me for the three dozen lures I brought in. "Tell John to keep 'em coming. I can barely keep the things in stock. Word's got out about how much the fish like your grandpa's lures."

I grinned. This was the second batch of lures I'd made and passed off as Grandpa's work. "I'll let him know." The last word caught in my throat. I tried to cover by nodding, then turned away. Grandpa had been gone almost two weeks and still hadn't called. When Cecilia stopped by last week to check on Queenie, she told me to stop fretting. After labeling Grandpa a 'trouble magnet,' she said, "Whatever kind of fix John's gotten himself into, he'll outrun it eventually. And, once he does, he'll call." I hoped she was right.

Even though I didn't mind living alone with Queenie at the cabin, I missed Grandpa. Missed his funny sayings. The way he approached each day. And the way he saw me.

I browsed the shelves until another customer came in and claimed Dennis' attention. Then I scooted over to the payphone and plunked in my coins. The phone rang twice before Dad picked up.

"Hey. It's me."

"Nicki. Hi. It's good to hear your voice." His voice crackled down the line.

I thought I'd planned for every possible direction this call might take, but the surge of anger that swept through me caught me off-guard. My pulse started racing while my thoughts whirled. Did Dad really hit Mom? And what about MJ? Why didn't he tell me that candles had started the fire that killed her? My sweaty palm slipped against the receiver. I tightened my grip and took a deep breath. I had to keep it together. If I got pissy, Dad would never agree to what I wanted. "It's good to hear you, too. I'm sorry about that call a couple weeks ago." I gulped some air. "When I woke you up. When you were in France."

"You didn't know I was in a different time zone."

"Right." How would I know? It wasn't like Dad ever really talked to me. I sucked in another lungful of air. The silence stretched. Sounded like Dad wasn't planning to tell me more – like who was in his room with him at midnight. "You're home now?"

"Yes. Um, I've got some news." He cleared his throat. "I met someone. We've been dating for a few weeks now. I think you two will hit it off."

I guess that meant Ms. Midnight-in-France was someone special. Maybe that could work in my favor. I wrapped the curlicue phone cord around my index finger. "I'm glad. Really. Kind of makes what I want to ask easier."

"What's going on, Nicole?"

Uh-oh. Calling me Nicole meant Dad was putting up his defenses, but I was ready. I hadn't rehearsed this call over and over again for nothing. "When I phoned you before, the messages I left… I know I came off kind of frantic. But I was scared."

"Why were you scared? Is everything all right up there?"

I checked to make sure Dennis wasn't in earshot. I might need to use this lie on him later. "Grandpa broke his leg. I got freaked out about taking care of him. It seemed like too much responsibility."

"Is he doing better now?"

"Yeah. He's cranky. Getting a little cabin fever. But he's doing all right. We both are."

"Good. That's not exactly the type of responsibility I was looking for you to take on, but good for you."

"The thing is, it's going to be a while before he can be left on his own. Once the cast comes off, there's rehab. Even then he's going to need help with the vegetable garden, with hunting and fishing."

"He won't leave that cabin of his or those woods."

"I know."

Dad sighed. "Guess I'll have to hire someone to look after him."

"I'd like to do it."

"I think you're a little young to handle interviewing and hiring a caregiver."

"No. I mean I want to look after Grandpa. Myself. I want to stay here." I pulled my finger free from the curl of phone cord. "There's still plenty of time to enroll in the high school for fall. That way I can be here to help him before and after school."

"Did your grandfather put you up to asking to stay?"

"No." Once again I wondered what went wrong between them. It had to be more than the living in the wilderness thing like Grandpa told me. "It's my idea." More like my lie. "I like it here. I want to stay." At least that part was true.

"What about your birthday?"

"What about it? I'd be celebrating it here in the woods whether or not Grandpa broke his leg." Man, the lie came easier each time I said it.

"Seventeen's a big one."

"Yeah. The Wilders are going to help me celebrate."

"The Wilders?"

"Yeah. I met your friend, Bill Wilder."

"Wild Bill still lives up there?"

"Yeah. He and his sons have a farm here."

"Huh. When we were kids, he was busting to get out of that town."

"He seems dug in now." Silence greeted that statement, but the line wasn't dead. "I know me staying up here would be a huge change, but I think I need it."

"Why do you say that?"

I took a deep breath. Explaining the next bit was crucial. Luckily it was both true and the part Dad would like hearing. "Coming up here has made me look at stuff differently. I mean, even before I lost my cell phone, I started feeling like I didn't have anything to say to Gemma. We used to talk all the time, but never about anything real. I feel like real life's what I'm getting here. It's not always fun. And sometimes it's hard work. But, like Grandpa says, you've got to take the pits with the peaches. I feel like I'm becoming more 'me' here – if that makes sense."

"I guess."

"I'm afraid if I come home now, I'll go back to being the old Nicki and I like the new one." More silence filled the line. "Dad?"

"Your grandfather told me you were doing well there. Still, this is unexpected. You really want to stay?"

"Yeah, I do."

"Well, if it keeps you out of trouble..." A deep sigh came down the line. "I could talk to the school about getting you enrolled. And maybe I can take some time off and come up there over Thanksgiving. Come celebrate with you and your grandfather."

"That sounds good. So, can I stay, Dad?"

"Yes."

My grip finally relaxed on the receiver. I'd debated whether or not to mention running into Mom up here, not sure if that would be a good or bad card to play. Seemed like leaving her out had been the right decision. "Thanks, Dad."

After we finished talking, I walked back outside to Todd's truck. Mr. Wilder had told me to keep it – for saving his and his boys' lives. Turned out without Grandpa around, Mr. Wilder seemed protective rather than scary. He said a girl living by herself in the woods ought to have some sort of transportation. He said I'd be safer that way. Of course, the woods were a whole lot safer since a combined task force from the sheriff's department, Mendocino County SWAT, and BLM rangers raided the cartel's pot farm. Fortunately for me and the Wilders, no one had figured out the identity of the anonymous caller who reported spotting the bodies of two uniformed men in the pot field. The cops tracked the call to the roof of the general store, but the trail ended there. The rumor was whoever called had used a throwaway phone.

I climbed into the cab of the truck. Queenie nosed my arm and I stroked the thick fur behind her ears. She still favored her good front leg, but the fur was already filling in around her stitches. I looked at my bare arm and the burn mark snaking from wrist to elbow. Dennis hadn't seemed to notice it. For too many years, I'd kept the scar covered and by hiding it, let it define me. But no more.

Before coming to the Mendo, I spent most my energy trying to fit in, trying to be someone — anyone — besides myself. That had been part of Gemma's appeal. Gemma and her endless chatter, her schemes and parties — they helped crowd out the constant feelings of guilt. Even going out with Scott had been Gemma's idea — until she decided she wanted him for herself.

Hard to believe only six weeks had gone by since Dad quick-marched me to the car and drove me to meet Grandpa. Back then, I dreaded a whole summer in the woods – couldn't wait to escape and get back to my friends. If anyone predicted I'd want to stay in the Mendo, I would've said they were crazy. So much had changed. So much about me had changed.

Dad would never have agreed to let me stay here if he knew Grandpa was gone. If I hadn't crafted my lie, Dad would've come to get me and I would've gotten to ask all the questions eating at me. About MJ. About Mom. But, if I went home, Dad would hear my screams. How could I explain my nightmares? How could I hide what I'd done? Lucky for me, each time I awoke shivering, picturing Santa's buckshot-riddled body or Walt's bloody stomach, Queenie was there by the sofa, ready to be hugged.

Between nightmares and daydreams, I'd explored every possible outcome for that day at the Wilders. And even in the versions where I didn't shoot at Santa, he always wound up dead. Deputy Walt was a different story. But after ten days of 'what if'-ing, I'd stopped trying to imagine how things might've gone if I hadn't followed Mr. Wilder up that hill. In a weird way, I'd been preparing for this most of my life. For almost eight years, guilt ate at me over a fire I never started. And though Walt's death sat securely on my shoulders, I didn't feel the old grizzly in my gut. I wished I hadn't killed him, but couldn't image a scenario where I wouldn't have shot him to protect Queenie.

But I didn't see how I could ever shoehorn myself back into my old life. Not after what I'd seen at the Wilders' farm. Not after what I'd done. I'd brought Manuela to safety, but I'd also wounded one man and killed another. So what did that make me now? How did it all balance out? Was some kind of balance even possible?

Was that what happened to Mom? Did she travel so far down her own rabbit hole she couldn't see a way back home? Was that happening to me right now? Maybe this was something I could talk to her about. Some day. If I let go of my anger. If she was willing to see me again.

I kissed Queenie's forehead. "But, I'm not the center of the universe am I?" She thumped her tail. Staying here was good for the dog. This was her home. She would heal better in the woods she loved. And when Grandpa came back – hopefully before Dad's promised Thanksgiving visit – Queenie would have everything she needed.

A beat-up looking truck pulled in front of the general store, bringing with it the smell of burning toast. I flashed on the fire that killed MJ. Finding out I wasn't the one who started that blaze had unlocked something inside me. It cast off some of the guilt I'd carried because I was the one who got out, the one who survived. If my afternoon at the Wilders' farm taught me anything, it was that the past couldn't be changed. All I could do was try to learn how to live with the choices I'd made.

I touched my forehead to Queenie's. "You're a survivor, aren't you, girl?" I breathed in her doggy scent. "We both are. And that's a good thing, right?" I sat up straight and stared into her deep brown eyes as I rubbed the fur behind her ears. "I'm done with scrambling to fit in. You and me, we're gonna be like rocks in the river. The world can shape itself around us for a change."

When I pulled onto the road, Queenie stuck her head out of the passenger window, tongue lolling. The smell of pine poured in with the breeze and I smiled at the dog. Within minutes, we were back beneath the tree canopy heading towards Grandpa's cabin.

Heading home.

The End

Evernight Teen ®

www.evernightteen.com

34848606R00161

Made in the USA
San Bernardino, CA
08 June 2016